A Saving Solace

By DS Bauden

II

Copyright © 2002 by DS Bauden

All rights reserved. No part of this publication may be reproduced in any form or by any means, electronic or mechanical, including photocopy, recording, or any information storage and retrieval system, without permission, in writing, from the publisher. All characters are fictional. Any resemblance to persons living or dead is coincidental and quite unintentional.

ISBN 0-9744037-3-3
Second Printing 2003
Cover art and design by Anne M. Clarkson
Photos by Limitless Corporation

Published by:
Dare 2 Dream Publishing
A Division of Limitless Corporation
Lexington, South Carolina 29073

Find us on the World Wide Web
http://www.limitlessd2d.net

Printed in the United States of America by

Lightning Source

IV

Acknowledgements:

I'd like to give thanks to some special people in my life.

To my partner, Lori - You give me inspiration with every breath you take. Thank you for loving me.

To Day – Thank you seems so trivial for the work you did on this story, but thank you. I'll be forever grateful to you.

To Diane – Your endless help throughout this tale was more than appreciated. I'm so grateful for our friendship.

To Heather – You have been a blessing in my life. Thank you for being my friend.

To my loyal readers in the Baudom - You guys ROCK! Thank you so much for your endless support of my writing.

To Kim Williamson – You've given me incredible insight to the people you face day in and day out. You are a rock star.

To Sam and Anne – Thank you for believing in my story. I'll never forget this experience.

**For
Sara Ann McKenzie**

A beautiful soul, taken
far too soon.

May you shine brightly
in the night sky;
Now your beauty can
be seen by billions.

Preface

In the words of Ebenezer Scrooge, 'Christmas, bah, humbug!'

Kelly Cavanaugh sat at her desk, her auburn head bent over the stacks of paperwork that threatened to engulf her. It was her least favorite part of the fourth quarter business. Everything was due yesterday: supply orders, expense reports, labor disputes - the list was endless. The thought of actually having time to celebrate the holiday was strictly out of the question, and in her frustration, she wondered anew what it was that kept her in the retail world. The answer was simple: she enjoyed the interaction with people. As messed up as some of them were, she really enjoyed it.

There were only a few weeks left until Christmas, which brought out a whole new breed of shopper. People who hadn't left their homes since the previous Christmas came out of the woodwork, making all sorts of unreasonable demands on retailers - who gave them what they wanted, no questions asked, as long as they had cash or credit. So the last minute buyers kept coming back, and the cycle repeated every year. Resulting in the backlog of paperwork and overtime hours for the regional director of Maxine's clothing store.

Kelly grinned wryly. *Who am I to complain? I get my best stories from this time of year.*

Nice life, Kelly, the truly annoying little voice inside of her said.

Hey, who asked you, anyway? she challenged back. **Don't you want something more from your life?**

A Saving Solace

I want a lot of things. But one thing my momma taught me was, 'Get used to disappointment.'

And she had dealt with the disappointments that had come her way, but she also had a lot to be thankful for. She had a nameplate on her desk that read: Kelly Cavanaugh, Regional Director, a title for which she had worked damn hard. She owned a nice home and a wonderful dog, and yet... the loneliness that filled her, she'd never get used to.

With a sigh, Kelly walked over to the window of her office and stared out onto the cold streets of Northshire, her eyes glued on the old Salvation Army building a couple of blocks away. A new outfit had taken that spot, but did basically the same thing for people - helped the needy, fed the hungry, all in the name of caring. She admired the people that spent their lives doing that sort of work. However, truth be told, her fascination with ForOthers, Inc. had less to do with charitable sacrifice and more to do with the young woman who worked for them who she had seen on a nearby corner every day.

The young blonde sat there in the biting cold of the Midwest winter, ringing a bell, silently asking people around her for a few bucks to help out the cause. Her beautiful brown eyes had inveigled Kelly into dropping in a few bills on more than one occasion. In fact, her visits to the corner had become almost a daily occurrence. It was ever her intention to strike up a conversation as she made her donation, but then the bell ringer would smile at her and the words she had rehearsed would vanish, leaving her to drop her money into the kettle and walk away without saying any more than hello. *Some women have more power than they give themselves credit for.*

Kelly sighed again and turned back to the plethora of papers cluttering her desk. Perhaps today would be the day she worked up her courage and went beyond the perfunctory greeting.

Six weeks... it's only six weeks. I have to remember that. As cold as she was in the suburbs of Chicago, Susan McGovern's assignment there was only going to be for the Christmas season. ForOthers, Inc. had asked many others before her, but they had all said no to that particular assignment. Fortunately, Susan was more tractable, and though she was wishing she was in a warmer place, from her vantage point on the corner she had seen many interesting people bustling about their preparations for the holiday.

The people in the suburban area seemed pretty self-absorbed. It was a whole new perspective for Susan, who had become used to working with people in the city. Though she had once been a part of suburbia herself, she had no desire to be so again. *Good thing, as I'm not likely to get the opportunity. Heck, not only couldn't I afford to live in the burbs, the company even has to pay for my commute.* She shook her head at her reduced circumstances, dislodging a few snowflakes as she did so. *I'm sure my parents would love to see me now. They could probably see me from their window if they looked hard enough.*

A gust of wind swept blonde hair away from Susan's face. Pulling her arms across her chest, she reminded herself to wear more underclothes in the future. The harsh November wind made her eyes water, leaving her to blink wildly to restore her vision. Returning to her people-watching, she noted a familiar patron coming her way. *Nice suit. Nice body in the suit,* she noted appreciatively.

Nice everything, said Susan's irritating inner voice.

A Saving Solace

You aren't kidding. Maybe this gig isn't so bad after all.
Wouldn't mummy and daddy love you appreciating a woman?
Like I care, she spat back.
You don't?
Do I?

Chapter One

As the cold wind blew against her face, Susan was loath to focus on the realization that her shift still had six hours remaining. The bell in her hand was virtually frozen to her mitten as the snow continued to fall.

It's cold out here. I really hope that next year finds me in a better place. God, if you are out there, please send me to the sun.

Clink

She acknowledged the patron that dropped some change into her bucket. "Thank you, ma'am. Happy holidays."

Shivering, she remembered Christmas mornings in her parents' house. They started the day with a huge warm breakfast - everything one could imagine, from eggs to pancakes. Even when it wasn't Christmas, she had never wanted for anything. Her parents watched over her and took care of every need she ever had. *Who knew my life would end up like this?*

It seemed like a lifetime ago, when in actuality, it had only been five years since Susan had seen or talked to her parents, Jonathan and Elise McGovern, the two people that had meant the world to her. Her pampered upbringing had never given her a clue that they could be so cold hearted. When she was 20 years old, circumstances had forced her to come out to her parents. When she stumbled through telling them about who she was, the look in their eyes was one she would never forget. If she'd taken a knife and driven it through their hearts, she would have seen the same horrified expressions. She had never meant to hurt them; she just couldn't lie anymore. She was the only child of their marriage of 35 years, and still they chose to abandon her, erase her from their lives.

So, there she sat in the cold winter air, earning her

living by asking other people for money. It's not that she minded the job, she liked helping others; she'd just never gotten used to it. Every season contained a challenge from the elements, from the rain to the blistering sun; but winter was her least favorite time of year. Anyone who had ever been in Chicago in November could readily imagine why that was.

Raising her jacket sleeve just enough to uncover the wrist, Susan looked at her watch. She knew that the immaculately dressed woman would be coming soon; she always did and was always generous. With milky white skin and eyes as blue as the sea, she was by far the most striking woman Susan had ever seen up close and personal. On more than one occasion, when the wind was chill and the foot traffic was slow, Susan had let her thoughts take her away, centering on the mane of auburn hair and the beautiful donor, who appeared at noon like clockwork.

Figuring that she must work in the area because she was around so often, Susan idly wondered what the woman did for a living, then she smiled ruefully at her own presumption. *I'll bet she's never had to ask for money in her whole life. And if she has, I'm sure it was given to her. No one could deny her anything. I know I never could.*

Looking past the two taxis queued up on the street, Susan saw her mystery woman approaching, noting by her walk that she seemed a confident sort. *Probably in control of her life, unlike me. Our worlds are so different. She's wearing Armani; I'm wearing the K-Mart blue light special.* The woman was drawing nearer and Susan sighed – both in hope and in hopelessness. *Perhaps she'll speak today. I can see in her eyes that she wants to say more than hello. Who knows? Stranger things have happened. I certainly wouldn't mind getting to know her.*

Among other things, her inner voice piped in.
Don't you ever go away?
Nope.
Halfway down the block from her, Susan heard someone call out a name, and her donor turned and smiled. *Her name is Kelly; a beautiful name for a beautiful woman, even more entrancing with that smile.*

~~*~*~*~*

Making her noontime pilgrimage to the kettle on the corner, Kelly's eyes were fixed on the blonde a long block up the street. Feeling the icy wind stinging her cheeks, she wondered how the woman braved the cold weather day after day without batting an eye, where she got her motivation. *God, I don't think I could do what she does. I see a whole different world, the people that get to come in from the cold. Working retail is no prize, but working outside ringing a bell to make money for the less fortunate... well that takes some gumption.* She glanced down at the suit she was wearing, considered appropriate attire for her position, and conjectured that the charity worker probably needed to be wearing long johns and several layers of warm clothing. *I wonder if she'd like to have coffee sometime and swap stories.*
Among other things, her annoying voice chimed in.
God, don't you ever go away?
You know the answer to that question.
Kelly noticed the blonde looking her way and felt a flash of guilt as she wondered if the worker had noticed that she walked past her every day at noon. Although she had done nothing wrong, she felt a bit like a predator. Feeling ridiculous, she reconsidered her decision to ask her out for coffee.
God, do I need another headache?
Shit, Kel, get a grip; it's just coffee for Chrissakes.

I need another lover like I need a hole in the head.
You need something.
Shut up, already. The last thing I need is to have my conscience telling me what I need.

"Kelly? Kelly!" a voice shouted.

Temporarily diverted, she turned around to find a co-worker from two years previous smiling at her. "Sheila, how've you been? You liking your position?" she asked, smiling back.

"I'm loving it, thanks to you and your reference," she said.

"Yeah, well, what can I say? You deserved it." Kelly pointed towards the store. "Are you going in?"

"Yeah. I thought I'd check out my old haunts for a bit and pick up some tips from the master," she teased.

"Well, don't go recruiting from under my nose. It took a lot of work getting the right people into that store!" the regional manager kidded.

"Oh, don't worry, Kel. I'm here to look, not touch," she promised.

"Good. Well, I won't keep you. Thanks for stopping me. I hope you have a happy holiday!" she said cheerily.

"You too, Kelly. Take care. It was good to see you."

Kelly waved at her departing figure. "You too, Sheila. Bye!"

Running into her former employee was a nice surprise. She hadn't seen Sheila since she had assumed the position of regional director. In fact, it had been a disappointment to find out that Sheila wasn't going to be a part of her team. Still, she was glad that the woman seemed happy in her new division.

The pleasant distraction was over, and Kelly's focus returned to her mission…and her pending decision – to invite or not invite. *I have to pass the bell girl now. My stomach's in knots, and I feel like I'm gonna puke. I can't believe I'm feeling like this. I don't even know her.*

Before you even chime in, yes, I know I want to. When the charity worker's eyes rose to meet Kelly's, she gazed into the blonde's beautiful brown eyes, and the butterflies started flitting in her stomach again. *I need to say more than 'hi' today. I've got to get up the nerve to give her the business card that I've been carrying in my pocket for weeks now.* Deciding that she would offer her business card and leave the next step up to the bell ringer, Kelly thrust her hand into her pocket to grasp the card and strode determinedly toward the corner. *Okay, take a deep breath, Kel. You can do this.*

Susan watched as Kelly said goodbye to her friend and made a beeline for the corner. It certainly looked as if she were going to put money into the donation bucket again, and Susan could not repress a wisp of a hope that making a charitable donation was not the only reason the woman was coming by.

Jesus, Susan, get a grip on yourself.

Unwelcome as always, her bolder inner self chimed in. **Susan, talk to her! Be a big girl.**

Shut up! I have to do it my way. Breathing deeply, she steeled herself to make the most of the impending encounter.

"Hi," they said simultaneously. They both laughed and looked shyly at each other.

Kelly found the courage to speak first. "Snow, sleet, or sunshine, I've seen you here every day ringing that bell. You've got to be cold," she said with a tentative smile.

"Yeah, but I've got a warm coat, so I'm okay. You

come by here almost every day, do you work nearby?" Susan asked.

"Yeah, my office is in the Maxine's building a block up, on the corner." Kelly pointed it out.

Susan nodded. "Oh, I see."

The conversation lapsed into silence, and the two women stood there and stared at each other for what seemed like several minutes.

"Were you going to make another donation?" Susan queried, directing her stare at Kelly's hand in her pocket.

"Um... not exactly. I mean... I will, but actually I was going to give you my card." The woman looked surprised and Kelly inhaled sharply and plunged on, worrying belatedly that the woman might think she was being patronizing, and hoping that would not be the case. "I thought that maybe if you aren't busy after your shift, maybe you would like to... That is, I was going to ask you if you wanted to grab a cup of coffee or something to eat. You know, to warm up after being out here all day," Kelly explained, a slight blush adding even more color to her wind reddened cheeks.

Caught completely off guard by the invitation she had not even dared to consider might come, Susan replied truthfully rather than observing social convention which would have dictated that she decline. "I'd like that very much. When would you like to go?"

Relieved that she had not been rebuffed outright, and charmed by the woman's ingenuous honesty, Kelly smiled. "Well, tonight, if you'd like, but if you have other plans then we can make it for another time," she offered tentatively.

Even if I had plans, I would rearrange them to get the chance to know you a little better. "Thank you, I'd love to," Susan accepted eagerly.

"Wonderful. What time should I pick you up?" Kelly asked.

"I'm off at seven o'clock and I'll be just up the street, out in front of the old Salvation Army building. Does that work for you?"

"Yes, that'll be fine. I'll meet you then," the taller woman replied, much more relaxed now that the die had been cast.

"Great, I can't wait. See you tonight!" Susan smiled her enthusiasm, turning her focus back to ringing funds from the passing masses.

Kelly turned to go, then chuckled and turned back. "Say, can I get your name?"

The bell ringer laughed. "It's Susan."

"It is nice to meet you, Susan."

"You too, Kelly."

Kelly looked puzzled. Out of habit, she glanced down to where her nametag was, but of course it was covered by her coat. "How did you know?"

Susan gave her an enigmatic look. "Let's just say I do a lot of people watching here."

"I bet you do," Kelly smirked. "So do I. I'll pick you up around seven o' clock then, and we can swap some of our better stories about the people we've encountered."

"I'll be there," the smaller woman promised.

Elated by the fact that she had mustered the courage to talk to Susan and things had progressed to the point that they were going to spend some time together, and yet not quite allowing herself to believe that success was so readily achieved, Kelly walked away saying quietly, "I sure hope so."

Susan sat mechanically ringing her bell, numbed not by the cold but by the realization that she had accepted an invitation to have coffee with a complete

A Saving Solace

stranger, something she had not done since ForOthers had her life turned around. *God, my brain must be frozen, going off with a stranger... At least she's a good-looking stranger. Mama always said I had good taste.* Thinking of the family that had been lost to her, she grew sad. *She just never knew I'd have good taste in women, never banked on having a gay daughter. Who plans for that, anyway? Obviously, she didn't.*

She shrugged off the sorrow with practiced discipline and turned her thoughts toward her coffee date. They were not much more comforting. *What am I going to say to Kelly? We probably have absolutely nothing in common. What will we talk about, the weather?* She grimaced at the banality of that. *Oh, God, tell me we'll find more to talk about more than that.*

Clink.

"Thanks, sir. Happy holidays!" she said to the man walking away from her bucket.

Oh, Christ, don't let this be a mistake!

~~*~*~*~*

Kelly could have danced her way back to her office, but mindful of appearances, she merely walked briskly back in the direction she had come. She was proud of herself for finally speaking to...Susan, and very happy that her invitation had been accepted. Suddenly realizing that she did not feel one bit like going back and delving into the work that awaited her, she debated over what to do with the next several hours before she was to pick up her new acquaintance.

You've got to go home and take a sedative or something. She's not going to want to see you again if she thinks you're neurotic.

Good idea; no more coffee today. I'll catch a cab home and try to calm down a bit before our date. Date?

Jesus, I haven't had a date in forever. Do I even want a date? I've got some baggage that she doesn't need to deal with, and I'm sure she's got plenty of her own. We all do.

"Hey, cabby!" Kelly shouted at the slowing taxi. Standing close to the curb, the cab almost took out her shins. "Pine and Churchill, please," she directed the driver.

He cranked the arm of the meter. "Yes, ma'am."

Kelly sat back and tried to relax as she thought of topics of conversation that she and Susan might have a common interest in.

Susan. What a beautiful name to go with that beautiful face. I could look into those eyes forever. I'm looking forward to getting to know her better; I guess I need to come up with something more to say than talking about her eyes all night. She snorted at her anxiety, dismissing it out of hand. *With the holidays coming, we'll find plenty to talk about. I hope.*

A Saving Solace

Chapter Two

Lifting the sleeve of her coat, Susan glanced down at her watch for the fifth time in the last half hour, hoping that it had sped up since last she looked.
6:20 p.m.
She couldn't believe how nervous she was, all too aware that she and Kelly were from completely different worlds. That hadn't always been the case. When she was young, she'd had the clothes, the money, the education, even the social position. As it turned out, her mistake was in thinking that those things were hers when actually they were her father's. He was the wealthy one, not her. And she was reminded of that every day she'd spent away from hearth and home.

Enough of that 'feeling sorry for yourself' shit, Susan. You've got a date with an incredible woman in forty minutes. Just think about what you're going to say to her when she comes to pick your ass up.

Thanks a lot. When I lose my nerve and can't think of a damn thing to talk to Kelly about, I'd better have some suggestions coming from you, Bigmouth.

Clink

"Thanks, ma'am. Happy holidays," she chimed.

Just ten minutes more and she could turn in the damn bucket. It had been a good day, actually. People had been very generous. Usually she just got stares, or people walked around her, pretending they didn't see her. Some actually mimed having blinders on their eyes; it was just priceless. It made her laugh. She wondered what had motivated them to change their behaviors so drastically.

Beep beep

A Saving Solace

The car horn interrupted Susan's musings, and she looked around and saw Kelly pulling up to the curb in a black BMW. She knew that car cost more than what she'd make in five years, but she swallowed her insecurities and smiled as she waved. "Hey, Kelly! I'll be done in about five minutes or so."

"That's fine. I just wanted to let you know I was here. I'll go park by the Salvation Army office. See you soon!" Kelly shouted back through the car window.

Susan shook her head as she started to gather up her kettle and her chair. *God, she's beautiful. Why would she want to take me out? I'm so out of my league here.*

Kelly's car idled at the curb in front of the Salvation Army building, waiting for Susan to finish her shift and turn in her proceeds for the day. *She looks so damn cute out there, but what I wouldn't give to get her out of the cold. Maybe I could get her a job at Maxine's,* she mused.

Yeah, but is that what she wants? I believe you made the mistake of making decisions for someone else once already.

Thanks for bringing up that happy subject. It was only a thought; I wasn't going to offer until I was sure, anyway. Get off my back, dammit.

As she waited, Kelly worried about whether Susan would like the restaurant she had chosen. It had been difficult to select an appropriate place, as she was torn between a desire to wine and dine her, and a fear of intimidating her with a choice that too sharply showed up the difference in their apparent circumstances. Kelly shook her head in frustration. *I don't know what's come over me, and I don't think I even care what it is. I just hope that whatever it is, it doesn't go anywhere soon.*

Knock knock

She looked up to find a smiling face staring at her through the window. Susan's eyes were just so incredible, they left her breathless, unable to think straight.

After waiting for an invitation that did not appear to be forthcoming, Susan shouted through the closed glass, "Can I get in?"

Kelly swore at her oversight as she opened her door and escorted Susan around to the passenger seat, closed the door and returned to her place behind the wheel. She smiled at her new passenger and asked quickly, "All done for the night?"

"Yep, thank God. It was starting to get really cold out there."

"Are you up for some dinner?" Kelly asked hopefully.

The smaller woman bit her lip, as if in thought, then asked nervously, "So, you don't want to get coffee?"

"Well, we could get coffee, but I thought you might like to grab some dinner, as well. Maybe get some pie for desert and wash it down with a good cup of coffee. What do you think?"

Ended before it's begun. Susan flushed, embarrassed. *Might as well go with the truth.* "That sounds really great, but I'm on a pretty tight budget and I don't really have the money to eat out," she answered.

Immediately sensitive to the difficulty, Kelly tried to put her guest at ease. "Hey, I asked *you*, remember? It's my treat. Don't think another thing about it, okay?"

Susan looked puzzled and then posed her question. "Can I ask you something?"

"Sure."

She was practically whispering as she said, "Why me?"

Kelly wasn't sure what she meant. "What?"

"Why ask *me* out?" Susan clarified.

"Why not you?"

"Don't answer my question with a question," Susan said with a hint of asperity, sounding unsure of herself. "I really hope that it's not a charity thing, because... "

"Okay." Kelly placed a gloved finger on Susan's lips to stop whatever might have been coming next. "What I meant to say was... why shouldn't I ask you out? I've been seeing you almost every day, and you intrigue me. I would like to get the chance to know you better, and just thought it would be nice to have dinner together. Don't you want to have dinner with me?" she asked, as she put on her best puppy dog eyes to try and dispel the tension.

Susan's eyes rolled as she caught on to Kelly's ploy. "You know, you could probably get away with robbing a bank with that look," she kidded. After considering for a bit, she looked up. "I would love to have dinner with you," she finally answered.

"Great. There's a wonderful crab house a few miles from here. Do you like seafood?"

Susan smiled. "I love seafood."

"I figured you for a shrimp lover."

"Hey, that's not a height joke, is it?" Susan asked, pretending anger.

"Not at all," Kelly replied.

Good humor restored, Susan relaxed. "Good, I wouldn't want our first date to start out on a bad note."

Okay, she said date... you need to calm down, Kel.

"Kelly?" Susan's voice brought her hostess back to the present.

"I'm sorry, what did you say?"

"I asked if the restaurant had a dress code." She gestured at her clothes, designed to keep her warm on a cold street corner, not win any fashion contests. "I'm not really dressed for an elegant meal."

Kelly smiled and winked at her dinner partner. "You look great. Don't worry about it, okay?"
"Okay. Thanks."
"You're welcome. Now, let's go eat!" Kelly said, pulling out of the parking space.
"Sounds good," Susan agreed.

~~*~*~*~*

Susan was extremely nervous as Kelly pulled the car up to the crab house. She knew Kelly had said not to worry about paying for the meal, but she couldn't help it. She realized it was not within her means to eat in a place like that. *I sure hope I'm not just a charity case to her. I couldn't take that. I won't take that pity shit from anyone. Not even her.*

The engine was turned off, and Kelly smiled as she got out of the car, walked around, and opened the door for Susan. "All evidence to the contrary, chivalry is not totally dead," Kelly said as she handed her guest out of the car.

Susan smiled. "Thanks."

Kelly smiled back. "You're welcome. I hope you're hungry."

"Very."

"Good, then let's get in there, because I'm starving!" she exclaimed.

They walked into the restaurant, where the maitre d' smiled at Kelly.

"Ah, Ms. Cavanaugh, how nice to see you again," he said with a welcoming smile.

"Nice to see you, too. My regular table available?"

"Absolutely! As soon as you called, we made sure it was ready for you," he assured her obsequiously.

She must tip really well, Susan mused.

Kelly motioned towards the table. "Lead the way,

Leonardo."

They walked past several diners, and heads turned as the pair walked by. Susan didn't blame them one bit. She assumed they were looking at Kelly, since she was undoubtedly a knockout. *What the heil am I doing here?* she marveled anew.

"Susan?"

Uh oh, I definitely missed something. The host seated the young blonde and she looked blankly at Kelly. "Yes?" she said softly.

Kelly smiled. "Would you like something from the bar?"

"I'm not really much of a drinker..." Her train of thought was derailed by Kelly's smile. *God, how does she do that?*

"Come on, it's the holidays. You sure you don't want some eggnog or something?" Kelly persisted.

At that urging, Susan capitulated. "Well, alright. I'll have a glass of Chardonnay."

"Two, please," Kelly instructed the hovering waiter.

"Yes, right away, Ms. Cavanaugh," the waiter said as he practically ran to get their drinks.

She really must tip very well.

Chapter Three

During dinner Kelly was transfixed by Susan's recounting of the many different cities and locales she'd been to in conjunction with her job with ForOthers Inc. She'd done everything from feeding the hungry to staffing shelters for the homeless. Intrigued, Kelly watched as Susan related her tales between bites, as she happily ate every morsel of food in front of her. Every now and then, the sparkle in Susan's eyes was shadowed, and her voice was tinged by a longing that made Kelly wonder what it was that plagued her so. And who might have been the cause.

Susan broke into her reverie. "Kelly?"

"Yes?" she replied with a smile.

"I've had a wonderful evening. It's been a long time since I've enjoyed someone's company as fully as I have tonight with you," Susan admitted.

"I feel the same way. I wasn't sure if you'd feel comfortable eating with a stranger, but I'm glad I took that chance that it would work out."

"You weren't exactly a stranger," the blonde challenged. "I've seen you almost every day for weeks."

"Well, I guess that's true in a sense, but we didn't actually speak until today," Kelly reminded her.

"Well, I've spoken enough tonight for the both of us." Her brown eyes sparkled with amusement. "Don't you think it's time to tell me a bit about you?"

Kelly experienced a moment of fleeting panic, trying to think of something to share about herself that she actually wanted to talk about.

Well, that ends this conversation, her ever-present commentator sneered.

Oh, shut up!

"Well, I work for Maxine's, down from where you work. I've been there a long time," Kelly began.

"That must be why you dress so well." Susan's cheeks flushed as she realized she had paid her hostess a personal compliment.

"Yeah, I have to look the part, I guess," Kelly agreed.

"What do you do for Maxine's?"

The auburn-haired woman shrugged in self-deprecation. "I'm a regional director."

"Wow, you are in charge of a lot of people then?"

"Yes. I'm responsible for about fifty stores, and the fair number of employees working in each store, as well. It's been quite a challenge." A note of pride crept into her voice. She really loved her job.

"I bet it has. It's great that you seem to really like your job. I can't say that I always feel that way," said Susan honestly.

Kelly was somewhat confused. "After listening to you speak this evening, I would've thought that you were really happy in your work."

"It's not that I don't like the job, per se; sometimes it just gets to be too much. There's so much sadness in people, especially the ones that I see. The ones that have the courage to keep going are the ones that I hope to model myself after. I really look up to them, if that makes any sense whatsoever." Susan paused and then started up again. "There was a time when I would have scoffed at people like the ones I work with," she said softly.

That genuinely interested Kelly. "Really? That surprises me. What happened?"

"My life did a one eighty," Susan said with noticeable bitterness.

Quickly backtracking, Kelly apologized for her inadvertent miscue. "I'm sorry, I don't mean to be nosy. We can talk about something else." She looked at her watch and realized they had been sitting at the table for almost four hours. "Susan, it's getting kind of late, and as much as I really want our night to keep going, I have an early meeting tomorrow morning," she said regretfully.

"Sure; it's okay. I have to work in the morning, as well. You can just drop me off by my work. I can catch a train from there," she suggested.

Kelly looked at her in disbelief. "Susan, it's after eleven. I wouldn't feel right sending you home on the train at this hour. Let me take you home," she offered.

"Well, I live just outside of the city. It'd take you about 30 minutes or so to get there. Are you sure you don't mind?" she asked shyly.

"No problem at all," Kelly assured her, happy for them to have the opportunity to spend more time together. *I'd drive all night for you. I don't want our night to end.*

Do I hear warm fuzzy tones coming from you? her obnoxious inner voice sneered.

Oh, fuck off! I'm enjoying her company. A lot.

She could be good for you, Kelly.

No one should have to be that good. I have way too much baggage.

They left the restaurant and headed back to the car. Susan walked slowly in front, and the wind was blowing her distinctive scent into Kelly's nose. She decided that she wanted to get to know Susan more than she'd ever wanted to know anyone.

What is it about you?

Susan sat in the plush luxury car in silence, wondering what was wrong with her. Thoughts tumbled through her head, none of them pausing long enough for her to wrap her mind around. *I can't stop wanting her to stay up all night with me. I can't believe she offered to*

A Saving Solace

take me home. *Watching her all through dinner was making me twitchy. I can't tell how she feels. Is she looking for a friend...or a friieennnddd? I am hoping for the latter.* She sighed. *Kelly is simply incredible.*

Although Kelly had seemed interested in her tale of woe, Susan didn't know if she wanted to dredge up those long-suppressed feelings again. *My parents abandoning me is just not the kind of talk to precede foreplay.* That gave her pause. *Did I just say that?*

Yes, ma'am you did. Ho.

Am not. She's just causing me to have feelings I haven't had in a very long time. I could use some casual sex in my life.

Yeah, because that's what you're all about, that damn casual sex girl.

Shut up! I know I'm not like that, but I'm feeling things for her that usually take weeks to surface.

Just admit that you really like her.

Yes, I do, very much. I could get lost in those baby blues.

The car was very comfortable to sit in; the leather seats in the BMW hugged Susan. She had forgotten how much she'd liked such cars. Her dad had had a couple that she remembered in particular. *Too bad he loved his cars more than his own kid,* she thought sadly. *I'm pretty sure he made Mom's decision for her. I really thought that we had a better relationship than that. She always said she wanted me to be happy. No one said that being gay wasn't allowed to be a part of the equation.*

Kelly's voice interrupted her reminiscences as they hit the split in the highway. "Where should I turn?"

"Take a left and get on Touhy," Susan directed.

"Okay, just keep telling me when to turn." Kelly smiled her beautiful smile and Susan felt a warmth even more welcome than that coming from the heated seat.

Oh, God, I'm so whipped.

"So, do you have any plans for Christmas?" the blue-eyed woman asked as she focused on the roadway.

Susan had no one she wanted to spend the holidays with. "No, not really. You?"

"I usually go to the movies," Kelly admitted.

Susan couldn't believe she didn't have someone to share the holidays with. "Alone?"

"Yes, alone," Kelly replied sadly.

"Don't you have any family?" From the expression on the driver's face, Susan could tell that she had hit a nerve. "I'm sorry, you don't need to answer that. I didn't mean to pry," she apologized.

"No, don't worry about it." Kelly drove in silence for a while, then finally she spoke again. "My dad left when I was a little girl, I don't really remember him."

Nice going, Susan. Why don't you see if you can rub some more salt in her wound? "I'm so sorry, Kelly."

"Thanks," she said quietly. "My mom died when I was seventeen. I've been on my own since then. I've actually worked for Maxine's since then," she revealed.

Susan mentally kicked herself. "Oh, God, I'm sorry, Kelly. Remind me to remove my foot from my mouth sometime later, okay?"

"Hey, you didn't know. Besides, I figured if I told you something about myself, you'd open up a little about what makes you so sad," she said softly.

"Oh..." Susan didn't know what to say. No one other than Carol had ever really cared about her or her life. "Turn into the next drive and we'll be at my place. If you'll come up for a drink or something, we can talk more. I mean, if it's not too late for you?" she added, pointing out the parking lot.

"Sounds good to me," Kelly said agreeably.

Susan swallowed. "Alright then." *She's coming up... Oh, God.*

A Saving Solace

Chapter Four

They walked from Kelly's car towards the building. Susan had never expected that Kelly might be her guest, and she hoped that her new friend would not be put off by the tiny studio apartment. Carol from work had found the place for her when she was down and out and things were at their worst. She'd never forget how the rescue worker had fostered her in those times that seemed so long ago.

~~*~*~*~*

"Hey, you okay?" the large woman asked.

"Who are you?" The young woman was shivering, and her teeth chattered when she spoke.

Carol smiled. "A friend. Can I get you something to eat?"

"Why? What do you want in exchange? Been there, done that. I won't do nothing for it; I'd rather starve," the smaller woman spat. "And don't tell me you're my friend. I don't have any friends."

"Sure you do. I'm here, aren't I?" Carol attempted.

"So you've said. I also told you, I'm not interested," Susan said, her posture stiff and rigid.

"Well, there's a group of us willing to give you, and any of your friends around here, some food. We have a van around the corner. It's good and warm too, if you are interested," the larger woman finished.

The street urchin just continued to stare at the elder. "Why are you doing this? You some sort of good deed doer? I'm not a charity case." Aware that her circumstances belied her statement, she eyed the floor of her cardboard home.

"I didn't say that you were; I'm just offering a little

A Saving Solace

Christmas *spirit around here. If you're interested, we're right over on Lincoln Avenue."* Carol *pointed back in the direction of their center.*
"Yeah, whatever. Give my best to St. Nick," Susan *said bitterly.*
Carol *smiled down at the frail woman in front of her. "See you later, honey."*
"I'm not your honey," she muttered back.

"God, I was so mean to her. Hell, I was mean to everyone. I just didn't want anything from anyone. That's how I had been learning to live," Susan said, finishing the beginning of her heart to heart with Kelly as they sat on her couch.
"I'm so sorry, Susan. It must've been awfully lonely and scary out there," Kelly whispered, glancing around the small apartment. "Can I ask you a really personal question?"
"You can ask... but we'll see if I can or want to answer it." She was unsure what Kelly might want to know.
Like it matters. You'd tell her anything, piped in the voice.
"What put you out there? The streets, I mean. You're so young. I guess I'm just really naïve about the idea of young people in the city living in boxes. You read about this stuff all the time, but... I don't know... I guess I haven't a clue as to how it actually happens."
"Hmmm..." Susan paused, uncertain as to whether she really wanted to talk about that particular subject. *As much as it hurts to bring up, maybe it would make me feel better to share it with someone.* "Well, I don't know if this is going to bother you at all," she began hesitantly, "but I'm gay. I've known I was gay since... Well, shit, I

can't remember a time when I wasn't." She smiled at Kelly's nod and grin.
"I can relate. Please, go on," she urged.
"I was nineteen when I kissed my first girl. Compared to some, I was a slow learner, I'm sure. I finally found out what all the fuss was about." Susan paused to take a sip of tea that she had made for them when they'd arrived. "I mean, I had kissed many guys, but I never felt any kind of hoopla or fireworks, like my friends were saying happened to them all the time. Nothing. I thought I was defective or something." She chuckled along with Kelly.
"Believe me, Susan, I puzzled over the same things. I thought that I just wasn't doing *enough* of the kissing and touching thing. Well, before I knew it, I'd slept with some guy and I *still* had no idea of what pleasure was all about. Coming to terms with your sexuality is a really hard process. I wouldn't go through that hell again if you paid me," Kelly said matter of factly.
"Yeah, well, neither would I. It amounted to more than that in my case, though. I started seeing this girl, Cindy. She was really wonderful. I thought I'd found the person I would grow old with. We were really good friends first, which made me happy. I wasn't the kind of girl to jump in the sack with just anyone. Maybe things wouldn't have been so bad if I had just slept around for a bit." Her tone of voice in that last statement indicated that she didn't believe it, even now.
"Unfortunately, I can't say that I haven't had any one night stands. They don't leave you feeling much of anything, though. I always felt so empty after them," Kelly admitted quietly.
"Do you still do that?" Susan asked, her interest piqued. She noticed their bodies were touching slightly, as they continued to speak as if they'd known each other their whole lives.

Kelly blushed. "No... um... I uh... let's just say that it's been a while."

"It's alright, Kelly," Susan said as she touched her leg. "You needn't be embarrassed with me, I won't tell anyone." She smiled reassuringly.

"Why wouldn't I be embarrassed with you? We barely know each other and here we are talking as if we've been friends since birth!" Kelly joked.

"I know, it seems odd to me as well," Susan agreed.

"Hey, I'm sorry. I get off on tangents. Please tell me about Cindy."

"Oh, yeah. Well, we dated for about three months or so. We had it made, for the most part. Her parents didn't care if I slept over there, and mine loved to have Cindy come over. That is, until they inadvertently found out we were lovers." She paused.

Blue eyes widened. "Oh no."

"Oh yes," Susan affirmed.

"What happened?"

"I told my mother and father that I was gay. I knew that I couldn't lie to them anymore. Like good, loving parents, they said it was a phase and that I would get over it. Well, I didn't get over it. I told them that it was who I was, and I wasn't going to change. They insisted that it was nonsense, that the McGovern women got married, raised their kids, and lived like their parents did. I told them I wanted all of that, just not with a man. They weren't at all happy." She paused and took a deep breath. The feelings coursing through her were ones she had kept shut away for so long, she had forgotten how much they hurt.

"They told me that something was wrong with me, and they would get me some help. My father was just horrible about it. He called me a mistake, and said that I should never have been born. All the things that I never expected to hear out of my father's mouth."

"I'm so sorry, Susan. That must have been incredibly difficult for you," Kelly comforted as she put her hand atop Susan's.

"Yeah, well, I saw my father's true colors that day. My mom and I had always had a great relationship, or so I thought. I think she really wanted to understand, but my father wouldn't let that happen. In his opinion, she either agreed with him or she was no better than I was. It's obvious which choice she made." She took a deep breath, aching at the part of the story that was coming next. "They told me that if I was going to be a McGovern, I would get help, medical help, to heal the homosexual inside of me."

"Oh, Christ!" Kelly blurted.

"I know. I couldn't believe it either. I was just about twenty years old, I had one year of college under my belt, and I had never had to work a day in my life. I knew I had no options at the time, so I agreed to go away on retreat with a group of other people 'like me' to get the help that I supposedly needed.

"Later that evening, I told Cindy what was happening. I knew she wasn't going to do anything about it; she was scared to death to tell her parents, too. We cried and cried, knowing that we would be apart for about six weeks or so. I guess my parents paid for the 'extra cleansing' package." She laughed bitterly. "Then I told my folks that Cindy was gonna sleep over before I went away, and they didn't think twice about it." She shrugged. "Why would they, right? Cindy and I had been friends a long time.

"Cindy came over that night. I had twin beds in my room, in case of sleepovers and the like. Well, we wanted to sleep together in my bed. We thought my parents were asleep, and I really wanted to hold her. I knew that I wouldn't get to do that for a long time. Cindy climbed into my bed and we started kissing. It got really

A Saving Solace

hot; our hands were all over each other. We stripped off our clothes and started to make love. Cindy tended to get a bit vocal when she reached, well, you know." Susan blushed in spite of herself.

"Mmhmm." Kelly giggled and sipped her tea, almost snorting the liquid out of her nose.

"So anyway, my mom was up watching TV in her room. She heard Cindy moaning and thought something was wrong. When she burst into my room, she found me on top of Cindy, naked and sweaty and still inside of her!"

"Oh, Jesus! What a visual!" Kelly cried.

"Yeah, unfortunately, it was the beginning of the end for both of us." Susan slumped back on the couch.

Kelly leaned back with her. She turned to face her, placing a hand on her knee. "So, what happened to you?"

"After my mom screamed, my father burst into the room. I asked my mom to close the door so we could get dressed, but she didn't, so my dad saw us both naked, too. It was really humiliating," the young woman continued. "She finally closed the door, and Cindy and I were crying because we didn't know what would happen next. It was all happening so fast."

"God, I can't even imagine dealing with that," Kelly said sympathetically.

"My parents called Cindy's parents, and they came to get her. I wasn't allowed to see her again. All of a sudden, *I* was the one who'd changed her. It was all *my* fault; *I* was the perverted one. My parents kicked me out without any more than the clothes on my back. I had no job, I had no money, I had nothing," she said, tears threatening to spill. "I went to everyone I knew to see if I could stay with them for a while until I got a place of my own. I thought, 'No problem, I'll just get a job and get my own apartment.' It wasn't that simple. Every house I went to, my friends were either away at school, or their parents called mine to find out what had happened, and then they wouldn't let me stay there. I was fucked with no kiss. Up shit creek with no paddles. You get the idea."

"Unfortunately, I do," she said. "I'm so sorry. I wish I could say more. I just..."

"Hey, don't worry about it. I'm still alive, I'm breathing, and feeling pretty good about myself now."

"How? How can you go through that and be alright?" Kelly was genuinely concerned.

How indeed? came the smug voice.

"After my resources ran out, I started getting into a bad scene: drugs, sex, the usual. I never thought that I'd let someone fuck me for money," she said with self-loathing. "I didn't have any choice. I couldn't get a real job. No food, no clothes other than the ones I'd left with, and I hadn't had a shower in forever. It was hell. Luckily for me, it was summer going into autumn and it wasn't that cold outside. I found a group of people that pretty much brought me down to a place they called home, the 'Heights'. I never knew why they called it that until I found out what kind of heights their drugs took me to. It was outside of the city and it was pretty safe. We hung out together and tried to take care of each other as much as possible. You'd be amazed how fast your morals go down the toilet when you are scrounging for food. I stole when I could, from whomever I could."

Kelly sat with her head against the cushions of the couch, unshed tears in her eyes. Susan heard her sniffle once or twice, but it was very hard for her to look at her guest as she recounted what had happened. This was the first time she had told the story in over two years. Kelly listened silently as her fingers brushed softly against the fabric on Susan's pants.

"I continued to get high, a lot. It took away some of the pain. Not enough, unfortunately. I started to need more and more drugs to keep the highs going. I lied to too many of the people that I considered my friends, and they told me to get lost and to stay away from them if I knew what was good for me. Not knowing better, I went back begging for a hit... for anything. They beat the shit out of me. I was left bleeding in an alley. Death would've been better than what the next years had in store for me.

"I lived in a cardboard box. I ate only if I could find something in the trash out in the back of some restaurants. I never thought that I would be eating someone else's garbage. I grew up in the North Shore for Chrissakes!" she shouted as she waved her hands around. "I was a savage, for lack of a better term. I did what I had to do to survive. As fervently as I prayed the sun wouldn't come up on some days, it always did.

"Like I told you earlier, Christmas time about two years ago, a woman came around. She was from ForOthers, Inc. They had a food van and were driving around giving food to those of us that needed it or just wanted to eat real food for a change. I was reluctant to take their offered help, to say the least. The last time I'd hooked up with anyone, I'd gotten the shit kicked out of me. There was no way I was trusting anyone else." She paused to drink her now-cold tea.

"What changed your mind about... um, Carol? Wasn't that her name?" Kelly asked, her eyes pinning Susan to her seat.

"Yeah, Carol. There was just something in her eyes that told me that she wasn't going to hurt me; she really was there to help. I finally gave in to her kindness. It only took about four weeks. Every day she came up to me and asked how I was and if I wanted anything to eat. She was relentless. I swear she was an angel in disguise. She came to me at a critical time in my life. Shortly after I met her, I was hit with pneumonia. I thought for sure my number was up, but Carol was right there for me. She got me into the clinic off Randolph Lane. Normally, they wouldn't look twice at someone like me. Carol told them that I worked for her, and they took me in, no problem. I was there for two weeks. I couldn't breathe without feeling like I had a brick for a lung. I lost more weight, if that was possible. They were afraid that I was gonna die just from malnutrition. Carol would have none of that. I didn't know why, but she took me in. She cared so much. She took care of me as if I was her own."

Kelly smiled. "She sounds like a wonderful woman."

"Yes, she was. She died last year after suffering a heart attack. She was overweight, but we never saw it coming." Susan could no longer hold back the tears that had been seeking release all night. "Before we could get her some help, she was gone." She started to cry. Kelly reached around her and pulled her close. Susan rested her head on Kelly's shoulder, and Kelly rubbed it tenderly.

God, that feels wonderful. I haven't been held like this for as long as I can remember.

"Shhh...it's okay, Susan. It's okay... I'm right here," she soothed.

"I'm sorry, Kelly." The young woman sniffled back more tears. "I can't remember the last time I felt the need to cry."

"It's all right. You go ahead, I don't mind," she said softly.

Susan heard her humming as she rocked her gently, felt herself begin to calm. She pulled back and wiped her face in embarrassment.

Kelly cupped her chin in her hands and smiled. "You're a very beautiful woman, Susan, inside and out. Carol saw that, I'm sure of it. That's why she took care of you. She saw what I see."

A Saving Solace

"And what is it that you see, Kelly?" she quavered.

"I see a very strong and caring woman who has fought to be the person she is today. You sacrificed your comfortable life to be the person that you knew you were, even though that meant that you were put in harm's way. You fought to stay alive, and you won! She saw the fire in your eyes that I see. That fire keeps you going, Susan. It's the reason you weren't defeated. It's the reason that you help the people that you do on a daily basis. You are truly incredible." She smiled as she shook her head in wonder.

"I can only help the ones that will accept my help. There are so many people out there that are stubborn like I was, and won't take any handouts. Those are the ones I worry about. They are the ones that might not make it. I hate knowing that, and I'll do what I can to change their minds. I want to be for them what Carol was for me. After I was well, she gave me a job with ForOthers, Inc. She had been on the streets, as well. It's amazing how life comes full circle, you know? Knowing that there might be someone out there like I was, that I can help, I can't stop doing what I do," Susan said as the tears rolled down her cheeks.

"What about your parents? Have you heard from them at all?" Kelly asked, wiping her cheeks with gentle fingers.

Susan couldn't keep the anger from her voice. "Fuck them!" she spat. "They didn't want me; they kicked me out. She chose to stay with him instead of helping her own child, just because I was gay! What the hell kind of mom was she?"

"Shh... I'm sorry. I shouldn't have said that," she said as she pulled Susan close to her again.

God, she smells so good. Her arms around me feel as natural to me as my own skin. She could be the one that Cindy wasn't.

Susan felt Kelly kiss the top of her head and rest her cheek there. She feared that she might have said too much, but Kelly was so easy to talk to she couldn't help it. Once she'd started, she just couldn't stop. She hoped she wouldn't become just a sad story line character to Kelly. *I couldn't take that.*
She isn't like that and you know it.
How do I know? We just met!
Ask your heart. She knows, too.
My heart?
Yeah, you know, that thing that's beating incredibly fast because you're in Kelly's arms.
Oh, shut up.
"Susan?" Kelly said softly.
"I'm sorry, what?" she said in a husky voice.
"It's almost three a.m. I hate to do this, but I really have to get going," Kelly said as she continued to rub circles on Susan's back.
"Oh, my God. I didn't mean to ramble on the way that I did. I'm sorry. I didn't mean to make this out to be the 'Poor Susan Show'."
"Hey, I wanted to know about you, remember? I asked."
Susan felt Kelly's voice vibrate into her body. She pulled back to look into her eyes, seeing only sincerity and compassion.
"Thank you for sharing your story with me. Now, before I take off, what are you doing tomorrow night?" Kelly asked.
"Nothing. It's Friday. I'm off all weekend. I usually just do laundry and run some errands."
"Not tomorrow. I would very much like for you to come out with me again. This time, I'd like for you to come to my home. I'd love to cook for you." She smiled that beautiful smile.
Susan grinned back at her. "You cook, do you?"

"Yes. I make homemade pasta and a killer Alfredo sauce. You game?" She arched her eyebrows and hope filled her eyes.

"I'd love to. But next time the conversation is all about you. Deal?" Susan asked, hoping Kelly knew what she meant. They untangled and stretched their cramped muscles as they stood for the first time in hours.

"Deal. It's my turn to share a little bit of me with you. I feel very honored that you shared your story with me, Susan. I'll take this with me to the grave. I won't ever break the confidence that you've placed in me. Thank you for inviting me up. I really had a wonderful time tonight."

"Me too. Thank you for coming here. I hope it didn't feel too cramped for you. There's barely enough room in here for me," she joked, gesturing around the one-roomed space.

Kelly smiled. "It is very homey. There's a lot of you in this little place; I like that. You do a lot with what you are given. That's a rare gift. It's really nice to see."

Susan walked into the kitchen and rinsed their two mugs out in the sink, then walked Kelly to the door. "You want me to walk you to your car?" she asked.

"Nah, I'm a big girl. Besides, it's cold out there and you're nice and warm in here." She leaned closer and Susan felt her breathing hitch a bit. Kelly reached out and Susan fell into her arms as if it were a well-established habit. They fit so well together, it was if they were two halves of a whole. Well, an uneven whole, being that their heights were a bit different. Neither cared; it felt more right than anything either had ever experienced.

They pulled apart and Kelly gave a lopsided smile. "I'm going to pay for this tomorrow morning, that's for sure. I think my meeting is going to be in the Guinness book for 'world's shortest board meeting,'" she laughed.

"Yeah, well there's no way I'm gonna fall asleep on the job tomorrow. I'm sure the wind will keep me wide awake!" Susan laughed back.

"Oh, God. How do you stand the weather?" she asked.

Susan pulled up her sweater so Kelly could see her underclothes. "Long john's save my life." They grinned together.

"I bet they do." They paused and just stared at each other for a little longer. "Well, I guess I should get going."

"Yeah, it's late. Tomorrow night, then?" Susan asked, trying to hide her excitement.

"Count on it." She winked. "Good night, Susan. Thank you for a wonderful evening."

"I don't know how you could say it was wonderful. I talked your ear off," Susan quipped back.

"And you have a beautiful voice." Kelly leaned down and placed a gentle kiss on her cheek. "See you tomorrow."

A bit taken aback, she stuttered, "Y…yeah… I'll see you tomorrow. Goodnight, Kelly. Please drive safely."

"You got it. Bye," she waved.

With that, Susan's mystery woman walked down the hall and out of the building. She closed the door and rested her body against it as it shut, drawing a deep breath and sighing contentedly. For the first time in her life she thought she'd found someone to fill the hole in her heart that'd been there since Cindy and she were last together.

I told you so.
Arghh!

Walking into her bathroom, Susan started getting ready for bed. She brushed her teeth and washed her face, smiling at her reflection. Returning to the living room that doubled as a sleeping area, she pulled her bed out from underneath the couch cushions, and threw the blankets on the wrinkled sheets. Lastly, she grabbed her pillows from behind the couch and flopped her body into bed. As much as Susan wanted sleep to claim her, she knew it wouldn't come anytime soon. She closed her eyes and uttered a small prayer of thanks to Carol, who was truly her angel, and definitely still working hard at her job.

Chapter Five

"So, after looking at the operational performance for last year, everyone can see the need for the departmental quotas for this year to be increased by thirteen percent." The room groaned. "Is there something wrong, Baxter?" Kelly leaned her tired frame against the wall of the boardroom.

"No. I can see our performance is on an upswing, and we should be able to achieve that goal," he conceded.

"Thank you. I was sure you would see it that way. We need to get better results from our labor investment, as well. There should be better productivity from our managers. God knows we pay them more than most retailers do; we should at least get our money's worth here. Our turnover was under thirty percent last year, which isn't bad actually, but we should try and get even better retention of our floor people. Does anyone have any ideas on how we can bring that about?"

Kelly looked over the table of district managers on her team and saw many faces that she had hired off the street. It was nice to know they were happy in their positions and didn't want to work for anyone else. A small, redheaded woman raised her hand.

"Yes, Marta?" she called out.

"I think if we made our bonus program an annual one versus a quarterly one, our managers' efforts might be more consistent, and they would receive a greater pay out in the long term."

"Very good, Marta. In fact, here is a blueprint for exactly that plan. I'm glad you and I both recognized this. It was something I brought up with my bosses as well, and they liked the idea. So, here you go: annual bonus incentives for this fiscal year for our store

A Saving Solace

managers," Kelly repeated, passing out the new plans to everyone.

"Please look these over and keep a copy for yourselves. The individual stores will receive these in their next mail packs. Any questions about this?" Looking around, she saw no hands being raised. "All right, then, this meeting is adjourned." Famished, she rubbed her stomach in sympathy, looked up at the clock and saw that it was nearly two. Shaking her head ruefully, Kelly realized that she was also really tired, and hoped that she would be able to stay awake up for her dinner engagement with Susan. *I remember when I could pull all nighters, one after the other.*

It's your age catching up with you, came the snide thought.

Thanks, I needed that ego boost right now.
Any time, babe. I'm here for you.
Whatever.

Gathering her things from the boardroom, Kelly went back into her office. She hadn't seen Susan on the corner when she'd arrived at work that morning, and hoped she wasn't late on account of the previous night.

I'm sure she's just as tired as I am. We can make it an early night tonight. As far as I'm concerned, I'm finished for today. I need to go the grocery for some last minute items for tonight, and maybe, just maybe, I can catch a nap before I pick her up.

Looking around one last time, she locked her office, walked through the store, and went outside to catch a cab. Where she saw a familiar face atop a shivering body. Crossing the street to the coffeehouse, she bought some hot cocoa, anxious to provide some warmth and comfort for her new friend.

"Hey, I didn't see you earlier. I hope you weren't late this morning because of me," Kelly greeted.

"Hey, how are you?" Susan beamed. Her eyes were

a bit dark from lack of sleep, but still had lots of sparkle to them as she spoke. "I missed my train by like two minutes. Then it took forever for the next one. It's my own fault. I thought my snooze button was a house fly; I kept swatting it over and over." She smiled.

Smiling back, Kelly replied, "You still up for tonight? We can make it another night if you are too tired. I'd certainly understand if you prefer to do that," she said, giving Susan a way out if she wanted it.

"And miss the story of Kelly Cavanaugh? Not on your life! I wouldn't miss this for anything in the world." Susan stopped for a second. "Unless you are too tired, and *you* want to postpone dinner. If you're beat, I'd also understand."

"Listen to us... Jeez! No, I want you to come over for dinner tonight. If you'd still like to come, I'll pick you up after work. What time do you get off?" Susan's face took on a mischievous look, and Kelly hoped to remember to ask her what she was thinking.

"I'll get out of here at around six o'clock tonight. Does that work for you?" Susan asked.

"Six is great for me. I'm going to head out to the grocery store and pick up some last minute ingredients and then head on home. I may even have time for a quick siesta," Kelly said with a guilty smile.

"You big cheater! God, I'd give my left eye tooth for a nap right about now," Susan whined playfully.

"I'm sorry. How about some nice hot cocoa for you instead? It'll keep you warm and give you a sugar boost all in one." Handing her the steaming cup, she had to laugh at Susan's response.

"Oooh!" Susan squeaked. "Thank you so much! God, it's really cold today, this is just perfect. Thank you, Kelly. That was very sweet of you."

"Yeah, well, don't let that get around," she smirked.

"Don't worry." Susan smiled as she sipped her

cocoa. "Boy, this hits the spot."

"I'm glad. Listen, I don't mean to run off, but I've got some cooking to do for a very special friend of mine, so I've got to get going," she teased.

"Oooh, a special friend eh? What's she like?" Susan teased back.

"You'd hate her - she's hairy, she drools, and she chews with her mouth open," Kelly elaborated with a straight face.

"What?" Kelly could tell Susan was a bit confused. "I don't do that!"

"I know, but my dog, Mattie, does!" Kelly couldn't help but laugh at the bell ringer's incredulous expression. "You do like dogs, I hope," she continued.

"I love dogs. I had a few when I was living in the great outdoors. Many strays kept me warm at night. I welcome most four legged animals... well, except rats." Susan grimaced.

"Ew, I'm not big on them, either. Don't worry. She's a yellow lab that looks nothing like a rat." Kelly beamed. "All right, I'm gonna get going. I'm really looking forward to this evening, Susan."

"Good, so am I," the brown-eyed woman replied.

They chatted until Kelly was able to flag a cab. Waving as she got in the taxi, Kelly smiled a giddy smile. "Tonight is definitely going to be fun."

Chapter Six

"Pine and Churchill, please," Kelly said to the cabby.
"Yes, ma'am. I know the way. I take you many times before," the foreigner explained.
"Thank you."
She was really nervous about how the evening might go, hoping that her house wasn't going to be too overwhelming for Susan. *She's had such a hard life and my house isn't exactly small. I could fit six of her places into my house. She came from money, though, so hopefully she won't think I am trying to show off. That certainly isn't my intention.*
The cab pulled into her driveway and she got out and paid her dues, with a healthy tip for the driver.
"You live so close, miss, why you don't drive to work?" the driver asked.
"You've seen the cars on the street down there, right?" Kelly asked.
"Yes."
"So you've seen the condition of them, then."
"Yes."
"There isn't a parking garage near my office."
"I see," he agreed.
"Well, it's pretty obvious why I don't drive to work then," she smiled.
He smiled back and just nodded as she opened the garage with the remote on her key chain and her BMW came into view. "I see your point. I would take a cab, too."
"Good man. Thanks for the ride," she said as she paid him.
"Have a good day, miss." He waved with a wink.
"Thanks," she replied, walking through the garage

A Saving Solace

and into her house.

~~*~*~*~*

"Woof!"

"Hey, girl! How are you?" Kelly said, rubbing Mattie's head. "You have to go out?" she asked, knowing full well what the answer would be.

"Woof!"

"Come on, let's get out back." Kelly led her pup out the kitchen's back door.

Looking around the kitchen she took note, probably for the first time in a long while, of how large her home was. Having seen Susan's the night before made her realize how fortunate she was. Even after her mom had died, she hadn't had to worry about money. She'd inherited some, but her job paid well and it just wasn't a problem. Kelly had worked her way up the corporate ladder and made a bit more in salary with each rung that she reached. She counted her blessings; so many people never even made it *to* the ladder.

She watched Mattie running around without a care in the world; she was beautiful when she ran. *I wish I had a dog's life. What would there possibly be to worry about?*

When you are going to take your nap? the niggling voice provided.

I think I could handle that.

"Mattie! Stop digging!" Kelly shouted through the screen door.

The dog looked up at her like, 'oops, busted' and started running back towards the house. "Come on in here, girl." Kelly laughed at her expression. Some people would say that canines don't have expressions, but Mattie did. She'd smile, she'd frown, and she could even say 'fuck you' with her eyes, if she felt the need. That was usually around the time when Kelly would wake her from one of her naps to go out for the last time of the night. That was always amusing.

"Good girl, Mattie. Are we going to have company tonight? I'm going to introduce you to a wonderful woman named Susan. I think you're really going to like her," Kelly continued as she petted her baby. "She's blonde, just like you; and come to think of it, she has dark brown eyes like you, as well. No wonder I'm attracted to her." Kelly laughed as Mattie looked at her and rolled her eyes.

"Let's see what we need to get to put dinner together, okay?" she asked her tail-wagging friend, inspecting her cabinets for the ingredients for her Alfredo sauce. Scanning the refrigerator next, she saw that she needed whipping cream and more butter. Opening and closing three or four more cabinets, she found the pasta maker that her cleaning lady must have hidden. *I love her to death, but she likes things her way, and sometimes it makes me crazy when I can't find anything.*

She made a list of the things that she needed from the grocery, and grabbed her coat and keys. Mattie's tail stopped wagging when she realized her companion was leaving again.

Kelly rubbed the dog's head as she spoke. "It's okay, girl, I'll be back in less than half an hour, I promise." She walked into the garage, got into her car, and left for the store.

A Saving Solace

Chapter Seven

Preparing the last of the pasta, Kelly danced around the kitchen. The only thing left was the sauce and that needed to wait until they were ready to eat. She looked up at the clock and saw it was almost five thirty.

"Holy shit! I have to get ready and pick up Susan. Damn, time got away from me," she cursed as she ran from the kitchen upstairs to her bedroom and straight to her closet. She pulled on a pair of loose fitting jeans and a burgundy V-neck sweater, threw on some socks and her Doc Martens, and ran into the bathroom. She brushed her hair and teeth and applied a small amount of make up, looked at her flushed reflection and realized that she was actually nervous about the upcoming night.

What if she doesn't like me like that?
You mean, what if she does?
I don't know what I mean; I just know that I want her to spend time with me. I'm comfortable around her. I...
You like her.
Yes. I like her. So what?
So nothing. Just let things go at their own pace. You may find that you want her around for longer than a couple of nights.
No more matchmaker talk. I've gotta go, I'm gonna be late.

Kelly sprayed the tiniest mist of Picasso on her neck and ran back downstairs. She clicked off the stereo, grabbed her leather jacket and ran out the door to pick up her date.
Your date?
Yeah, my date. That's enough out of you. I mean it.

Oh, yes, ma'am.
She groaned, knowing that wouldn't be the end of the conversation. She just wished she knew when the talks with that annoying inner voice would end. She got in her BMW and backed down the driveway on her way to pick up Susan.

Driving towards town, Kelly's stomach was twisted in knots. She was quite nervous about Susan hearing her life story. She wasn't entirely sure how much she wanted to tell, but guessed that she'd find out soon enough.

Parking the car out in front of the ForOthers building, Kelly homed in on Susan's shining smile the minute she looked up. Getting out of the car, she walked over and greeted her with an answering smile. "Hey."

"Hi there," Susan replied with a large grin.

"I hope I didn't keep you waiting long. I got caught up with dinner preparations. How are you feeling?" Kelly asked.

"I'm feeling much better, now that I have the next couple days off," she said with a beaming smile.

"I'm with you there." Kelly motioned towards the car with her head. "Are you ready to go?"

"Absolutely! I'm really hungry. I can't wait to try out your culinary masterpiece," Susan teased.

"Trust me, you'll eat like you've never eaten before." Kelly paused, hoping that statement wasn't actually true. *Although it probably is, for the recent past anyway.*

"Well, what are we waiting for?" Susan asked excitedly as she got in the car.

"Me, I guess." Kelly laughed as she ran around the car to the driver's side.

They drove out of the uptown area and back

towards Kelly's house. Out of the corner of her eye, she quietly watched Susan eyeing the streets they passed, and wondered what she was thinking. "Penny for your thoughts," she said softly.

"My uh... my parents used to live around here. I was just wondering if they were still in my old house. I don't know why. I could really give two shits," she said with a bite in her voice.

I think she cares more than she wants to admit, but I don't want to go there right now. There's plenty of time to explore that. No need to ruin our night. "Oh, really?" she responded lamely.

"Yeah. If you took a right at this next road you'd be on my old street," she remarked with a notable sadness.

"Do you want me to drive down there? We don't have to stop, we can just drive by," Kelly suggested.

Susan was stunned by the suggestion and looked at Kelly with amazement. After they had almost passed the street, she squeaked out, "Could we?"

Without screeching the tires too badly, the driver managed to slow the car enough to make the turn. They drove down a lovely street, and Kelly was quite impressed with the houses they passed. "Which one is it?" she asked, unsure whether Susan would respond.

"It's two twenty. The mailbox is the little log cabin on the left."

Kelly heard her friend's breathing hitch as she slowed down for her to be able to see her childhood home. It was a beautiful house, almost qualifying as a mansion. *Her folks must have a lot of money.*

"It's a beautiful house, Susan." Kelly turned to find her passenger with tears in her eyes. "Oh, Susan, if I'd known this would make you cry, I never would've suggested we drive by. I'm so sorry," she said as she took Susan's hand, feeling an answering squeeze.

"I didn't think I would..." She paused. "I honestly

didn't know how I was going to react. It's been so long since I've thought about this house as my own, that I don't really know how I'm feeling at all," she admitted.

"I can understand that," Kelly said as they paused a bit longer to take a good look.

"Thank you."

"You're welcome, Susan. Let's leave any sad thoughts behind and go home." The words were out of Kelly's mouth before she could stop them.

She didn't seem to hear me.

Lucky you.

Go away!

Bitch.

Bite me.

"Kelly?" Susan's tiny voice intruded on Kelly's internal sparring match.

"Yes, sweetheart?" she said before she thought. *I've gotta stop doing that.*

"I really appreciate you taking me there. I've wanted to see the house for a while; I just didn't have nerve to go back. I guess I was afraid I'd see one of my parents and go off the deep end again," she admitted.

"Hey, don't worry about it. If I can help you work through that at all, please know that I'm here for you," Kelly said earnestly.

"Thank you... thank you for being my friend." Susan smiled, her eyes bright with unshed tears.

"You're very welcome. Now let's go eat!" Kelly said, trying to lighten the mood.

"I'm all for that. Drive on!" Susan gestured with her hands.

They drove the last couple of miles in comfortable silence. Kelly knew the rest of the night would be much easier for them once they got out of the car. Food was always something with which she could make people smile. She couldn't wait to see Susan's expression when

she took her first bite.
Bite of what?
Oh, for the love of Mary...

A Saving Solace

Chapter Eight

As they pulled up slowly into the driveway, Kelly could feel the tension in her passenger had subsided some. She was grateful that their little trip down memory lane hadn't been too upsetting for Susan. *I would've felt like total shit for upsetting her like that.* Turning off the engine, she faced her guest and smiled. "You ready to meet the other woman in my life?"

For a second, Susan looked at Kelly with uncertainty and then smiled back. "Yes. I forgot for a second who you were speaking about. I can't wait to meet... Mattie, was it?" Susan hazarded.

God, I love a woman with a good memory.

You just love a woman with big...

Don't say another word.

"Yes." She smiled back. "Her name's Mattie. You've a good memory."

"Yeah, well, I do my damndest." She fluttered her light brown lashes at Kelly, who almost sighed out loud.

"Let's go in, shall we?" Kelly suggested.

Susan smiled. "Lead the way."

Stepping out of the car, Kelly circled around to the passenger side. As Susan started to get out, Kelly reached for the door handle. "Hey, allow me." She smiled sweetly at Susan's surprised expression.

Susan bowed as she stood from the car. "Thank you, gracious lady."

They giggled like mischievous children and headed towards the door leading into the house. As the door was opened, wonderful smells from the kitchen filled her nostrils.

"Oh, that smells heavenly."

"I'm glad you think so. I can't wait for you to taste it," Kelly said with anticipation.

A Saving Solace

They heard the clickity clack of Mattie's nails on the wood floor as she approached. When the Labrador saw that her mistress had brought company, her tail started flailing around.

"Hey, girl! I told you I had someone I wanted you to meet!" Kelly said in her mommy voice as she scratched her pup behind the ears. "Susan, this is Mattie. Mattie, say hi to Susan."

"Hey there, girl, your momma's told me all about you. I'm so glad to meet you," Susan said as she let Mattie sniff her. As soon as Mattie sensed that Susan was all right, she rubbed against her as if she were a cat. Susan smiled and crouched lower to pet Mattie, unknowingly not a smart move on her part. Mattie thought that anything near the floor was fair game, so Susan went down and was assaulted by a wet, slimy tongue.

That unfortunately isn't mine. I can't believe I just thought that.

You know you meant it, too.

Go away!

"She's beautiful, Kelly." Mattie was clearly enjoying the attention; they both were.

"Thank you. You hear that, you big lug? She likes you. I guess your kisses helped." Kelly smiled at the two girls, hoping against hope that she too would get the opportunity to kiss that beautiful face.

Oh yeah, you're in trouble.

Stop!

Kelly shook her head as if to clear her thoughts, and remembered the sauce that needed to be made. "Would you like a tour of the kitchen? There's some wine in the refrigerator," she offered.

"That'd be lovely, thank you. Come on, girl, let's go see what your momma has conjured up in that kitchen of hers." Susan smiled as Mattie stayed at her side.

Traitor.
Yeah, but look who she gave you up for.
True. Now go away. Please?
Fine...
After the tour, the two went to relax in the family room and Kelly watched as Susan looked around appreciatively. The sunken room was Kelly's favorite part of the house. It held her entertainment center and a large leather pit group that had afforded her many nights of utter bliss in its comfort.

Susan smiled. "This room is beautiful, Kelly. I bet you spend most of your time in here. God knows I would."

"Yeah, it's my favorite room in the whole house. I've spent many nights on this couch. It swallows you up before you even have time to put up a fight," she laughed.

"So what can I help with? Is dinner nearly ready? It smells just wonderful," Susan commented.

"Well, I just have to finish the sauce, and the pasta is in its warmer, so I guess if you'd like to toss the salad, we'll be all set."

"I can do that. But first, how about that wine you mentioned." She waggled her eyebrows, and Kelly was unable to restrain a laugh.

"You looked absolutely adorable when you did that," she said, hoping Susan wouldn't be offended or embarrassed.

Her face flushed and her smile broadened as she shyly replied, "Thanks."

Heart lurching with emotion at that display, Kelly hoped that she could make it through dinner without choking or being busted for staring too long at her guest.

Susan tossed the salad with accomplished familiarity, and Kelly finished with the rest of the preparations then strolled into the dining room to put the finishing touches on their dining ambiance. Poking her head back into the kitchen, she asked, "Shall we eat?"

"Please. It has been torture for me to wait with all of this food around me." Susan chuckled and Kelly couldn't help but giggle along with her. Susan started towards the kitchen table, but Kelly stopped her and motioned towards the dining room right behind them.

"I thought it would be cozier to eat in here." She paused. "I hope you like it," she said, biting her lower lip in anticipation. Kelly watched Susan's face as she slowly walked towards the dining room doorway.

A small gasp escaped her lips as she saw the candles burning on the table, set intimately for two. "Wow... Kelly, this is beautiful. You didn't have to go to so much trouble... just for me," she said meekly.

Her hostess walked up behind her and whispered in her ear, "But I wanted to do this... just for you." She gestured at the table. "Please, take a seat." As she placed her hands on Susan's shoulders to direct her to her chair, Kelly felt a tremor run through the slight body. Whether it was voluntary or not, she was glad to know she wasn't the only one with a sea of feelings racing through her veins.

They sat down and Susan immediately dug into the pasta. Kelly watched her face as she seemed to savor her first bite with much passion. It was thoroughly arousing to watch her eat like that.

Susan closed her eyes and groaned with pleasure "Oh... my... God... I have never tasted anything like this before. Oh... Kelly..."

Kelly's heart raced as she heard Susan moaning her name. "So... you like it?" she joked, knowing full well what the response was going to be.

"Like? Oh, nononononono... It's way beyond that point. This is just obscene! This is the best pasta I've ever eaten. God, it just melts in your mouth." Her body and voice were getting extremely animated as she praised the food Kelly had made for her, and she proceeded to eat with gusto.

Seeing her so open and comfortable is something I could really get used to.

A Saving Solace

Chapter Nine

Dinner filled them completely and they sat with their empty plates in front of them for several minutes, waiting for the meal to start digesting.

"Oh, I can't move! I can't remember ever enjoying a meal so thoroughly. I have to say your gift for narration is exquisite," the chef joked.

"I'm sorry, Kelly. I've always had the gift of gab, especially when something affects me deeply. That food was incredible. Thank you again for going to so much trouble," Susan said, looking deeply into Kelly's eyes.

She grinned. "You're welcome. I'm very glad you liked it so much. I would've been afraid to ask you out again if you thought I might poison you with my culinary skills."

"No way; that was terrific. Would you mind if we went into the next room to sit for a bit? I'm feeling a little overstuffed," she admitted with a grin.

"Sure, I'll turn on the stereo and we can just relax with some music or whatever," Kelly suggested.

Susan nodded as she stood. "That sounds great. Should I worry about what music you have available?"

"No, I think you'll be all right. I have a wide variety, so if you'd feel better, you can make the selection," Kelly offered.

"Oh, no, I trust you. You go ahead. I think I need to visit the restroom, though. Could you give me directions?" Susan teased.

"Of course. Go down the hallway, and it's the second door on your left. I'll be in the family room," Kelly replied, as she started removing the dishes from the table.

"Oh, please, Kelly, let me help you clean up."

"Absolutely not! I'm not cleaning; I'm putting

dishes into the sink. That's all, I promise. I'm too full to do anything else," Kelly laughed.

"All right, I'll see you in a bit."

Kelly smiled. "Okay."

Watching Susan walk down the hallway, she continued to smile. She was really enjoying herself. It'd been a while since she had spent an evening with someone when she was thinking about more than just sex, allowing herself to *feel* anything.

After taking the last of the dishes and depositing them in the sink, Kelly went into the family room and crossed down to the stereo to decide what to listen to. She was a fool for the classics and old jazz, and hoped Susan liked them as well.

She turned on the stereo, then leaned back on the leather sofa and threw her feet up on the coffee table, feeling the food work its way through her body.

Susan returned from the bathroom to find Kelly with her eyes closed and resting, with Louie Armstrong coming from the stereo. He sang of green trees and red roses. *What a wonderful world indeed.*

"I haven't heard this song in so long. My parents loved old jazz," she said with a small smile.

"It doesn't bother you, does it? I can change it if you'd prefer," Kelly offered.

"No... it's fine. It just took me by surprise to hear it," she replied, sitting next to her on the sofa. She wriggled to get comfortable and her leg touched Kelly's. Neither woman moved away.

Kelly felt more comfortable with Susan than with anyone else in many years. *How does one person, who was no more than a stranger to me before yesterday, affect my emotions on such a deep level? I haven't felt this open and content with people I've known for much longer!*

"So, how long have you lived here, Kelly?" Susan

asked as she turned her head to look at her hostess' face.

"I've lived here almost two years. I moved here after I got my promotion to regional director."

"How exciting for you. You must really love what you do to take it to the level that you're at," Susan observed.

"Yes, I do. I've always loved working with people. Retail gives you more than one opportunity to do that." She chuckled. "I like the interaction. The perks that go with the position are pretty good, too." She waggled her eyebrows. Belatedly, she hoped that hadn't sounded like bragging. She hadn't invited Susan over to do that at all; and Kelly made a mental note to watch what she said about money.

It seemed as though her guest was okay with the comment, as she responded, "I can see that. This house is beautiful. I could bathe in the sink in your powder room," she laughed.

"I think I'd pay to see that," Kelly said out loud before she could stop herself. She realized she had no idea what reaction to expect from her friend.

"Would you?" Susan asked in a deep tone with her eyes focused on Kelly's.

Kelly found it very sensual. "Indeed I would," she said, not looking away at all. She matched the sensuality, and saw Susan's face redden as she turned away.

"So, how about telling me a bit more about you?" Susan requested, no longer meeting Kelly's gaze as the coloring of her face went back to normal.

"Ah yes, this was the Kelly show tonight, right?" She laughed quietly.

"Yes, that was the plan. I think I shared enough with you last night to warrant some insight into your life. What do you think?" Susan timidly raised her gaze to Kelly's.

The older woman nodded slowly and thought about

where to start. Leaning over to grab her wineglass off of the coffee table, she took a sip to moisten her suddenly dry mouth. "Well, what part would you like to hear about: my mom's death; my dad's departure; my love life or lack thereof? Actually, I used to have a string of love lives; perhaps you'd like to hear about that one? Pick a topic, any topic," she said, a brittle tone behind her playfulness.

Susan looked up into Kelly's eyes and took her hand. "It hurts you a lot to talk about those things, doesn't it?"

Susan's eyes were burning into her, she couldn't look away. She had known the street-wise woman was perceptive, but had not realized to what extent. "Yes," she whispered. "How did...?"

She spoke softly. "Anyone that makes light of things that serious tends to have a lot of pain behind the smile they show."

God, she's amazing. It's no wonder I'm drawn to her.

She's got your number, all right.

"Well, I guess I can give you a bit of everything. It all pretty much makes me who I am today." She rubbed Susan's fingers softly and threw some perception back at her. "You are very strong willed, Susan. Not many would call me on my cover-up like that; you didn't even flinch."

"I'm used to people with sadness in their lives. I see it every day, Kelly. And just like with them, I'd like to do whatever I can to help you; if you want me to, that is." She offered services the more affluent woman wasn't exactly sure she needed.

"What makes you think...?" she started.

"That you need help? I'm not saying that you do. I'm just offering an ear...and perhaps a shoulder. I bet you haven't entrusted your confidences to many, especially not about subjects like these," she guessed.

"There was one..." Kelly began. She couldn't believe she was about to talk about such an abhorrent topic. She had sworn she would never breathe that particular name again.

Susan's grip tightened around her fingers and Kelly was helpless to fight off the gentle gaze.

"We met at a work conference about seven years ago. Her name was Julie Adams. We both worked for Maxine's and were both moving up the same corporate ladder. We clicked immediately. We spent many hours that week just talking after meetings and such. We even stayed a few extra days in the hotel just to hang out and talk. I thought that I had truly met the other half of my soul. I know now that I was severely mistaken." She paused to take another gulp of wine. "I opened up to her more than I had with anyone in my life. I told her things that no one else knew. I told her about my mom, my dad... She even held me as I cried, retelling the stories. God, what a fool I was," Kelly said bitterly.

Susan's eyes never faltered. "What happened?"

"She fucked me, literally and figuratively... and yes, in that order," she said angrily.

Susan flinched. "I'm sorry, Kelly. How um... did she..."

"The figurative part?" When Susan nodded, she continued. "We'd become lovers only four days after meeting, but we knew our relationship was going to be hard. There were work ethics that were being compromised since we were heading towards the same ultimate goal. I told her that I didn't want to relinquish what we'd started, so I'd keep my mouth to myself, so to speak, and she agreed to do the same. Hell, I was in love with her! There wasn't much I wouldn't have done for her. The company wasn't very sympathetic to the 'gay element' working for them at the time, so we were discreet and pretty much kept our relationship a secret. I'd have her over to my house every once in a while, but she said she had a roommate that was against our relationship, so we never hung out at her place. She would just come over when her schedule allowed, and we'd make the most of our time together.

"We had been together almost a year when our next conference came up. I requested that we be roommates again. People used to do that all the time with people they knew within the company. Nothing's worse than spending four days with a complete stranger in a hotel room." Susan managed a tiny grin. "So, when I arrived in Seattle and walked into my hotel room, I was surprised when I found someone else there and not Julie. I looked at the woman and asked where Julie was or whether there had been a mistake, blah blah blah, and she said it was her room assignment and we were, in fact, roommates.

"I went down to the concierge of the hotel and asked which room Julie was staying in and whether she'd arrived yet. She hadn't, so I waited in the lobby for her. About an hour or so passed and I was getting antsy and very hungry, so I decided to get something to eat in the restaurant of the hotel while I awaited her arrival.

"I walked into the bar area, where I spotted her on a bar stool. As I approached her, I saw a man walk up and kiss her quite passionately." Kelly paused as she felt the same lurching in her gut as she had back then. Susan's fingers caressed her hand as she tried to compose herself. "Kelly looked at Susan with that long-ago disbelief in her eyes. "I thought I was going to throw up. I didn't quite know what to do. I watched their interaction a little bit longer, then left the bar area altogether."

"Did she see you?" Susan asked softly.

"No, she was a little distracted at the time," Kelly

answered. "I didn't say a word to her until later that night. There was an awards ceremony that evening. She showed up dressed to the nines, escorted by the guy from the bar. She was beaming until she saw me staring at her. She took one look at me and winked," Kelly said, feeling the emotions beginning to build.

"She winked at you? What the hell was that about?" Susan asked, a bit annoyed on her behalf.

"At first I wasn't sure what it meant. Later in the evening, I found out full well. In that intervening year, I'd been coaching her on her job skills and did everything I could for her. I was so over my head in love, I couldn't see the daylight in front of me. She really wanted to move up in the company, and I was going to do everything in my power to help her accomplish that. These award ceremonies were to showcase new talent or up and coming promotion opportunities, and so forth. I'd been up for the regional position and I knew it. They announced their candidates for the position. I wasn't on the list, but Julie was,"

"No fucking way! I can't believe that!" Susan exclaimed.

"It's true. Not only did she use my knowledge to move up in the company, but for the entire year she'd also been lying to me about her marital status. The guy on her arm was her husband. He had come to escort his lovely, *successful* wife to the dinner. It was the only event which the company invited spouses to attend. It suddenly became clear to me why we could never hang out at her place, or God forbid, pick her up from her home. I never once stepped foot into her home!" Kelly spat.

"Jesus! I can't believe her!"

"I'm not finished. The worst thing about all of it was, she lied to our vice president and said I'd been hitting on her to get where *I* was. It wouldn't do to have a gay regional director, you know." Kelly silenced Susan's outrage with a finger on her lips. "They believed her. I'd been their hardest worker for almost five years, and yet they believed this woman who'd been with the company for only two years, because she had what I didn't - she had an acceptable social lifestyle.

"I couldn't believe what she had done to me, after everything we'd been through. I never thought I'd want to hear the words 'I love you' ever again. She hurt me so badly on so many levels with those words, I just didn't know what to do next." She sighed and collected herself, wiping the now falling tears from her face.

"Here." Susan handed her a Kleenex from the box on the end table.

"Thanks." She blew her nose and took a deep breath.

"How could you work for a company that showed you no support whatsoever? You knew that what Julie told them was not what happened."

"Yes, but I wanted to have them hear my side before I made my final judgment about my bosses. Luckily for me, Julie fucked up big time before I had that talk with my supervisors. I was going to go under the lamp with Human Resources, too, because hitting on co-workers is not allowed, especially if it's an unwelcome advance. You know, the old sexual harassment?" Susan nodded. "Luckily for me, Julie herself inadvertently proved to everyone that she was a liar, so I never had to take a stand on that."

"What happened?" Susan asked, truly involved with the tale.

"The next week we were supposed to submit our figures for the upcoming year. I had implemented a plan in my area that was going to be considered for company-wide use. It's a huge accomplishment if corporate chooses one of your ideas to roll out within the entire company. I knew that my proposal had a very good chance of becoming that next 'new idea'. The day after I sent in my plan, my boss called me in to talk about it. I was really excited, so I sped right over to headquarters to see if my initiative was going to be considered. I sat in his office and he sat at his desk with a neutral expression on his face.

~~*~*~*

"Jack? Is there something wrong?"

"Yes, Kelly, unfortunately something is very wrong."

"Well, what is it? We don't pull punches with each other, what's going on?" Kelly asked bluntly, as she always had with him.

"I've been told something very disconcerting about your labor plan," Jack said, steepling his fingers together.

"What do you mean?" she asked, bridling at what was sounding like an accusation.

"My source tells me that you stole this idea from another leader in our division," he stated clearly.

"What? You cannot be serious, Jack!" Kelly's temper was rising quickly. "You've known me for five years! I've done nothing but help this company out however possible. It's bad enough I got passed over because of some lies, but now I'm being accused of stealing my own idea? I just want to get this straight," Kelly barked back at him. "Whose idea is this, supposedly?"

"The accusations in your outburst are directly related to what I'm talking about. You're angry with Julie since we decided to go with her as regional director instead of you. Now you've stolen one of her ideas to make yourself look better!"

A Saving Solace

Whose dick is she impaling herself on now? *Kelly thought. I think I'm looking at her latest victim.* "Jack, can I ask you a question?" she asked.

"Of course." His smile was not genuine.

"Where are the plans we sent you? Are they still on e-mail, or have you printed them out?"

"I haven't printed anything. I wanted to get down to the bottom of this before I gave anyone a hard copy of the proposal," he explained.

"Believe me, I welcome the opportunity to help you get to the truth of the matter. Where is Ms. Adams now? Is she nearby?" Kelly was smug; she knew she was going to derive a great deal of satisfaction from the outcome of the impending confrontation.

"Actually, she's in the building. I brought you both here to question you about this," he answered.

"Good. Bring her in here, now," she demanded.

His eyes went wide with surprise. "What?"

"I said, bring her in here now. I think I'll have your answer for you in a few minutes if you'll do me the courtesy," Kelly responded sweetly.

"Fine." He reached to his intercom and instructed his secretary to send Ms. Adams in.

Shortly thereafter, Julie strode cockily into his office and sat next to Kelly without even looking in her direction. "Hi, Jack, you wanted to see me?" Julie smiled confidently.

"Yes. I wanted you both here to get to the bottom of this discrepancy," he stated carefully, though his eyes gave him away.

Bastard, Kelly *thought.*

"Fine. What would you like to know?"

"First off, I want to know whether you can prove that Kelly stole this idea from you and not the other way around," Jack said with an encouraging smile.

"I just figured my numbers would speak for

themselves here. *My department's costs have gone down considerably with this plan of mine. How else could that have happened?"* she responded innocently.

"*How about by my coaching you for the last year? How about that, Julie! You'd never be where you are right now if I hadn't helped you!*" Kelly continued to present her case. "*My numbers are even better than yours!*" she finished, knowing her argument was going to net her no results.

"*Oh, Kelly, come on. A few helpful tips don't change things the way my labor development plan has. It's bad enough I had to deal with all of your advances during -*"

Kelly had had quite enough. It was time to play her trump card. "*Jack, let me ask you one question. What is my signature on every document that I send you via e-mail?*" She watched Julie shift uncomfortably in her chair.

Jack's eyes got as wide as saucers as the import of what she was saying to him sank in.

"*Print them,*" she snarled.

Jack turned to his computer and brought up Kelly's file, then brought up Julie's. He printed out both documents and instantly Kelly knew she had won.

"*What do you see, Jack?*"

Come on, I need to see her goddamned face! Kelly thought triumphantly.

"*Yes, Jack, what do you see?*" Julie asked nervously.

"*Kelly's watermark,*" he said, defeated.

"*Her what?*" Julie shouted.

"*My watermark, you lying piece of -*" Kelly stopped her words before she couldn't contain all she wanted to say to Julie. She threw the document in Julie's face and watched her stare at the page, knowing she was soon going to be out of a job. "*I put a watermark on every* document I send so that there's no mistake about who it belongs to. When you so lovingly stole that file from my computer, you took it in all its glory," Kelly gritted through bared teeth. "I hope you had fun during your brief fling at the top, or should I say 'on top'?" She whispered the last part in Julie's ear with controlled anger.

Redirecting herself to Jack, Kelly said, "I demand that a full investigation take place. I'll be calling Human Resources immediately to start the inquiry." She turned her head to look at Julie's forlorn face. It made her happy to see justice happen at her own hand.

"Bitch," Kelly whispered.

"I will call a meeting first thing in the morning. As for you, Ms. Adams, you are suspended until further notice. You may leave," he said as she stood without saying a word and quietly left the room.

"Yes!" Kelly muttered, mentally pumping her fist.

"I can't believe she did that to you. She really wasn't a nice person," Susan added as Kelly finished her walk down memory lane.

"Yeah, she was a peach all right. Even better, the company didn't approve of Jack's involvement with Julie, so he was terminated as well. When his position came open, there was a regional director's chair up for the taking. I didn't get it, though," she revealed.

"What? After all of that crap you'd gone through, they didn't even have the decency to promote you?" Susan asked, unbelieving.

"No, but I got a full apology from the vice president, the president, and all of my colleagues that had known that I would never have behaved in such an unprofessional fashion. And this time, I knew the person they did hire for the job, and she was more than qualified for the spot. I worked very closely with her and learned a lot more than I'd thought I needed to. They were right in not promoting me at the first opportunity; I really wasn't ready. I stayed in the field for another few years, and doing this job now, I know it was wise of them to wait. All in all, it was a very good learning experience for me. I learned a lot about my peers, and a lot more about how not to give away my heart. It hurt too badly when it was broken," she whispered.

Susan took both of Kelly's hands in hers and raised them to her lips and gently kissed her knuckles. "I'm so sorry that happened to you. There's been no one since Julie?" she asked gently.

"Well... that leads into a different tale. I've had plenty of companionship; let's just leave it at that. We talked about one night stands last night, right?" Kelly gazed into Susan's eyes.

"Yes, I remember. Is that what your life turned into - nights filled with faceless, nameless bed mates?" Susan asked with a sad smile.

It sounds better the way she says it. Most everything does. "Yeah, it's been that way for several years now. I just can't give my heart away again... I can't... " Kelly stuttered, knowing if they talked about the subject any longer she would start crying uncontrollably.

"I know it's hard, believe me. My own parents turned their backs on me. My heart hasn't healed from that experience, either. I am so thankful we've become friends, Kelly. I feel quite safe when I'm with you. And I haven't felt safe in a very long time," she said gently as she squeezed Kelly's hands, holding them comfortingly in her lap.

One of Kelly's favorite songs was filtering from the speakers. The violins began, and she instantly knew she wanted to hold the younger woman in her arms. "Would you dance with me, Susan?" she asked as she stood from the couch and urged her companion gently to her feet.

Susan smiled uncertainly and nodded as Kelly led her into the open area of the family room. She held one hand and placed the other on Kelly's shoulder, while Kelly's arm went instinctively around her waist. Susan looked into caring blue eyes and felt herself falling. *At last...*

They swayed to the music and slowly began to circle the room in tiny steps. Being in each other's arms felt wonderful. After a bit, Kelly pulled Susan closer and she welcomed the close embrace. Gentle hands caressed; scents were intoxicating, causing their breathing to hitch. Beyond the sharing of their most intimate feelings, something had changed between them.

Susan and Kelly glided across the floor as if they'd danced together a thousand times before. Etta James was singing their emotions. Kelly knew the person in her arms would never hurt her the way she'd been hurt before. She knew with all of her heart that she'd finally found what she was looking for. *At last...*

Chapter Ten

At last, indeed. God, I haven't felt this way in... Well, I can't remember, it's been so long. Kelly crawled into my heart so quickly I didn't even have time to tack up that 'Keep Out' sign. *Not that I would've.*
Nor would I have let you. Kelly's the one for you, Susan.
You may be right. I don't think I've ever felt this safe and right with any other person.
Looking into the bluest eyes in the world, Susan realized she had most definitely missed a question. "I'm sorry, Kelly. What did you say?" she stuttered.
"I asked if you would like to sleep here tonight. I have a guest room that you are more than welcome to use, unless you'd be more comfy at home," Kelly asked shyly.
She is absolutely beautiful. I can't feel my tongue.
"I... I would... um..." Susan couldn't believe she couldn't form an answer.
"Hey, forget it. I was just wondering. I don't want you to be uncomfortable in any way. I can take you home, Susan." Kelly looked like a child being reprimanded for asking something she shouldn't have.
"Kelly, wait. I didn't mean to... That is, I wasn't going to say no." Catching Kelly's surprised expression, Susan nodded and continued. "Really. I guess the offer kind of took me by surprise; I wasn't expecting it." Susan took Kelly's hand as they turned the music down and headed back to the couch. They sat down, Susan putting their hands in her lap. "I'd rather stay here. I'm sure your bed is going to be much more comfy than my sleeper sofa."
Kelly blushed. "*My* bed?" she asked softly.
"Oh crap, I didn't mean yours, per se, I just

meant..." Susan could feel her face getting hot and brighter red with each passing second. "I just meant here, with you, or, I mean, in your house... Ugh!" She put her head in her hands, determining to just be quiet for the rest of the evening.

Kelly's soft chuckle made Susan look up into the stunning face. She had a smile that could brighten the dullest of days. "My God, you're beautiful, Kelly. I know how often you've probably heard that in your life, but it's the God's honest truth." Susan felt her hands sweating, and knew Kelly could probably feel her nervousness.

"Yeah, I suppose I've heard that a time or two, but quite frankly, it never really mattered to me how people saw me. Not until now." Kelly paused and turned to face her companion. "You make me care about how I look. I want to be this way for you. Who wouldn't want to be beautiful for you?" Kelly asked in a husky voice, stroking Susan's cheek with her knuckles.

Each caress of her face made Susan's heart beat faster, each word heightening the emotion coursing through her. She dove into blue pools and before she knew it, their lips had come together in a brush of tenderness. It was a short, chaste kiss, but what followed packed a whole lot more. They kissed again, this time more passionately and with an urgency that couldn't be denied. Their tongues danced with their own private rhythm to music all their own. As they parted, Susan could see the smoldering desire in Kelly's eyes.

Kelly's lips tingled from the contact. *God, she is good at that.* "Wow, that was... incredible," she whispered.

Gooseflesh instantly broke out on Susan's body as she felt the warm breath near her ear. "Yeah... it was." She was quite pleased to have formed a coherent sentence.

Kelly nuzzled against Susan's neck and placed tender kisses along her jaw line. "You don't have to stay, if you don't want," she said in a low, sexy voice.

"I want," Susan said, her own tone low. She wasn't exactly sure what it was that she wanted; she just knew she wanted to stay the night.

"So do I," Kelly agreed as she continued her sensual assault on Susan's ear, who moaned in response. Their lips met again, and with each passing moment Kelly could feel her body responding, felt herself slipping out of control. Her heart raced faster than it ever had in her life. She wanted to possess Susan. Her hands wrapped around the slim waist and pulled the smaller body harder against her. Feeling Susan groan into her mouth sparked an intense wave of arousal in her belly.

"Oh, Kelly," Susan sighed, her body on fire. "You feel so incredible."

Kelly's hands started to roam down Susan's sides and outlined the sides of her breasts. Susan instinctively arched into the touch. Their bodies shifted so that most of Kelly was lying on top of Susan. She cradled Susan's shoulders with her arms and slid her leg between those under her.

"Oh!" Susan gasped.

"Mmm." Kelly groaned into Susan's ear as she began to slowly move against her, willing legs involuntarily wrapping around the probing thigh.

Susan could feel her center throbbing with need. *Oh, this is amazing! This is heaven! This is... too soon! I don't think I'm ready yet! Dammit!* Her thoughts raced through her head, stealing all of her pleasure away. "Wait!" she gasped, breaking their connection.

"Is everything all right, Susan?"

The concern that she saw in Kelly's eyes was enough to melt her heart. "I'm sorry, Kelly. As much as I want this with you, I don't think that I'm ready to jump right now. I'm so sorry." She looked away from the steady blue gaze, unable to bear the disappointment they were certain to show. Susan could feel the stinging of tears welling.

"Hey," Kelly whispered, gently cupping Susan's chin and turning her head to look into her eyes. "Baby, if you're not ready, then we'll wait. There's no need for you to be sorry; I'm glad that you stopped me. I would never want to make love with someone unless they really wanted to. Especially not with you, Susan. I know how much you've been through. I never want you to feel pressured by me, for anything. Especially this." She kissed Susan gently on the lips.

Susan smiled into deep blue orbs. "Thank you, Kelly. You're wonderful. What did I ever do to deserve you?"

"I should be the one asking that question." Kelly smiled and started to move her body from Susan's.

"Wait." She exhaled deeply as Kelly stopped and looked at her in confusion. Susan swallowed nervously. "Can I have one more kiss?" She was unsure as to whether she'd want to, hoping Kelly wouldn't think she was a tease, but needing to feel her again.

"You never have to ask that, Susan. I'll kiss you whenever you want." Kelly smiled and slowly brought her lips down in a soul searing, heart stopping kiss that took Susan's breath away.

"Wow... I can't wait for stage two," Susan sighed, hearing Kelly chuckling as she sat up. Susan sat up, as well, and ran her hands down her top to straighten it. She felt Kelly's breath against her ear.

"I can guarantee it'll be well worth waiting for," she whispered, sending gooseflesh down Susan's body.

I don't doubt that.
You can say that again.

Chapter Eleven

Kelly's heart was thumping just thinking about the contact she and Susan had shared, not believing what had almost happened. In a way, her bad side still really wanted it to happen; the grown up, more responsible and caring side was glad they'd stopped.
God, I wanted her. I still want her.
Bad.
"Would you like some more wine?" Kelly asked, trying to break the frustrated tension that hung between them.
"I'd better not." She looked up shyly at her hostess. "How about some tea?" she suggested, stifling a yawn.
"Sure, I can do that. Besides, I think we still have some talking to do." *I can't believe I just said that.*
Susan smiled. "Yeah, I was hoping you'd continue. I just didn't want to push any more tonight."
"Don't worry, talking will give me something else to do with my mouth," Kelly replied with a wink as she got up to go into the kitchen.
Kelly heard Susan laughing at her retreating form, and took a deep cleansing breath as she entered the kitchen. She knew the rest of the evening wasn't going to be nearly as fun as it could've been. *What was it my grandma always said to me?*
There's always going to be time for that later.
Smiling at the words, Kelly thought, *I need to call her. Her advice is always so priceless.* "You want green tea?" she shouted into the family room.
"Yeah, that'd be great."
Kelly put the water on the stove to boil. Even though she had most amenities known to a kitchen, Kelly thought water for tea should always be made using the teakettle; the coffee maker should only be used for

coffee.

Call me strange, I'm not sure if I'm ready to talk about the loss of my mom. That pain is still pretty raw. She knew that Susan would hear that story one day, she just wasn't sure she wanted to go down that road yet. She'd already spoken of Julie, which she really hadn't thought would happen ever again, but there she was - spouting away like there was no tomorrow. And Susan was so comforting and understanding about that whole situation. It was little wonder she could help people. Her soft eyes told you that you could trust her; she'd listen and she'd care. She'd make you feel as if she were there with you through it all. *That's a heart you don't find in many people. It's a heart I hope to win one day soon.*

Kelly reluctantly admitted to herself that Susan already had hers. *I never would have dreamed that I'd give it to her so quickly. Who knew that she'd have such an effect on me?*

You did, you big idiot. You knew it from the first moment you saw her ringing that bell.

Yeah, well, shoot me.

Don't tempt me.

Kelly sat and argued with herself until she heard the squealing of the teakettle. She put the kettle and cups on a tray with the tea and headed back into the family room.

"Here we are..." She stopped abruptly when she looked down into an angelic sleeping face. Susan had drifted to sleep on the couch with Mattie happily curled below her feet. Kelly melted, this woman having officially turned her into a marshmallow.

She didn't care one bit.

Returning the tray to the kitchen, Kelly considered that she should put her charge to bed, but was reluctant to wake her. *God, she looked so at peace. I'm sure she didn't always look like that while she slept. If she slept at all while she was on the streets. I only pray that I can keep her face looking like it does right now.*

Mattie looked up and thumped her tail against the couch as Kelly came back in. "Hi, sweetie, did we wear out our guest?" she asked, scratching the dog behind the ears. Mattie rubbed harder against the pleasuring hand. Kelly laughed at her antics and gave one final scratch before moving to wake Susan.

Leaning down, she brushed a few stray hairs away from Susan's face, her fingers caressing the cheek. She felt Susan move into her touch. *Even asleep, she responds to me. She is truly a find.* Kelly guiltily continued her touches until she felt her own body pleading its fatigue. She covered her mouth as a yawn escaped, then cupped Susan's cheek while attempting to wake her.

"Susan, sweetheart, wake up. It's time to go to bed," she said softly. There was no response.

Oh boy.

"Susan? Wake up, honey," Kelly said a little louder, as she moved her fingers tenderly across Susan's cheek.

She stirred and smiled into the touch.

"That's it. Wake up, baby. I'll put you to bed in a much softer place. I promise you'll find it much more comfortable," Kelly continued.

"Mmm... I like it here. S'warm," she mumbled softly. Her eyes flickered, then opened fully. Those beautiful brown eyes stared up at Kelly. At first they were uncertain of where they were, and looked a little scared.

"Shhh..." Kelly tried to soothe her panic. "Hey, sleepyhead, let me show you to your room,"

"Oh, Kelly, I'm so sorry. I can't believe I fell asleep! I'm so embarrassed!" she said, scrubbing her face with her hands.

"Hey, don't worry about it. I told you, this couch has no shame," Kelly chuckled.

"You weren't kidding. It totally sucked me in." Susan smiled sleepily and yawned.

"Well, as comfy as this couch is, it doesn't hold a candle to the bed. Come on, I'll show you the way." Kelly offered her hand. When Susan took it, Kelly guided her up onto her feet. She stretched while Kelly turned off the lights and the stereo.

"Are you sure it's no trouble for me to stay here, Kelly?" Susan asked.

"I wouldn't have offered if I didn't want your company. Besides, it'll be like a slumber party. God knows I haven't had one of those in years!" she chuckled.

"Slumber party, eh? The ones I went to always had all of us sleeping in the same room and laughing and talking until dawn." Susan smiled at the memory.

"We could do that if you wanted. I mean - if you want to share a bed with me," Kelly said, watching for her reaction.

For a long heartbeat, there was no response, then Susan smiled. "If you promise not to steal all the covers, you've got yourself a deal," she agreed, trying to stifle another yawn.

"From the looks of you, talking until dawn is out of the question, but it'll still be nice to sleep with you. Uh... if... if you're all right with that. I mean, I don't want to scare you or make you uncomfortable. We've already talked about this, so when I say 'sleep with you', I do mean sleep," Kelly assured her. "I'd just really like to hold you tonight," she confessed.

"I'd like that too, Kelly," Susan admitted shyly. "Very much."

"All right then." She smiled. "Let me get Mattie outside one last time, and then I'll show you where my room is. Okay?"

"Sure thing."

Kelly let Mattie out and the Lab decided to cooperate for once. Nighttime was usually her time for mischief; Kelly never expected her to come in until half the yard was dug up, perhaps figuring that Kelly couldn't see her in the dark. Luckily, on this particular evening, she did her business and made her way to the back door without tearing up the lawn.

"Good girl! You deserve a reward for that," Kelly commended as she walked to the cabinet and pulled out a treat.

Mattie eagerly took the rawhide and trotted towards the stairs leading to the master bedroom. She had a tendency to prance when she got a treat. She knew she'd done something right to get it, and she'd be damned if she wasn't going to show it off.

Feeling more content than she ever had in her life, Kelly took Susan's hand and led her towards the stairs, realizing that Susan was filling a chasm in her life that had been present for far too long. *I don't think I could ever convey to her how precious she has become to me. I couldn't find the words.*

As they walked into the master suite, Susan scanned the room with approval. "Kelly, this room is beautiful! God, your room is as big as my whole apartment!"

"I'm glad you like it. I hope..." Kelly looked at her guest, took both of her hands, and faced her. "I really hope you know that I didn't bring you here to um... be pretentious or anything. I know things have been hard for you the last few years and - "

Susan placed a finger on Kelly's lips to stop her ramblings. "Kelly, I know you're not like that, and believe me, I can tell. I've been around enough people that think their shit doesn't stink. You're nothing like them. You invited me here to see you, not to be impressed by the things you have. For that, I'm grateful, because I've had such a wonderful time tonight. I haven't danced in ages. In forever, I think. The last person I danced with was my father..."

She paused and sighed deeply. "Anyway, thank you for starting to say what you did, even though it wasn't necessary. You're not a fake, Kelly. You're an incredible woman, and I'm really proud to call you my friend."

Kelly was speechless, once again amazed by Susan's insight. All she could do was inch closer and pull Susan into her arms. Their bodies fit together perfectly, and felt so right. She rested her chin on the top of her head and took a deep breath. Susan's hair smelled like sunshine. That analogy made her smile. Only one other person had ever smelled like sunshine, and that was her mother. *I wonder if she sent her to me.*

Was she a gift, Momma? If she was, I really can't thank you enough. God, I miss you.

Kelly's eyes shed tears over which she had no control. She felt so vulnerable around Susan, but she'd never felt safer. She knew this woman would never hurt her, that she could be trusted with anything or anyone.

Susan heard Kelly sniffle and slowly pulled out of her embrace. "Kelly?" She looked up and noted the tears. "Sweetheart, why are you crying?" she asked as she brushed away a few tears with her thumbs.

"I'm sorry, Susan. I was holding you and I um... smelled your hair. It smelled like sunshine." She smiled a watery smile. "My mom was the only other person that I can say that about. I guess it just sparked something inside of me and I was missing her. It happens every once in a while. She was the world to me. When I was a kid, I thought she hung the moon," Kelly explained in a voice that was barely above a whisper.

"Oh, sweetheart, I can totally understand that. Never apologize for missing your mom. And even though you haven't told me much about her, I know that you loved her very much." Susan pulled Kelly back against her. "You can cry on my shoulder whenever you feel like it."

"Thanks, I really appreciate that. I haven't had anyone that I could share this with, other than my grandmother. It's nice to talk about my mom with someone else. I'd like to tell you more about her one day. I know she would've liked you a lot." *Like I do.*

"Do you see her often, your grandma?" Susan asked.

"Only once in a while. We've kind of drifted apart. She and I used to talk frequently, but she lost a lot too when Mom died. Maybe it hurts her too much to see me, I honestly don't know. I don't like to push her. She's a sweet lady. Funny as hell, too." Kelly smiled at the thought of her quick humor and one-liners.

"Kelly? Can we continue this, there?" Susan shyly pointed to the bed. "I'm a little chilly."

"Yeah, sure. Let me get you something comfy to sleep in." Kelly smiled and walked over to the armoire and opened the pajama drawer. She pulled out a pair of flannel bottoms and a long sleeved T-shirt. "Will you be warm enough in this, or would you like something else?"

She shook her head. "Oh, that's fine. I may even be a little too warm in that, but let's give it a shot."

"I have boxers, too, if you'd rather," Kelly offered.

"You know what? I like that idea better. I never could understand pants in bed. My sheets would always wrap around my clothed legs and I'd feel like I was trapped." She grinned and shrugged. "Thanks," Susan said as Kelly handed her the clothing.

"Sure. The bathroom is in there." She pointed to the door. "And there are new toothbrushes in the cabinet.

Feel free to use whichever color you like," her hostess offered.
"Again, thanks. Your hospitality is absolutely wonderful." Susan stood on her tiptoes and kissed Kelly's cheek before she sauntered into the bathroom to get ready for bed.
Kelly grabbed another pair of boxer shorts and a short-sleeved T-shirt to wear to bed. If she wore anything too warm at night, she'd get nightmares. And she had no desire to provide additional fuel to her overly active dreamscapes; they were scary enough on their own.

~~*~*~*~*

Susan marveled at the bathroom that was three times the size of the powder room downstairs. The place was just incredible. The bathtub had whirlpool jets and looked like it could seat at least four. *Not even my parents had a tub like that.*
Opening the medicine cabinet, she found several toothbrushes, and indeed they were in different colors.
Have lots of overnight guests, Kelly?
Oh, jealousy isn't a good look on you, darlin'.
I'm not jealous! Besides, she said she had quite a checkered past. I also believe she said that those days are over. Maybe she's just planning ahead so she doesn't have to rush out to buy a spare.
Are you trying to convince yourself or me, Suze?
Oh, shut up. Please?
She took the wrapper off the toothbrush and found some toothpaste. Looking at her reflection as she cleaned her teeth, she began to giggle at her appearance. Kelly's clothes were at least three sizes too big for her, but they smelled like her; therefore, it was all good. Susan spat the last of the toothpaste down the drain and

wiped her mouth on the towel hanging on the rod next to the vanity. She felt her heart go out to the woman in the next room. *She must've loved her mom a great deal. I wonder if she'll tell me what happened.*
Don't push, Susan. She'll tell you when she's ready. You've taken years to work through a lot of your issues; maybe she needs a bit more time before she can tell all.
For once, you're right. Thank you. Now, goodnight.
Goodnight, Susan.
She walked out of the bathroom to find Kelly pulling up her boxers and smiling shyly at her. Susan felt avid eyes taking in her body, and the gaze burned her flesh.
"Wow, you look absolutely adorable. You look better in my clothes than I do."
"Yeah, but I bet you look better out of them." Hearing herself say that out loud, Susan felt her ears turn red. *I can't believe I said that.*
Kelly's chuckling was her only response as she moved closer. Her head bent down to lightly touch Susan's and she whispered softly, "I very much doubt that. But ohh... I can't wait to find out who's right," she purred seductively in Susan's ear before she made her way to the bathroom.
Susan felt eyes on her back and slowly turned around to see if she was right. She saw Kelly wink and smile before she closed the door.
She's going to kill me. She's definitely going to kill me. "Whoa..." She exhaled breathily. "This is going to get more and more interesting, isn't it, Mattie?" she whispered to the dog, who was looking at her with the partly chewed rawhide sticking out of her mouth. Her tail thumped against the bed in agreement, and then she went back to work on her treat.

"Thanks, pal. You've been very insightful," Susan snickered at the beast on the floor.

Now that the internal heat had died down a bit, she was starting to feel chilly again, and decided to get into bed. She walked to the bathroom door and knocked quietly. "Hey, Kelly, which side do you sleep on?" she asked through the door.

"The right," Kelly mumbled through her toothpaste filled mouth.

"'Kay, thanks."

Susan crossed to the left side of the bed and turned down the sheets and comforter. She climbed between the cool sheets, feeling more at home in this bed than she did in the one at her own apartment. Kelly's scent was everywhere and it was a comfort to her. She decided that she liked that. A lot.

Chapter Twelve

Kelly came out of the bathroom to find her guest snuggling into the blankets on her bed. It warmed her heart, not to mention other parts of her anatomy. Susan looked up at her and smiled. She couldn't help but smile back. "Comfortable?" Kelly asked.

Susan smiled sleepily. "Oh, Kelly, I can't tell you the last time I've laid in a bed this comfy. It's heaven. Thank you for asking me over."

"You're welcome, darlin'. Even though the rest of our time will probably be spent sleeping, I didn't want to say good-bye just yet," she confessed.

"I know what you mean. I've had such a good time tonight. Thank you again," Susan said.

Kelly rolled back the sheets and blankets on her side of the bed and got in. She wrestled playfully with Susan for the covers, and then settled comfortably on her left side so she could look at her bedmate. Susan had done the same onto her right side, and they just stared at each other for many moments. Time passed slowly as Kelly registered every feature on her face, from the tiny freckles on her nose to what looked like a chicken pox scar next to her right eye.

Reaching up, Kelly gently caressed Susan's face, wondering at what this girl's childhood must have been like. It had to have been unimaginably different from the life that she was living at present. Kelly couldn't believe that someone's parents would actually throw their own daughter out because they were offended by her sexual orientation. She knew that she had been very lucky in that respect. She and her mom had had a very close relationship, and Kelly knew she could tell her anything and everything. So when she was fifteen and went to her mom and told her she didn't think she liked boys "in that way," her mom just smiled, opened her arms, and said, "I love you, Kelly, no matter what."

"Hey, you all right?" Susan asked, startling her a bit.

"Just thinking." Kelly's fingers continued to caress her, as she outlined the small scar next to her eye. "Where'd you get this?" she asked cautiously.

"Chicken pox. Six years old," Susan confirmed.

"That's what I thought. I have a similar one next to my eye. See?" Kelly pointed to where she thought the scar was on her face.

"Wow, look at that. We're twins," she giggled.

"Oh, God, I hope not. What we did downstairs wouldn't be acceptable in most family circles," Kelly joked.

"Ew, Kelly!" Susan laughed and swatted her shoulder.

"I'm just kidding." She grasped the retreating hand, interlacing their fingers. Taking a deep breath, she looked down at Susan. *Her eyes are incredible. They've seen so much more of this life than I ever will. They've seen places I've only heard horror stories about. I feel so incredibly blessed that I've never had to go through any of the things that she has. I hope that I never do.* Kelly caressed the palm of Susan's hand with her thumb.

Susan caught her staring and raised an eyebrow. "Something on your mind, Kelly?"

"Well, actually, I'm hoping that we can postpone the remainder of our 'heart to heart' for another day. I don't know if I'm up to going into another story tonight." She offered a small smile to her new friend.

"Oh honey, you don't have to tell me anything if you don't feel up to it. If you decide one day that you want to share that part of your life, then of course, I'll be more than willing to listen. Please don't feel pressured into telling me something you aren't ready to share. I would hate that." Susan held tight to Kelly's hand. "Let's just take this slowly; find a pace that we're both happy with and go with it. No pressure?" She smiled hopefully.

"No pressure," Kelly agreed. Relief instantly flooded her body and she squeezed Susan's hand. She wasn't really ready to reveal such intimate information so soon, but did want Susan to feel that she was willing to take an equal part in developing the relationship. She knew Susan had taken a risk when she accepted the invitation to dinner, and also at the apartment when she'd shared so much of herself with a virtual stranger without batting an eye. *I guess she sensed the connection as much as I did. God knows I've never felt it this strongly with anyone before.*

"Can we snuggle?" Kelly asked hesitantly.

"Of course we can snuggle. I was hoping you'd want to."

Kelly rolled onto her back and felt the bed shift as Susan rolled closer to her, rested her head on the nearby shoulder and wrapped her arm securely around Kelly's waist. Kelly's arm instinctively wrapped itself around Susan's shoulders and held her close. "This feels so nice," Kelly cooed, as she began rubbing her back.

"I have to agree. Your arms feel great around me," Susan said as she snuggled impossibly closer.

Kelly had never felt more secure. Or more cared for.

A Saving Solace

Chapter Thirteen

Susan could hear Kelly's heartbeat racing with every breath she took. *At least I'm not the only one who's nervous. I haven't been in another woman's arms since Cindy. God, it's been a long time. This feels too good to be true. I don't think I'll ever forget the sound of Kelly's heartbeat. It's so strong. I love the way that she holds me. Her hands are so soothing.*
I bet they'd feel great on other places, too.
Quit that!
Just thought I'd keep you posted on my thoughts.
Well don't!
Night, babe.
Go away!
If she never heard her shadow's voice again, it would be too soon. If she could just get over her fears, maybe the voice would go away.
"Susan?" Kelly whispered.
"Yeah?"
"Are you still sleepy?"
God, she's so cute. "Yeah, I am. Being all cuddled up like this makes me feel so safe, I could stay here forever," Susan said before she could stop herself. *Hell, who am I kidding? I don't want to stop myself. This is where I wanted to be. I'll be damned if anyone's going to take that from me again.*
"I'm glad you're comfortable," Kelly said softly against her hair. "I haven't felt this good in a long time."
"Mmm," Susan murmured. "I know the feeling."
"Good night, darlin'," Kelly said quietly.
"Sweet dreams, Kelly," Susan said as she looked up into dreamy blue eyes.
"You, too," she said as she leaned closer.

A Saving Solace

The kiss was soft and warm and it tingled Susan's body completely. Susan moaned into the invading mouth. Kelly's body coiled like a snake ready to pounce and she deepened the kiss. Their tongues met and they tasted the fresh toothpaste between them. Kelly was so good at the kissing thing; Susan's body really wanted to sink into her fully. She felt her lips being nipped as their kiss slowly came to an end. "Whoa," Susan breathed.

"Yeah," Kelly agreed.

Susan smiled at her. "You are so good at that."

"I'm glad you think so. You're pretty gifted yourself. My body thanks you, too. It's trying really hard to override my head," she giggled.

"I know the feeling," Susan mumbled. "I'm sorry -"

Kelly placed her fingers across pouting lips. "Shhh, don't go there. I told you I'd gladly wait to make love with you. I just thought you'd like to know what my body thinks of you."

"It's nice to know. It really is. It's been so long since I've wanted anyone to feel these things for me. I'm so glad you do, Kelly. You are an incredible woman. Thank you for breaking the ice yesterday. I doubt I ever would've had the nerve to approach you. It's hard to predict what kind of reactions people like me will get," Susan said sadly.

"God, it has to be so hard for you. I'm so glad your friend Carol got you off the streets."

"Yeah, she was the greatest woman I've ever known. She truly brought me back to life. I was so dead inside, I never thought I'd make it back to living a real life. I thought the rest of my life, short as that might be, was going be as it was in my own little world out there." Thinking back, she sighed, thanking God she was warm, clothed, fed, and cared for.

"Susan?" Kelly started. "What are your plans for Christmas? I know I told you that I go to the movies, but I'd love some company this year. What do you think? It's getting closer, and I thought we could spend it together," Kelly bit her lip anticipating the response.

"Actually, I am heading the yearly holiday food drive for the shelter. It's something I like to do; it reminds me of Carol. It kind of brings me closer to her, in a way. She did it for me and I really like giving some of that back," Susan said proudly.

"You need any help?" Kelly asked.

Susan looked up at smiling eyes. "Are you serious?"

"Of course I am. I wouldn't offer something like that if I wasn't serious," she insisted.

"Kelly, I'd love that!" Susan hugged her tightly. "You are an absolute godsend! Thank you; you don't know what this means to me."

"I see your face shining like I've never seen before. I have a pretty good idea what it means to you. I also know what you mean to me. There isn't much I wouldn't do for you." Kelly grinned shyly.

"Thank you. Thank you so much," Susan breathed against her chest.

Kelly's arms held Susan firmly, and Susan knew without a doubt that Kelly Cavanaugh was going to make it impossible for her *not* to fall in love with her.

"You're welcome, baby."

"Kelly?"

"Hmm?"

"Can I ask you something?" Susan asked quietly.

"Honey, you can ask me anything you want," she assured.

"Why don't you have a Christmas tree?" Susan felt her giggle.

"Funny you should ask me that. I have an artificial one that I keep in my garage. I haven't put it up yet, because I wasn't sure I wanted to. I never really celebrate Christmas with anyone, so I guess I figured, why bother?" she said matter of factly.

"Well, I'd love to help you decorate it," Susan offered, excited. "I haven't decorated a tree in a long time. My parents always had a huge nine or ten foot tree in the living room. It was always magical to me. Bing Crosby would be crooning in the background, and we'd dress the tree as a family... God, I miss that," she sighed.

"You miss doing the tree?" Kelly asked, sounding a bit confused.

"No, well, yes, but what I meant was, I miss having a family," Susan said sadly.

"I can be a part of your family, Susan. All you have to do is say the word. I know what missing family is all about. My mom was my world." Kelly started running her fingers through Susan's hair. "Even though it was just my mom, grandma, and me, it was very special for me. I knew if I needed anything, they would be there. If I was sick, my mom would take care of me. Even if I only needed a hug, she was there for me. And if I needed a good kick in the ass, they were *both* on me faster than lightning. Believe me, that happened way too often for my liking." Kelly chuckled along with Susan.

"I bet you were something else when you were younger," the younger woman giggled.

Kelly laughed. "You have no idea. I had so much energy when I was a child, my mom went to a preacher because she thought I might be possessed or something!"

Susan was shocked. "No way! Are you serious?"

"I'm quite serious. She was a very religious, hard core Catholic up until the day she took her last breath," Kelly said with a touch of sorrow. "God, she was a fighter."

Susan didn't want to press Kelly about her mom. She knew she would be told the whole story when Kelly was ready. In the meanwhile, she would take the bits and pieces. It indicated that Kelly was starting to trust her. That in itself was good enough for her.

"Anyway, I'd love to decorate the tree with you this year, Susan. It'd be great fun, I think. It's been a while since I've had anyone other than Mattie to enjoy it with," Kelly said wistfully.

"I'd love to. Thanks for asking me."

"You're welcome, darlin'." Kelly reached back and clicked off the lamp that rested on the night table. The moon was shining through the windows and the wind blew outside.

God, I'm glad I'm in here. The memories of freezing my ass off aren't far enough away yet.

Kelly kissed the top of Susan's head and settled down for a comfortable slumber. "Night, baby," she said into her hair.

"G'night, Kelly." Susan turned her head and kissed her neck, then snuggled deeper into her human pillow and happily let sleep take her.

A Saving Solace

Chapter Fourteen

"*Are you sure, Gram? I mean, could they be wrong?*" *Kelly asked hopefully.*
Connie said sadly, "No, sweetie, they've confirmed it with tests."
"*Is Mom there? Can I talk to her?*"
"*She's sleeping, dear. She's had quite a day. We'll be flying back tomorrow. She's going to need you to be strong for her, Kelly. The doctors have given me information about this illness, and I'm going to be honest with you, honey, it's going to get really hard on the both of you,*" *Kelly's grandmother explained. "She's eventually going to lose all of her muscle control. Slowly but surely this disease will take all of her abilities away from her - everything from her ability to walk, eat, maybe even her ability to talk."*
On the other end of the phone, Kelly couldn't seem to stop the tears. *"Is she going to be in pain, Gram?"*
"*I don't know, sweetheart. Typically, part of the mind is affected too, so she may not be aware of the disease and its progress. Sometimes the person is completely lucid, though. Everyone reacts differently; we won't know until it happens. We'll just have to wait it out." Kelly's grandmother sighed sadly. "She's strong, Kelly. The Lord will take care of her."*
"*How long, Gram?*" *Kelly sobbed into the phone. "How long does she have?"*
"*They say anywhere from two to five years. Again, it really depends on how badly it affects her. She could live longer than that or shorter. Only time will tell." Connie paused. "Listen, I'm going to get back to your mother. Try to pull yourself together for her. She needs you to be strong. For the both of you. I know you can do it, sweetie. I love you," Connie finished.*

"I love you, too, Gram. Thanks for letting me know. At least we understand why she's been acting so differently. God! This is so not fair!" Kelly screamed.

"I know, baby. I know. Shhh... We'll be home tomorrow. Will you be okay? Why don't you call a friend to come over to stay with you tonight," her grandma suggested.

"No, Gram, I don't want anyone around me right now." Kelly took a deep breath, stilling her tears briefly. "All right, Gram. Take care of her, and I'll see you guys tomorrow," she sniffled.

"All right, dear. Bye."

"Bye, Gram." Kelly dropped the phone onto the coffee table, tears and anguish accompanying every breath she took.

"WHY? Why, God dammit! Why her? Why'd You have to do this to her?" Kelly screamed up at the ceiling. "She's a fucking saint! She's been the kindest person to everyone! Everyone loves her. She's never done a cruel thing to anyone or anything in her whole life. Jesus..." Kelly collapsed on the couch and wept until she fell asleep.

~~*

Kelly peeked her head into her mother's room. Normally at that hour, her mother would be resting. "Mom, are you awake?" She looked down at the sickly figure and felt her heart constrict painfully. There she was, lying in the hospital bed the hospice had given them to use until her passing. Her frail form was curled on its side, a catheter tube running the length of the bed and into her body. Her breathing was shallow, but she was still alive and with Kelly and her grandmother.

Dorothy's eyes slowly opened. A bit glazed, they slowly moved around until they rested on her daughter, who was silently watching her. She made a slight noise to let Kelly know she knew she was there.

"Hi, Ma." Kelly ran her fingers through her mother's fine hair. "How was your nap?"

Her mother raised her eyebrows, trying to communicate with her only daughter.

"I hope I'm not disturbing you." Kelly took a deep breath. "Mom, I really want to talk to you." The tears began to roll down Kelly's cheeks. She reached down to her mother's bed and took one of her hands. The slight pressure she felt from the fingers in her grasp made her smile sadly. "Oh, Mom, this is the hardest thing I've ever had to do. I know I've only been around for seventeen years, but I think I've seen more in the last two years than I ever want to again. I know that soon we're going to be apart, and I think that maybe this is the best time for me to tell you all the things that I've wanted to. Somewhere inside of you, I know that you can hear me, and you can understand what I'm saying. I really hate that guy that comes in here and pretends like you don't know what's going on. I know you do!" Kelly paused to catch her breath.

"I just wanted to let you know, that I think you're the most wonderful woman that God put on this earth. You've been the best mom and the best friend anyone could ask for. You've worked hard to keep me fed and clothed, and you kept me in better schools than most kids get to go to. You let me go the popular school, just because I asked to go there. I could've easily gone to Winston High down the road, but no, I wanted to go to South with all my friends. You never even said a word when you had to work longer hours to make sure I was able to go there. You drove me every single day, too. I don't know of anyone else that didn't have to take the bus to school." Kelly wiped her nose and eyes with her drenched Kleenex. She could feel her mother's hand tighten ever so slightly in her grasp, and knew her mother could hear every word she spoke. "You did so much for me, Mom, in the short time that we've been together. I'm truly blessed that I had you in my life. Even though my father, whose worthless ass I could kick right now, is nowhere to be found, he gave life to me and therefore brought me to you. That's the only thing I could ever thank him for. Lord knows he doesn't deserve shit from anyone." Kelly felt her mom tighten her hold a bit more. "Sorry, I know you hate when I curse." The grip loosened. "I don't want to waste my time talking about him anyway. This is all about you, Mom. The words 'I love you' don't mean nearly enough right now. I wish you could see inside of me to know how much you mean to me, Mom. You're my life; you've always been there for me, even when I told you that I was gay. I thought for sure you'd disown me or beat the tar out of me until I changed my mind, but you didn't. You opened your arms to me and told me you loved me, no matter what. I will always remember that day, Mom. Always."

Kelly began to cry in earnest and had to try to calm herself to finish what she needed to say. "I hate with all that I am to see you like this. You were such an independent woman. You've never asked for anything in your whole life. Now you can't. What kind of divine love is that? Why did God do this to you? You've gone to church almost daily since I was born. Is this the gratitude He shows you? I will never understand the justice in all of this. You serve Him, so He knocks you down with an incurable illness? What the hell is that? I know you've served God your whole life, and you believe that He chose you to endure this trial because He knew you were strong enough to handle it. Well, I don't buy it! You're too good of a person for this to happen to. I just don't understand that kind of love." Kelly stopped to sob against her mother's side. "I'm so sorry this happened to you, Mom. I'm so sorry..."

Her mother uttered a sound, and Kelly got closer to her mouth so she could listen better. "What, Ma? I didn't hear you."

"Laaa you," her mother's voice stretched.

"I love you too, Mom," Kelly sobbed.

She walked around to the other side of her mother's bed, climbed into bed with her, and held her spooned tightly against her. They lay there together silently crying until they both fell into a restless sleep.

~~*

Kelly watched as they removed the oxygen tube from her mother's nose. She didn't want any respiratory help once her lungs began to fail. Her mother had slipped into a coma and was breathing in quick, short gasps. The nurse was watching as Kelly and her grandmother waited for the inevitable. Dorothy's breaths evened out, until finally, she took one last breath then was taken silently into the heavens. The color faded from her cheeks, as did the warmth from her skin. Kelly hung on to her mother during the whole process. She sobbed endlessly until she heard the word 'coroner'. She looked up into the dark, loving eyes of her grandmother and wordlessly asked for a few minutes alone with her mom.

Connie rose and took the nurse into the kitchen to give her granddaughter the privacy that she herself would ask for shortly.

Kelly clung to her mother's nightgown, rested her head on her mother's chest. She heard nothing beating or moving inside, finalizing everything in her own mind. She cried and murmured words of love and longing, until she finally whispered her good-byes.

A Saving Solace

One of the nurses from the hospice was called to help prepare the body for transport to the funeral home, and even though it was the middle of the night, came right over before the coroner arrived. Pat had been Dorothy's favorite nurse and vice versa. She wailed against Dorothy's lifeless body. Seeing Pat hunched over her mother sent a cascade of new tears down Kelly's face.

The doorbell rang and Kelly knew it was the coroner's office to pick up her mother's body. She didn't want to answer the door, believing if she didn't let them in, her mother wouldn't leave. Realistically, she knew better, and opened the door to find two pairs of warm comforting eyes.

"Miss Cavanaugh?" Kelly nodded and let the two gentlemen into their home. "We're so sorry for your loss. Is she in there?" Kelly nodded dumbly and watched as her grandmother readied her daughter for removal.

Kelly heard the words "expire" and "patient" in the same sentence. She'd never heard someone's death referred to as them expiring. It was a world of language she never wanted to learn.

They wheeled her mother's body out of her room on a gurney. It would have been fairly tolerable, but her mother's remains had been put in a body bag. Kelly took one final look at her mother's form being wheeled from her life, and collapsed into the waiting arms of her grandmother.

"No! I can't believe she's gone, Gram. No! Mommy! No!" she sobbed over and over.

~~*~*~*

Susan felt movement under her and started awake, momentarily wondering where she was. She heard

Kelly moaning in her sleep and it was getting louder.
"No..." she heard Kelly whisper. "No."
"Kelly?" Susan hoped she wasn't one of those people that couldn't be awakened from a nightmare. "Kelly, honey, it's okay. I'm here with you. Everything's fine." She tried to soothe her back into consciousness, holding her close and caressing every body part she could reach.

Still crying, Kelly jerked awake and clutched at Susan desperately.

"Shhh, baby. I've got you," the smaller woman said as she rolled to her back, taking Kelly with her. Kelly's head rested on her chest and she could feel tears soaking through the material of her shirt. She ran calming fingers through her hair and lightly scratched her scalp. "It's okay now, sweetheart. No one can hurt you now," she soothed.

Kelly was sobbing quietly, and Susan was unsure whether or not she was really awake. "Kelly? You want to talk about it?" she asked.

Kelly shook her head like a small child and Susan's heart broke for her at that moment. It was obvious by her reaction to the dream that it must have been about her mother. Susan held her closer and rocked her with all the will and strength that she had. She might not like her own mother, but at least she was still alive. As far as she knew, Kelly had said she was only seventeen when her mother died. Susan had surmised that it must have been from cancer or something. She hated not knowing. She could try to help if only she knew what she was talking about. *This patience thing is truly virtuous.*

Kelly's sobs lessened with every deep breath she took. She raised her head and softly kissed Susan's cheek. "I'll be right back. I just need to use the bathroom for a second," she said quietly.

"Are you going to be all right, honey?" Susan's

heart was breaking at the sound of her sad voice.

"Yeah... I just um... I haven't had a dream like that in a long time." She sighed and got up off the bed and walked into the bathroom.

Susan heard the faucet turn on, then the splashing of water. She assumed Kelly was rinsing off her face. She would just have to wait until Kelly was ready to talk about it.

~~*~*~*~*~*

That was a bad one. I haven't had one of those dreams in a long time.

Kelly rinsed her face with cold water, trying to shut out the images of her mother on her deathbed. The straining of her last breath would always be a visual she could've lived without, although having been with her during her last moments on earth made it as good as it could have been. *I'm glad she didn't die all alone. No one deserves to go that way.* When it came to her mother's dying, the fact that she had been there with her was the only thing she was grateful for.

Poor Susan. I don't think she was expecting our first night together to be quite like this. Hell, I had no intention of this happening. The peace that she brought to me was just so reminiscent of my mom, it simply brought it into my subconscious, I guess.

Kelly looked at her reflection and saw red puffy eyes staring back at her.

Susan'll help you through this. You know she will. Let her in, Kel.

I will, but not tonight. I just don't have it in me tonight.

She used the toilet and washed her hands and face one last time. She brushed her teeth again for good measure, then went back towards the bedroom. The light on the nightstand had been turned on, and Susan and Mattie were nowhere to be seen. Kelly's heart began racing.

"Susan?" she called.

"I'll be right up!" Susan shouted from downstairs.

The whistle of the teakettle brought a smile to Kelly's face. *She is really something,* she thought. *I don't know what I did to deserve her, but I'm thankful. Thanks, Momma.*

Kelly heard the padding of several feet heading her way. She sat on the bed and was greeted by Mattie and Susan, who was carrying a tray that had their tea from earlier in the evening.

"Hey." Susan smiled.

Kelly smiled back. "Hey."

"I thought you might want something warm to drink to try to help you fall back to sleep. I saw that there was no caffeine in this, so I made the tea you brought out earlier. You think you could handle some?"

Susan's beautiful face lit up when Kelly nodded. She handed her a cup of tea with the tea bag's string resting over the brim and onto the saucer. Kelly bobbed the bag up and down until she got the water to the color and flavor she desired, then pulled the bag from the cup and rested it on the saucer. Taking her first small sip, Kelly felt the warmth of the liquid seep into her body, giving her solace.

"Thank you, Susan. This is exactly what I needed," she said graciously.

"I'm glad. I know when I've had a bad dream or I can't sleep, a nice cup of tea usually does the trick. I'm glad that's the case with you, too." Susan smiled into her cup.

"I'm so glad you're here," Kelly said quietly. Reaching for Susan's hand, she led her to the bed to sit next to her. "Thank you for being here."

Susan smiled softly at her. "There's no place I'd rather be right now."

They drank their tea, then sank into the warmth of the bed linens. Kelly held Susan in her arms and breathed in her scent. Her voice was warm with emotion when she said, "Good night, baby."

Susan squeezed Kelly's mid section and kissed her clothed breast. "Sweet dreams."

Kelly truly hoped her dreams were over for the night.

Chapter Fifteen

Christmas Eve arrived before Kelly knew what hit her. That time of year was always so damn busy, she never had time for anything except work. All she did was check on the stock levels in each store, make sure each schedule had been made properly, and call her managers to make sure they didn't have any needs that hadn't been met. *Only two more weeks of this and it's over, and I can get back to my regular life.*
With Susan.
Susan. What a difference a name makes. I just hear that name and my face lights up, regardless if it's indeed my Susan that's being thought about.
Your *Susan*?
Oh, hush!
You've come a long way, Kel.
Don't jinx it!
I have *no* intention of doing that. She's the best thing to happen to you, ever.
Don't I know it.
Their time together had been wonderful. The last couple of weeks had been kind of quiet, though. Kelly knew the reason and she hoped Susan wasn't feeling ignored. *It's impossible to get in touch with her since she has no phone. Of course, that just gives me a reason to go and see her every day. I didn't see her this morning, though. I was running late; perhaps she was, as well.*

Kelly was looking forward to spending the evening with Susan. They were going to decorate the artificial Christmas tree that had been lying abandoned in Kelly's garage forever and a day. She couldn't wait to watch Susan's face light up when they plugged in the lights for the first time. That was always Kelly's favorite part of

A Saving Solace

tree trimming - when she got to see the finished product: tinsel glistening against the ornaments that reflected the light from the thousands of strings of lights she'd wrapped around the branches. It was definitely going to be a night to remember.

Not that the weekends they'd spent together hadn't been wonderful. They had truly been some of the best that she could remember. Even though her nightmares had recurred, on the nights Susan stayed over, she'd been incredibly soothing. *She has such a huge heart; I can't imagine hurting her, ever.*

You hope you don't hurt her.

You're right... I hope I never do.

~~*~*~*~*

God, it's freezing out here today. I cannot wait until I can stop with bucket detail. It's not that I mind the work; I'm just frozen like a Popsicle. Only a few more weeks, then it's paperwork month. Oh joy. She pulled a face at the thought of the mountains of paperwork, then smiled. *It's better than being out here, though.*

She was anticipating the evening with Kelly, expecting it to be great fun, as she hadn't decorated a tree in years. *I hope I don't break any of her family's ornaments. I'd never forgive myself.* Her thoughts flitted to the meal they would share. *I have dinner duty tonight, and I'm going to make her spaghetti. It's really the only thing that I can cook well. I know how to make anything from a box, but I want to cook Kelly a real dinner to celebrate our first Christmas together.*

Thinking of Kelly made her smile. *God, she's incredible. She makes me feel so special, so beautiful. I'm the luckiest woman on the planet. I'm so completely smitten with her, I forget my name while looking into her*

eyes. *It's an abyss I fall into without hesitation... every time.*
Clink
"Thanks, ma'am. Have a happy holiday!" Susan shivered as she spoke.
Trying to think warm thoughts, Susan's returned to Kelly. *I'm so sad her nightmares have hit her so hard. I feel badly for her. I know she sleeps poorly the rest of the night, because I can feel her next to me, trying not to wake me with her restlessness. I'm quite a light sleeper, so that doesn't work at all. For either of us.*
When the morning after came, Susan was never sure what to expect Kelly's mood to be. Some people would hide in their shells when they thought someone had seen too much of their inner being. Not Kelly. She was sweet and kind, even though Susan knew she had to be as tired as all hell. She herself certainly was.
Saturdays had been spent just hanging out and watching movies. Susan thought that she could get used to watching movies like that. *Her family room is a theater all its own! I could really get used to that way of living again.*
Don't get too comfy.
Oh, now you don't like Kelly?
Sure I do; what's not to like? I'm just playing devil's advocate. I know she won't hurt you, at least I hope she won't. Just make sure you don't take her for granted. There aren't many people out there that would've approached you like she did.
I know that! Jesus! Kelly isn't like everyone else! Go away!
Hey, I'm just trying to protect you.
No, you're my fears trying to rebuild themselves again. Well, just stay out, because I haven't got any room in here for you anymore!
Susan shook her head as if to chase the voice away,

A Saving Solace

then pulled up her coat sleeve to check her watch, and thanked God her break was due. She needed to put on a second pair of long johns.

Chapter Sixteen

By midday, Kelly was sitting in her office trying to put out every damn fire her managers had thrown at her. *I'm gonna kill them, I swear to God. Not everything is an emergency!* She shook her head in frustration, wishing that she could be out on the sales floor with the customers. She quite enjoyed that part of the job, not like being stuck on her phone. Grimacing, she dialed another number.

I'm almost done. One more call and I'll be able to get out there and feel a little of the positive holiday spirit.
Until the next page comes.
Arghh!

~~*~*~*~*

"Can I help the next guest in line, please?" Therese said with a smile.

A short, dark haired man who was sorely in need of a shave walked up to the sales counter and slammed a fur coat down on the counter.

"I want a new coat! I special ordered this one for my wife for Christmas and it has a rip in it! I don't have another three weeks to wait, either, so don't even think of suggesting that!" he shouted at the saleswoman.

Attempting to placate him, she said, "Sir, please calm down, and I'll help you as best as I can."

"Don't tell me to calm down! I waited three weeks for this coat and it's fucking ripped! I want a new one and I want it NOW!" he exploded.

"Could I see your receipt, please?" Therese asked politely.

The man threw the receipt at the nonplussed

A Saving Solace

woman. "Here!"

"Sir, let me look this up on the computer and see if we have another one in stock. I'll just be a moment." She smiled.

"You'd better have one. This is bullshit!"

"Sir, I'll ask you once again to please lower your voice. There are children nearby that don't need to hear such language," Therese said calmly as she typed information into her computer.

"Whatever," he said indifferently.

"Well, I'm sorry to tell you that we are out of stock on that item. I can look..." She stopped when the man in front of her interrupted her.

"I told you I didn't want to hear it! I want a new coat for my wife, and I want it now!" he bellowed.

"Sir, I can't give you what I don't have. I'm very sorry. I will call around to our other stores..." Her eyes went wide when she saw the knife in his hand.

"I'm not gonna tell you again. I want that coat for my wife and you're gonna get me one or I'm gonna hurt you," he snarled.

Kelly had heard the shouting from her office and after completing her phone call, went out to see what the problem was. She saw the man threatening her employee with a knife. Tripping the silent alarm for Security to come, she quickly ran to Therese's aid. Joining the other woman behind the counter, she smiled innocently and said, "Hi there, I'm Kelly. How can I help you today?"

"Look! I bought this coat for my wife... I had to fucking order it and it's ripped! I can't give her that! I want a new one, but Miss High and Mighty back there won't get me one, so I'm gonna take it out of her ass!"

"Now hold on a minute. I know you don't want to hurt anyone. Just give me a chance to call some other stores, and I will find you what you want." She froze when she saw the man grab the woman behind him and place the knife at her throat.

"I'm not waiting any longer. I want something done, and so help me, I'm gonna get what I want!" he screamed into his victim's ear. The small woman in his grasp started crying desperately for help. "Shut up, bitch! Not one more word, or I swear I'll gut ya like a trout," the out-of-control assailant hissed.

Kelly captured the gaze of the frightened woman, staring into her eyes and trying to will her to be calm. As she saw the security guards approaching, she quickly moved in front of the armed man, hoping to keep him distracted long enough for the guards to act.

"What are you, fucking stupid? I should just kill *your* ass while I'm at it," he said, taking a swipe at Kelly. As the armed man blindly lunged for her, the security guards made their move.

Kelly sidestepped the man's attack and watched as the security guards subdued and disarmed him, then handcuffed his hands behind his back. Immediately going to the woman hostage to comfort her and make sure she was unharmed, Kelly directed, "Therese, call the police!"

"We already did," the burly security officer said. "They should be here in a few minutes."

"Good." Kelly sighed. "Ma'am, are you sure you're okay?" She directed her gaze at Therese and then to the queue of customers. "Is everyone okay?"

The woman who had had a knife to her throat just moments before said, "I'm fine, young lady, thanks to you. That was either the bravest or the most stupid thing I've ever seen anyone do. He could've hurt you," she said in an awed voice, watching the security guards control the belligerent man who was trying to escape.

"Nah, he was too upset to be effective." Kelly smiled warmly at the customer. "I'm glad you're all

right, though. I'd never have forgiven myself if something had happened to you." She glanced around. "To any of you. Once you walk through those doors, you're all my responsibility."
"You must be the manager here, then."
"I'm the manager for this region. This just happens to be the base store where my office is located, and I'm very glad I was here to help," the blue-eyed woman said, downplaying her intervention.
"You're a hero, is what you are, Miss... Kelly, did you say your name was?"
"Yes, ma'am, Kelly Cavanaugh," she confirmed. "I feel awful that this happened. Please let me know if there's anything I can do for you."
"Don't worry about it. I'm not going to sue you or anything because of this. You've already done quite enough: you saved my life. Thank you, Kelly Cavanaugh."
Kelly blushed at the woman's outpouring, "You're very welcome." She turned to check on her employees and saw the police entering the building, rolling her eyes when she saw a camera crew for Channel Four News right behind them.
Oh, Christ, here comes the media circus. Merry fucking Christmas! Kelly thought to herself.

~~*~*~*~*

Susan watched as the police cars screeched around Lawrence Avenue towards Maxine's, the sirens on both cars blaring loudly. She saw the Channel Four News truck right behind them. All of the vehicles raced up to the clothing store and stopped, then several people got out and ran inside. *Jesus! What's going on in there?* Susan thought to herself as she felt her throat constrict.
"Oh, my God, Kelly's in there!" she shouted with

sudden realization, and grabbed her bucket and ran for her office. She dropped the bucket off with the woman at the office, with a fleeting explanation that she had to leave. The woman at the desk looked bewildered at the whirlwind entrance and exit.

"I've got to get to her," Susan panted as she ran towards Maxine's. "I don't know what I'd do if I lost her."

Susan ran until she got to the front door, where she waited as the police brought out a man who was struggling and screeching threats and curses. She looked in through the display windows, frantically searching for any sign of Kelly. Her eyes filled with tears and her heart thumped rapidly in her chest. She turned to one of the officers exiting the building and tried to speak calmly.

"Officer, I have to get in there. My partner works in there! I have to know if she's all right."

"No one's been hurt as far as I know, Ma'am," the young officer said.

"Can I please go inside? I really have to find her. Please?" Susan pleaded.

"Let me make sure you can go in." The officer turned and spoke to his superior then returned to her and smiled. "He says it's safe for you to go inside."

"Thank you!" Susan exclaimed as she ran inside. Beyond anxious to find Kelly, she headed directly towards the group of people with the camera crew.

"Kelly?" she called, her eyes frantically searching the gathering. She finally saw what she was looking for: a tall, auburn haired beauty that had won a place in her heart faster than the speed of light. "Oh, Kelly!" she cried, running towards her.

Kelly was answering questions for the Channel Four News when she spotted the teary eyed woman running at her. She smiled and turned towards her to absorb the impact of Susan's body against hers, then held the woman against her.

"Oh, Kelly, I was so worried!"

"Hey," she soothed. "I'm fine, sweetheart, I promise."

Susan held very tightly to Kelly until she was certain she was fine. "What happened? Why are the police in here? I saw them dragging out some scary looking dude. Did he do something?"

"Yeah, He was a bit unhappy with a gift he'd gotten for his wife, and he snapped. It happens this time of year. Not usually so violently, but still..." Kelly smiled reassuringly.

"What did he do?" the brown-eyed woman asked.

"He pulled a knife on one of my customers." Kelly paused, unsure if she should tell the whole story. "Then he um... tried to stab me," she said quietly, hoping Susan wouldn't freak out. The camera was still facing in their direction.

"What?" Susan cried. "Did you get hurt?" she asked, trying to take a full inventory of all of Kelly's parts.

"Susan, I'm fine. Please, believe me. Besides, I think we've given them quite enough news already." She blushed, and Susan finally realized the scene was being captured for the world to see.

"Oh, screw them." She leaned up and kissed Kelly solidly on the mouth. "I'm so glad you're all right."

Kelly laughed at Susan's forthrightness. "Me too, darlin'. Me too." She trailed her fingers down Susan's cheek. "Let's get out of here. I've had enough attention for one Christmas Eve. What do you say? Can we start celebrating early?"

Susan couldn't deny that expectant face any more than she could live without breathing. "Okay, let me just finish up at the ForOthers office and let them know that

I'm leaving because I have an emergency to take care of." She winked. "Besides, we'll be working there most of the day tomorrow. They'll be okay without me for a few hours today."

"Great. Let me just grab my briefcase from my office and I'll be ready," Kelly said.

Susan smiled. "Okay, come to the office and I'll be there."

"All right, sweetie. I'll see you soon."

"Kelly... I... Bye," Susan stuttered as she waved. *I love you,* she thought to herself, not being able to say the words.

"Bye," Kelly responded as she watched her friend walk towards the exit.

"Miss Cavanaugh, who was that?" the news anchor asked.

With a look of admiration on her face, Kelly stared at the retreating figure. "Only the most wonderful person who's ever walked into my life. Are we finished?" Kelly asked, now anxious to leave.

The reporter smiled. "Yes, thank you, Miss Cavanaugh. Merry Christmas to you."

"Yeah, you too," Kelly said absently, as she headed towards her office.

"Wow, did you see that?" the cameraman asked the correspondent.

"Oh, yeah, a Christmas story for the New Millennium," she smiled. "Tell me you got all of that," she said sternly.

"All of it," he said with pride.

"Good man."

A Saving Solace

Chapter Seventeen

Kelly was very glad to be out of the limelight and on her way to being with Susan. She hoped Susan was all right; she had looked so distressed when she first ran into the building. However, Kelly knew that she would have been just as upset if their roles had been reversed. *That was as close to being killed as I'd like to come.*

All right, Kelly, tonight is going to be fun. Let's not think bad thoughts any more than we have to. I'm sure Susan's going to want the whole story, but after that, it's all about celebrating your first Christmas together.

Thank you. Yes, it's going to be great. I'll hold on to that thought. Wow, our first Christmas together.

It was hard for Kelly to believe she was actually sharing a holiday with someone. She'd been very lonely without her mom. Her grandma had come for holidays the first couple of years after Dorothy Cavanaugh had passed away, but it was just too hard for her. *I buried my mother; she buried her daughter. I'm a reminder of that, I think. Hell, I don't think I could bury my own child. I pray I never have to find out what that's like.*

Christmas was always especially hard for Kelly. In four days it would be the anniversary of her mom's death. *At least I got one last Christmas with her before she was taken. It was always such a special time for us.*

~~*~*~*~*

Walking in a winter wonderland...

"Isn't this great, Momma?" Kelly asked as she placed the tinsel on their artificial Christmas tree.

From her wheelchair, Dorothy glanced quietly at her daughter. Kelly could see a little of the woman she knew as her mother staring back at her. Her grandma sat on the couch, coaching Kelly on where to put the rest of the tinsel.

"Honey, there's a blank spot towards the back. Can you get it?"

"Sure, Gram, I got it." She circled around to the bare part of the tree and hung some tinsel, as well as rearranging the ornaments to fill the area better.

"Perfect," her grandmother beamed.

Her mother managed an approving peep, letting Kelly know that she agreed.

Pat, Dorothy's nurse, rubbed her shoulders with affection. "It's a beautiful tree, Dot," Pat smiled.

"I have to agree. Must be the trimmer," Kelly said confidently.

Her mother peeped again at the statement.

Kelly smiled lovingly at her mother. "So, Mom, do you want to put up the last of the tinsel?" the teenager asked.

Dorothy reached for Kelly's hand and she draped the tinsel over her mother's arm. Pat wheeled the frail woman closer to the tree and watched as Dorothy tried desperately to loop the tinsel onto the tree branch. Kelly watched painfully as her mother persisted at trying to get her hands to cooperate. Dorothy had lost her dexterity in her right hand, but still had some movement in her left. With a victorious gleam in her eye, the determined woman placed the last piece of tinsel on their tree.

"Oh, Momma, that's beautiful! This is the best tree we've had yet!" Kelly's face shone as brightly as the Christmas lights. At the first smile from her mother in days, Kelly's heart flooded, as did her eyes. She looked away so her mother wouldn't see the sadness.

They all knew Dorothy didn't have much time left. She could barely keep any food down. Her body would purge anything it was fed. Her breathing had become increasingly shallow, and she needed more sleep now than she ever had.

Kelly moved to change the record. She found one of her mother's favorite Christmas songs.

It's the most wonderful time of the year...

Andy Williams sang in the background as Kelly composed herself. She took deep breaths and told herself that she needed to show her mom that she'd be all right. She thought her mother had hung on so long because she was worried about her. As much as Kelly didn't want her mom to leave her, she wanted her to be at peace.

Kelly moved to sit next to her grandma on the couch. Pat wheeled Dorothy close to them as they all looked at the tree.

"Ready?" Pat smiled.

"Do it!" Kelly shouted.

Click

The tree lit up brilliantly when Pat flicked the switch. All four of them just stared at it, each lost in her own thoughts. Smiles were wide, even Dorothy's. Kelly leaned over to her mom's wheelchair and reached for her hand. Dorothy grasped Kelly's hand with as much strength as she could muster. Connie reached over the chair and placed her arm around her daughter's shoulders.

"Picture time!" Pat shouted as she walked to the kitchen table to grab the camera.

The three women looked up at Pat and put on their best smiles. As the flash went off Kelly sobered, knowing this was the last Christmas she would have with her mother. She leaned over and placed a kiss on her cheek. "I love you, lady," she rasped as she felt her hand being *tenderly squeezed.*

~~*~*~*

Tracing the picture of the trio with trembling fingers, Kelly waited for Susan to change clothes. She kissed the photo and returned it to its place on the mantle of the fireplace.

"Penny for your thoughts," Susan chimed, startling Kelly who had forgotten her presence for those moments she had spent in memory.

"They're not worth that much sometimes," she said blankly.

"Honey, what's wrong? Are you still reeling from today?" Susan asked with concern.

"No, just feeling a bit sad, I guess. I promised myself I wasn't going to feel that way this year, but it always hurts so damn much," Kelly said, trying to swallow the emotions she could feel building. She reached out and handed Susan the picture.

"Is this your mom?" she asked in a muted voice.

"Yes, it was the last picture we had taken together. Christmas Eve, eleven years ago. She died four days later."

"Can I ask you what she died of?"

"ALS," Kelly answered stiffly. She watched Susan's brows furrow and figured she should just get it out in the open. Susan deserved to know the truth. She'd earned that trust and then some.

"Amyotrophic Lateral Sclerosis or Lou Gehrig's disease. It's a progressive, fatal neuromuscular disease that attacks nerve cells in the brain and around the spinal cord. Basically, the motor neurons die and can't send signals to the muscles. The brain just stops working in that way. The muscles get no nourishment, so they turn to mush. All voluntary muscle movements are affected and the person eventually becomes completely paralyzed. The lungs give out, and that's what actually kills them. They suffocate, and then die. It's just brutal," Kelly finished hoarsely.

Susan handed the picture back to her. "Thanks for showing me the picture. She was very beautiful, just like her daughter."

"Thanks," Kelly said, feeling the tears brim in her eyes.

"I think I have a good idea about why you don't like to celebrate Christmas. I'm so sorry, Kelly," Susan said as she looked compassionately into tear-filled blue eyes.

That was all it took, Kelly felt the floodgates open and suddenly Susan's arms opened wide. "C'mere," Susan whispered.

Kelly fell into her arms and began to cry. She hadn't felt so out of control in years. It'd been over a decade since her mother's death and she still had a hard time dealing with the reality of it. Probably always would. After several moments she stood straighter and wiped her eyes. "I'm sorry. This is supposed to be a fun night for us. Let's start that fun, shall we?" she asked, sniffling.

"Yes, let's. I'll get dinner started, and you go turn on the tube or something until it's ready," Susan directed.

"Are you sure I can't help?"

"You can help by eating everything on your plate. How's that?"

Susan smiled a beautiful smile, and Kelly knew she couldn't refuse her. "I'll be in here until you call then," she acquiesced.

"Good girl." Susan winked and patted Kelly's behind as she turned towards the couch. Smiling, she walked towards the kitchen, where she stayed to fix dinner.

A Saving Solace

Chapter Eighteen

God, how awful for her! Susan only had bits and pieces of knowledge about ALS, but knew that it must have been impossibly painful for a seventeen year old girl to watch her mother die like that. *How does anyone watch someone they love die at all? Jesus.*

She turned her thoughts to the spaghetti with a desire to make the best damn pasta she'd ever made. Now more than ever, she wanted the night to be special. She hoped that once they started trimming the tree, they'd both fall into a fun rhythm and begin to create new and happier memories. *I'll do everything in my power to make this a special time for her again, for both of us.*

She'd found some eggnog at the grocery. It had been ages since she'd had the traditional Christmas drink, and she hoped that Kelly liked it, too. *I could get used to working in this kitchen; she has every amenity I've ever seen! I bet she's used every appliance in here, too. The way she's cooked for me, I'd bet my last dime on it.* "Ten more minutes!" she shouted into the family room.

"Okay!" she heard Kelly call back. She smiled in response and stirred the sauce a little more. Taking a spoonful into her mouth for a taste, Susan hummed in pleasure. It'd been a while since she'd cooked for anyone, Carol having been her last taker. Every once and again she still felt the presence of the amazing woman. *I know she'll always be a part of me.*

~~*~*~*

"Hey, you asleep?" Susan called from the sleeper sofa.

"Not anymore. What's the matter, darlin', can't sleep?" Carol asked from her bedroom.

"No. I never could sleep the night before Christmas. I guess I'm wondering what my parents are doing," Susan admitted softly, staring at the small tree in Carol's living room.

"Get your butt in here. This old bird can't hear you from all the way in there. If you wanna talk, then assume your position," the older woman chuckled.

Susan was already three steps into Carol's room before Carol finished issuing the invitation. "You sure you're not tired?" Susan said as she snuggled into Carol's bedding.

Carol turned to face her bedmate. "What's on your mind, kiddo?"

Susan was on her back with her hands behind her head, looking at the ceiling. "Do you think they still think about me?" she asked shyly.

"I can't answer for them, darlin', but I know that if you were my kid, I'd be sick over not knowing where you were," Carol said honestly.

"If I was your kid, you'd never have tossed my ass out in the first place," the bitter woman spat angrily.

"You're right, my dear. You're absolutely right on that," Carol said as she fingered Susan's pillow-mashed hair. "They had their reasons, though."

"Their reasons were bullshit, Carol, and you know it! How could they throw away their own child because they didn't approve of her sexual orientation? That is just ludicrous! I would never do that to my child. It's not like I invited them into my bed, for God's sake!" Susan cried. "It was a mistake the way they found Cindy and I. I never meant for them to see me that way. I never meant to hurt them."

"Shh, honey. No one can explain their reactions except for your parents. They must've grown up believing that two women being together like that was wrong. Some people just can't deal with change," she explained softly.

Susan began to cry in earnest. "Why didn't they love me enough to keep me?"

"I don't know, honey. I just know that I've been blessed to have you in my life. You're a strong woman, Susan. You've come a long way in a short amount of time," Carol soothed. "When I met you, you were so full of piss and vinegar, I couldn't get anything nice to come out of your mouth for weeks." The woman chuckled in memory.

"You had such a tough skin when we first met, I thought I'd never get in. I'm so glad I kept at you, darlin'." Carol turned to lie on her back.

Susan followed her movements until the larger woman was cradling her. "So am I. I was so angry all the time, I'd forgotten how to feel anything else. You came along and changed all of that. Thank you for letting me feel loved again." She snuggled deeper into the woman. "Sometimes I wish you were my mom."

"I'd be the luckiest woman on this planet if I had a daughter half as wonderful as you, darlin'," Carol sighed, feeling the tears spring to her eyes. "Thank you for letting me in."

Susan smiled. "Thanks for knocking."

"Merry Christmas, Susan," Carol softly whispered into Susan's hair.

"Merry Christmas, Carol," she said, and giggled to herself at the way that sounded.

"Ha, ha, very funny. Now go to sleep," Carol mumbled.

"Yes, ma'am." Susan smiled. "Good night."

"Good night, darlin'."

~~*~*~*

Susan wiped her tears at the memories flooding through her, then heard the timer on the stove ring. *God, she was special. If she hadn't found me, I shudder to think where I'd be right now. Certainly not here. And certainly not with the beautiful woman that's waiting for me in the next room.* She felt very lucky. *Thanks, Carol.*

"Hey, Susan, come quick! We're on TV!" Kelly shouted.

Susan raced into the living room where the five o'clock news was just beginning.

~~*~*~*

"Kelly Cavanaugh, regional manager for Maxine's, an up-scale clothing chain, spread a little bit of her own Christmas cheer today when she saved a woman's life right here in her own store." The interviewer turned to face Kelly. "Miss Cavanaugh, can you tell us what happened today?"

"Well, I was in my office when one of our customers came in, unhappy with a purchase. He kind of got out of hand with a sales clerk and another customer."

"Can you describe what happened?"

"He was shouting about his dissatisfaction with the product, then he pulled a knife from his pocket and pointed it at one of my employees," Kelly began.

"Then what?" The interviewer shoved the microphone back into Kelly's face.

"At that point I'd come out of my office to find out what the shouting was all about, and saw him brandishing his knife. I tried to intercede and help with the transaction, but he got impatient and grabbed the woman in line behind him and put the knife to her throat. I'd called for Security and when I saw them arriving, I made a move to distract him; which is when he jabbed the knife at me. The guards jumped him, and the rest is history." She smiled shyly.

"Oh, don't let her fool you! She's a hero!" a woman in the background cheered as the camera focused in on her. "She saved my life and who knows who else's here today. Kelly Cavanaugh is a hero."

The camera panned back to show Kelly's flushed face, and then focused on her turning towards Susan who was running towards her and crying out her name.

Susan ran into Kelly at full tilt as the camera continued to roll. "Oh, Kelly, I was so worried!" Susan cried.

"Hey," she soothed, "I'm fine, sweetheart, I promise."

The camera cut to Susan's kiss on Kelly's lips, then Susan's voice was heard. "I'm just so glad you're all right."

Kelly laughed. "Me too, darlin'. Me too." The camera and the viewing audience watched as she brushed her fingers down Susan's cheek. "Let's get out of here. I've had enough attention for one Christmas Eve. What do you say? Can we start celebrating early?"

Then the film cut to:

"Okay, come to the ForOthers office and I'll be there."

"Alright, sweetie, I'll see you soon."

"Kelly… I…Bye," Susan stuttered as she waved.

"Bye," Kelly answered as she watched her walk towards the exit.

"Miss Cavanaugh, who was that?" the journalist asked.

With a look of admiration on her face, she stared at the retreating figure. "Only the most wonderful person who's ever walked into my life." A moment passed. "Are we finished?"

"Yes, thank you, Miss Cavanaugh. Merry Christmas to you."

"Yeah, you too," Kelly said as she walked away.

"A Christmas story for the New Millennium. I'm Tina Simkins reporting. Back to you, James."

~~*~*~*~*

Kelly turned down the volume on the next news story as the two women looked at each other in awe.

"I can't believe they showed me kissing you on national television!" Susan exclaimed.

"Me neither!" Kelly smiled. "You looked pretty good, I have to say."

Susan felt her face flush in embarrassment. "Thank you. You're not so bad yourself, Miss Hero."

The woman of the hour modestly changed the subject. "So, how's dinner coming?"

"A couple of minutes and it should be done." Susan smiled. The news broadcast had given her a sudden burst of energy. "God, I want to call someone to see if they saw us on TV!" she shouted.

"Well, I'm sure plenty of people saw it. Besides, it had a happy ending. What better story can you tell on Christmas, right?" Kelly beamed.

At that moment, Kelly looked more beautiful to Susan than she ever had. She knew without a doubt that she and Kelly had a future. A very happy and loving future. At that point, she could've forgotten all about the newscast. The entire known world could've seen them for all she cared. She just wanted to spend Christmas with the woman that had stolen her heart. "Let's eat!" Susan exclaimed.

Kelly smiled. "I'm right behind you."

~~*~*~*~*

"...*I'm Tina Simkins reporting. Back to you, James.*"

The TV was muted as a trembling hand covered the mouth that hung agape. Hazel eyes filled with tears as the realization hit like a ton of bricks. "Oh, my God... Susan..."

A Saving Solace

Chapter Nineteen

Kelly's mouth began watering at the tantalizing aroma as Susan set her plate before her; and when she took her first bite, the reality even exceeded the expectation. Susan was an incredible cook. Kelly had never eaten spaghetti that tasted anywhere near as delicious. They settled in to enjoy the meal and the company.

When the last bite had been ingested, getting up from the table, Susan started collecting the dishes and bringing them to the sink.

"Just what do you think you're doing?" Kelly asked gently, but sternly.

"I usually call this 'doing the dishes'. Why, what do you normally call it?" she answered teasingly.

"Very funny. Since you cooked, I insist on doing the dishes, okay? The cook shouldn't have to clean up as well."

"That's very sweet, but you've had quite a day, honey. Let me take care of everything, okay? Go sit in the family room and take a load off." With Kelly's stare burning into her, she tried another tactic. Giving Kelly her best puppy dog stare, she said, "Can't I do this for you? Please, let me. I want to."

"Fine, you win," Kelly capitulated.

"Thanks, I won't be but a minute." Susan kissed her cheek and went off to finish cleaning up their dishes.

Settling back in her chair after losing the discussion, Kelly gave her thoughts free rein. *God, I could get used to seeing her at my table every day. At my table, on my table, under my table...*

Getting a little ahead of yourself, aren't you, Kel?

I don't think so. Why do you ask?

You guys haven't even, well, you know, done the world's most favorite horizontal activity.
What? Fly like Superman?
Oh, very cute, Kel. You know what I mean.
Yes, I do. That's not the most important thing, though. Although, the way she makes me feel when we kiss, I know there won't be any problems in that department.
Maybe not for you.
What are you implying? She won't enjoy making love with me?
I'm just saying, don't set your expectations too high. Dinner's one thing; that next step is another.
A girl can dream, can't she? Don't rain on my parade. This feels more right than anything I've ever experienced. I'm not going to hurt her, dammit. And I know she'd hurt herself before she'd hurt me; she's got a heart of gold,
Okay, if you're sure.
I am sure. I've got this under control. Beat it.
Yes, mistress...
Smart-ass.

Susan finished up with the dishes and finally joined Kelly on the couch.

"Thank you again, sweetheart. Dinner was fantastic. It was the best meal I've had that I didn't cook myself." Kelly chuckled and leaned over to kiss her cheek.

Susan smiled and turned a becoming shade of red. "I'll take that as a compliment, I guess."

"You're blushing. You are so beautiful when you do that," Kelly observed.

"Thank you," Susan replied, her features becoming even a darker crimson. She smiled shyly. "I told you that I didn't have enough money saved to buy you a Christmas present, so I figured I could cook you a wonderful meal and just be with you. Merry Christmas, Kelly."

"I couldn't have asked for a better gift. I would put you on the top of my tree if I could. You're my angel, Susan; you really are," she whispered.

Susan's eyes shone with unshed tears. "That is the sweetest thing anyone's ever said to me."

Kelly smiled and their eyes locked. "Yeah, well, I've only just begun."

"Yeah, you and the Carpenters," Susan teased.

Elbowing her in response, Kelly asked, "Are you ready to start the tree?"

"You bet!" Susan exclaimed as she wiped her eyes.

"Great." Kelly stood and pointed to the many boxes sitting on the floor next to the tree. "I brought down all the decorations from the attic. I swear one of the boxes actually groaned when I opened it. It's been a long time since I've pulled them out."

"I know, honey. I'm so sorry Christmas has been so hard on you," she soothed.

"Thanks. This year, I think, will be a little easier." Kelly caressed Susan's cheek with her thumb and pulled her into a tender embrace. "Thank you for being here." Their bodies melted together, with the smaller woman's head fitting perfectly under Kelly's chin. Susan looked up with love in her big brown eyes, and Kelly's heart felt like it would explode. *She has filled that part of me that has longed to feel this for so long.* Kelly lowered her head and their lips met softly; the taste of Susan upon her tongue was like nectar from the gods.

I'm sure that goes for other regions of her body as well, the impudent voice interjected.

God, she makes me so crazy! I'm so turned on by her kisses, I could just swallow her whole.

One kiss turned into several. Kelly could feel Susan's hips pressing into her. She slid her hands down to caress Susan's lower back, pulling her gently against her body. Their breathing escalated rapidly, and Kelly knew that soon they were going to spiral towards the point of no return.

"Mm..." Susan moaned into Kelly's mouth, sending jolts of electricity throughout her body.

"Oh, baby," Kelly whispered in response as their lips separated.

Susan's assault moved to Kelly's neck, and she continued to press herself against the soft body as her hands strayed lower down her back and began kneading the muscles in Kelly's butt.

Kelly started to repay the neck kissing in kind, and felt herself losing control. She knew she couldn't take much more without wanting to take what they had begun to its natural conclusion. She also knew if they continued, there was absolutely *no way* the tree was going to get decorated. *If anything is getting trimmed, it's going to be me!*

"Susan?" she croaked. There was no reply, just murmurs of pleasure. *Not good.* "Susan, honey... we need to stop. I... I can't take much more," she managed to grate out in a voice husky with desire.

Her face flushed with arousal, Susan pulled back. Her eyes were focused on Kelly's, and it looked as though her hostess was going to be her next meal, a fact that was both exciting and daunting. A few moments passed as they held each other loosely, and their passion slowly began to simmer down.

Susan's forehead was resting on Kelly's breastbone as she tried to get her breathing under control. "God, Kelly, you make me so crazy!" she said, frustrated.

Kelly smiled and kissed the top of her head. "I was just thinking the same thing about you a few moments ago."

Taking one last deep breath, Susan looked up at

Kelly with a beautiful smile. "Let's do this thing! We'll get back to the unfinished business later." She winked and walked to the corner of the room to get to the boxes.

"Oh, God..." Kelly breathed as she followed in her footsteps. *This is going to be the fastest tree trimming the world has ever seen.*

A Saving Solace

Chapter Twenty

Susan was thinking just the opposite, deciding to torment Kelly by stretching out the decorating and seeing how excited she could get her. *I want to try to take away all the bad memories she has and start fresh with our own. I really think I'm ready for her. I want to love her so badly that my body is literally shaking right now. Just those few minutes with her have made me a walking hormone.*

Directing her attention to the boxes, Susan said, "Holy cow, you have a lot of decorations. This would even compete with my parents' collection. This is going to be a beautiful tree." *And this is going to be the best Christmas ever.*

Kelly was watching Susan and trying to be subtle about it. The younger woman smiled at her to let her know she'd been busted. Kelly's eyes grew wide and she tried to look away but Susan took her hand and led her to the boxes, wanting to start the decorating before she totally lost her own resolve.

"So, where would you like to start?" she asked.

Kelly looked her up and down, and said, "Well, I could think of a few places I'd like to start on, right now."

Susan knew they weren't thinking on the same level at all. Though she was pleased at the comment, she cried with mock outrage, "The tree, Kel!"

Laughing, Kelly cleared her throat, then looked at the tree with serious consideration. "Well, you should start with the lights first, then the ornaments, then the tinsel." She smiled. "At least, that's how we've always done it."

"Well, lucky for you, it's the same where I came

from. Do you have a topper for the tree?"

"Yes. Actually I have a smaller version of you; I have an angel," She dug through a couple of boxes until she found what she was looking for. "It's from my childhood. My mom loved this thing," she whispered as she touched the angel reverently.

"It's lovely. I know your mom would be happy that it's making an appearance this year," Susan said guardedly, uncertain as to whether she should assume anything about Kelly's mother.

"Yeah," she breathed. "I think you're right. I think Mom's gonna be happy that I'm dressing the tree with someone special this year, too."

"Good. I know I am."

"Me, too." Kelly looked deep in thought, then looked back at her guest. "Would you like some music to go with our festivities?"

"Sure! I love the classic carols. Do you have Bing Crosby or Nat King Cole? Those are my favorites," Susan said, sounding like a child. She was actually excited about trimming the tree, even more than before.

"I think I can accommodate you." Kelly smiled, then flipped through her enormous CD collection and pulled out three. She placed the CDs in the player and closed the drawer. Within seconds, the room was filled with wonderful sounds, and memories pervaded Susan's thoughts.

She had always loved Christmas with her folks, and the music took her back to a time when she and her parents were trimming their tree together: they were laughing and singing, without a care in the world. *Who knew our lives would change because I didn't want to hide who I was? I'll never understand how they could forget me so easily.*

"Susan? Can we make a pact right now?" Kelly said seriously.

"Sure," she agreed, with a note of hesitation.
"Tonight is our night. No more sad thoughts or dwelling on things we can't change. Okay? Let's just enjoy each other and create some new magic. I think we both need that desperately."

Susan knew she had tears in her eyes again, but she didn't care. *She must've seen me drift off. Damn.* "Deal. I like that idea very much, Kelly," she agreed. "Now, let's get to work."

Bing crooned some of their favorites and Nat followed shortly after. Susan watched as Kelly wrapped the lights around the tree, branch by branch, with a practiced hand. "I think I know what duty you had," she said brightly.

"Yeah. I was the only one that could wrap the lights up on top without falling off the ladder. I've grown quite fond of this, actually. You have to have the lights just right, otherwise the whole tree is off, you know?" she explained, as she continued to wrap string after string of lights around the branches.

Susan smiled at her as she watched Kelly dim the overhead lights and squint at the illuminated tree. It was an old trick to make sure there were no blank spots on the tree. "You *are* a master, aren't you?" she teased.

"You hush. Just you wait, you'll see what a beauty this one's going to be," Kelly said with a smile.

"I see a beauty, all right. But she's not green and prickly," Susan shot back.

Kelly smiled such an amazing smile that it took Susan's breath away. It never ceased to amaze her how gorgeous Kelly was. *I could stare at her all night. Perhaps I will, just to make her nervous. She'll try to figure out what I'm thinking, I'll bet. I hope she knows how much she's come to mean to me.*

"Okay, I think we're ready for the ornaments," Kelly announced.

Susan bent over a box and took out a couple of crystal ornaments that were just stunning, as anything cast in crystal would be. There was one of the Virgin Mary holding a tiny Jesus. "These are gorgeous, Kelly. Are these new, or have you had them a while?" she asked.

"That particular one is old. I think it belonged to my grandmother. Which reminds me, I called her the other day to see what she was doing tonight."

"Really? How is she?" Susan asked, very pleased that her friend had made the effort to make contact.

"She's doing okay. There's still such a distance between us that I really hate. We used to be closer. I just wish we had that again," Kelly said with a sigh.

"You will, honey. How can she resist you? I know I can't," she stated honestly, moving to the tree to hang the ornaments that were in her hand. She turned to Kelly and willed her to see the passion that was in her heart.

They each took one step closer to one another, then their bodies crashed together. Their mouths met harshly and they began to suck wildly on each other's lips. The wet smacking sounds drove Susan's hunger to an even higher pitch. She wanted Kelly so badly. But there was the tree to be finished.

Before Susan knew what was happening, Kelly's tongue rushed past her lips and Kelly began to drink from her. Her tongue was soft yet determined in its exploration. Susan felt the fireworks go off once again, and her body was humming Kelly's tune. They both needed the loving so badly; and they would have it.

"God, I want you... so much..." Kelly said huskily into Susan's mouth.

"I'm yours, honey... no one else's..." the smaller woman whispered back.

Kelly's kisses slowed to tenderness, and then she pulled her head back to look deeply into Susan's eyes.

The words began to sink in, and she swallowed a few times before speaking. "Do you mean that?" Kelly asked, sounding like a small child who was amazed by a gift.

"I do, Kelly. I'm yours, if you want me. Forever, if you'd like." Susan almost whispered the last part, not sure if she'd asked for too much.

"I'd like that very much, baby. *So* much..." she growled, as she picked Susan up and held her tightly.

They giggled as Kelly spun Susan around the living room. Susan had never felt so light-hearted. She'd known this woman for such a short time, yet Kelly was filling a gap in her that she'd thought would always be empty. It was funny how things sometimes happened.

Kelly set her down and they went about putting all the ornaments and tinsel on the tree. It was just gorgeous. Kelly took the last strand of tinsel and draped it over her mother's picture on the mantel. Susan's heart ached for her, for the sadness she must be feeling intermingling with their joy.

"Merry Christmas, Momma," she whispered, as she kissed the photo again. Kelly turned to Susan as if to explain, even though it wasn't necessary. "The tinsel was her favorite part of the tree. She always did the tinsel. We covered her casket with it at the funeral." She paused and took a much-needed breath. "God, I miss her, Susan."

"I know, honey, I know. I also know that she's here with us, right now. She only left the physical world." Susan tried to lighten the mood. "I think God took her then so she could watch over you now. Maybe she can watch you better this way." Kelly was silent and Susan could tell that she was thinking about what she'd just said.

"Do you really think so? For the longest time I could never come to terms with why He'd taken her. She was the most beautiful person on this earth. She did anything for anyone, without hesitation. She even went to church every flippin' day! I was so angry with God that I stopped talking to Him altogether. I couldn't believe He'd taken someone that had shown such love for Him." Kelly started to pace around while she spoke.

It was the first time she'd really opened up about her feelings about her mother's death, and Susan was glad she trusted her enough to share it all.

"I was such an angry person for such a long time. I think that's why I slept with so many strangers; I just wanted to feel something other than the rage. Anything else. I wanted instant gratification, and I got it. I feel bad for some of the women I slept with, though."

"Why?" Susan questioned. "I can't imagine you were mean to them."

Kelly stopped pacing and crossed back to her, taking hold of her hands. She looked down and her blue eyes burned into Susan's soul, and she knew Kelly could never harm anyone.

"No, I wasn't mean, but some of them wanted to pursue a relationship. I wanted no part of that. I didn't want to love, because that would only mean it would hurt again the day that I lost it. I felt that loss with Julie's betrayal. You're the first person I've wanted in my life since her. It scares me to death, though, Susan. You have to know that."

"I think I have a good idea. What we have is very strong, and it scares me too, Kelly. I've never felt for anyone, what I feel for you. We've only known each other really for, what, a few weeks, right? But it feels like I've known you my whole life!" she exclaimed. "I know you're scared, but I'm right there with you, honey."

The grip that was holding Susan's hands loosened a bit as Kelly snuck one arm behind the smaller woman's back. They turned so her arm held Susan's waist and

Susan was leaning into her body, resting her head on Kelly's chest as they stared at their first Christmas tree.

"You do a pretty good tree, Miss Cavanaugh," Susan said, her smile evident in her voice.

"Thanks, darlin'. It is a pretty one."

They waited a few more seconds for the music to come to an end, and then the only sound to be heard was Mattie's panting from the couch. Kelly turned to face her pet and called to her, "What do you think, Mattie? Should we keep her?"

Mattie's tail thumped wildly against the cushions on the sofa.

"I think so, too," Kelly said as she kissed the top of Susan's head.

"So, should I assume that I'm in?" their guest teased.

"You?" Kelly's eyebrows shot up. "I was talking about the tree!"

Susan's feigned look of injury couldn't have held water if it needed to. Dancing with such love and mischief, Kelly's baby blues were too much for her. She couldn't even imagine being with anyone else.

"There's one more thing we need to do," Kelly whispered.

"Oh, yeah. It wouldn't be complete without it"

"Would you do the honors? I'll hold the stool for you."

Kelly could've asked for anything right then and the answer would have been yes. "I'd love to, Kelly. Thanks," Susan beamed. She reached higher than she thought safe, and rested the angel on the top of the tree. When they plugged her in, she lit right up, adding the finishing touch to make theirs the perfect Christmas tree.

"How's that?" she asked Kelly's upturned face.

"Perfect."

"I think so too," Susan said as she started to climb

down.

When she missed the next step down and started to fall, well-toned arms immediately shot out and caught her before she hit the floor. "God, I'm sorry!" Susan shrieked. "Thank you. You're my hero."

"It was no problem. You're a lightweight," Kelly chuckled, cradling her catch against her.

Susan nestled into her embrace for a few moments, then sighed loudly. "I feel so safe here, Kelly."

"I feel safe with you here, too. If I could, I'd hold you all day. Just like this." She kissed Susan gently on the lips and moved them to the couch, sitting them both down without changing their positions.

Susan sat cradled in Kelly's lap, strong arms wrapped around her protectively, and she knew there would never be another place that would feel like that. She would never have to look again.

Thank God.

"It really is beautiful. I'm so glad you convinced me to do this. Thank you, Susan."

"It was my pleasure. I really wanted to do this with you. I'm glad you let me in. We both have a lot to be thankful for, don't we?"

Kelly nodded. "Which reminds me…" she said as she gracefully tipped Susan off her lap. Going into the kitchen, she came back with a wrapped gift.

Susan assumed it was for her. "Kelly, I thought we said no gifts."

Putting her finger to pouting lips to silence them, she said, "This is more than a gift. Please, just open it." She sat down next to her guest and anxiously waited for her to open the package.

Muttering softly to herself, Susan took the lightweight gift into her hands and instantly turned back into a child. It'd been a long while since she'd opened a Christmas gift. She shook the box, hoping to guess what was inside. She put her ear to it and smiled. "Well, it's not ticking, so that's a good thing."

"Just open it!" Kelly cried.

"Fine, be a spoil sport," she grumbled playfully. Susan reached to the side of the box and tore open the tape and wrapping. When she pulled out the box, she saw that it held a cellular phone. "Oh, Kelly... this is too much... please...I can't..."

She interrupted, "Susan, please. Like I said, this is more than a gift; this is a safety thing for me. You don't have a phone at your place and frankly, it makes me crazy!" she laughed. "There were so many nights I wanted just to talk to you, and I couldn't. I hated waiting for you to get to work. Even then we could only talk for a couple of minutes. You use public transportation every day, and anything could happen to you. This way I'll know you're safe all the time. Please, just take this. Please?"

Big blue eyes were staring at Susan with such affection that she didn't have a chance in hell of denying her request. "Thank you, Kelly. I could never afford one of these. No one would've called anyhow, so I didn't think to bother."

"Well, it's paid for, and you have a year of service and about a million minutes; so, you'd better use them all on me!" she joked.

Susan reached over and threw her arms around the taller woman, starting to cry before she could stop herself. "Thank you so much," she sobbed. "You are so good to me. Thank you so much."

Snuggled into Kelly's arms, Susan cried for several moments. Being rocked slowly, she felt herself begin to calm. Her head lifted from the soggy shoulder, and Kelly wiped her tears with trembling fingers. Reaching behind her and grabbing the box of tissues off the table, Kelly gestured for Susan to blow her nose. She did as requested, and then Kelly took another tissue and wiped her face, clearing away all evidence of any sadness.

"Ahh, there's my girl," she said as she finished her task.

"I'm so glad that I'm your girl. I've never felt so cared for."

"I do care for you, baby. Very much."

Kelly held her close and softly brushed her cheeks with the backs of her knuckles. Her fingers reached further back and began to massage the back of Susan's head.

Tingles went through Susan's body as Kelly lightly scratched her scalp. "I'll give you six hours to knock that off," she giggled.

"I think I have six hours. In fact, I do believe, I have all night."

"Lucky me," Susan whispered, as Kelly's face got closer to hers.

"Funny, I was thinking the exact same thing," she said, closing the distance between them with a gentle kiss to soft, inviting lips.

Chapter Twenty-One

Kelly's heart was beating triple time, feeling Susan nestling in her arms and hearing her make the most sensual noises against her neck. *Between her quick breaths and her deep sighs, she is truly going to drive me insane. She can call the little men in white coats; I couldn't care less. She can wrap herself around me any time she wants.*

Considering Susan's responsiveness, Kelly wondered if the younger woman was ready to explore other facets of their relationship. *There doesn't seem to be any hesitation from either one of us tonight. I know I'm more than ready to show her how deeply I care for her. I'm pretty sure she's feeling the same for me right now.*

She continued her assault on Susan's neck as Susan purred happily. "Baby?" she said huskily.

"Yeah?" Susan sighed into the nearby ear sending jolts of desire throughout Kelly's body.

"Can we move this into my room? As much as I like playing pretzel on the couch with you, I don't know how much more my back can take." She smiled gently, hoping she wasn't presuming too much.

"I think I'd like you right over there," Susan said with a hand gesture as she wriggled her way out of Kelly's grasp and off the couch.

She reached down and grabbed Kelly's hand and led her confused but willing captive towards the fireplace and in front of the tree. She turned out the lights in the room, leaving only the tree and the fire in the hearth for light.

"Stay... " She smiled. "Don't move. I'll be right back," she said seductively as Kelly felt the air leave her

lungs.
This is really going to happen. Tonight. My God!
Susan crossed to the couch and grabbed two pillows and the blanket that was draped along the back of the couch. She took her booty and positioned it on the floor. "Sit," she commanded gently.
Kelly eagerly complied, reclining on the floor with her elbows resting behind her. Watching Susan in the firelight, she knew she'd never seen anyone more beautiful in her life.
"Are you ready for me?" Susan whispered sexily. "Because I don't think I can wait any longer for you."
Kelly knew her gulp was audible, but she didn't care. "Yes." It was the only word that she could make come out of her mouth. She nodded to reinforce her monosyllable. She hadn't really had any idea what power Susan held over her until that moment.
"I'm glad," Susan said with a saucy smile, beginning to slowly undress before transfixed eyes. She watched Kelly closely for any sign of reluctance. Kelly watched mutely; her brain had shut down.
"I want you to know how much I want you, Kelly," she whispered as she began to unbutton her blouse.
Kelly watched as Susan's fingers mastered each button with excruciating slowness. "I don't think I've ever wanted or desired anyone like I want you right now," she confessed honestly. "Please come down here." Kelly reached up to take Susan's hand, but she avoided the grasp.
"Soon, my darling; patience is a virtue." As Kelly's eyebrow raised, Susan's her hips started to sway as she pulled her shirttail from her jeans.
Kelly knew that she was in deep trouble. And Susan was her name-o.
She slipped the blouse off of her shoulders and Kelly watched as it tumbled onto the floor. Susan stood

before her in jeans and bra.
I don't think I'll ever recover from this torture.
Kelly couldn't wait to feel Susan's skin against her. She could tell from the expression on the temptress's face that she knew she was getting to her. Susan was confident and in control—a deadly combination, or so Kelly was beginning to think.

Susan moved her fingers to the button on her jeans. She undid the one fastener and slowly slid the zipper down its serrated path, then brought both of her hands inside her waistband and slid the material down her hips and thighs. She heard Kelly's gasp, and smirked at her with unbridled lust in her eyes. She knew she had Kelly's number, and Kelly was in no shape to argue.

Raising one leg to grasp at the ankle of her pants, Susan divested her leg of its encasement, then followed suit with her other leg, leaving her practically naked before Kelly's widening eyes.

"You are so beautiful, Susan," Kelly breathed.

"Thank you, sweetheart," she said as she knelt in front of Kelly at last.

Kelly sat up and let her eyes travel over the body clad only in undergarments. Susan was shapelier and stronger than she had imagined. The sandy blonde hair was brushed away from her sculpted face by a trembling hand, and it felt like silk against Kelly's fingers. Susan's shoulders and midsection were strong, but with a feminine softness. Kelly badly wanted to touch her, but she wanted to make sure Susan wanted that, as well. It seemed to be her show, after all.

"Do you want to touch me, Kelly?"

Kelly looked confused by the no-brainer of a question. *Who wouldn't want to touch her?* "More than anything," she replied with hooded eyes.

"You have to pay a toll first."

Kelly's eyes flared a bit at the request, but she

would've offered anything at that point and Susan knew it. "Whatever you want is yours," she said honestly.

"Your sweater. Off. Now," Susan commanded, and no sooner had the edict come from her than Kelly's sweater had been removed, leaving her in bra and slacks.

When she had been with other women, Kelly had always controlled the situation. Somehow, she had never imagined herself in the submissive position that she found herself in at that moment. It was a completely different role for her. It dawned on her that Susan wasn't at all like the other women that she'd slept with. She was more than a one-night stand, and always would be. *If she were like them, I never would've fallen in love with her.*

Love? Did you say love?

Yes, I did. Dear God! I'm in love with Susan McGovern!

Kelly's heart began to beat wildly at her discovery. Her hands hurriedly unbuttoned and unzipped her pants. She had never wanted anything so much in her life.

"Slow down, sweetie. We have all night, remember?" Susan cooed softly.

The older woman blushed like a schoolgirl. She was so out of control it was making her dizzy. Susan had her wrapped tightly in her web, and Kelly was sure she didn't even know she'd spun one.

"Let me get those," Susan said softly as she leaned over to pull down on the waist of Kelly's pants. "Lean back, honey. It's okay, I've got you."

She leaned back and watched as Susan slowly pulled the clothing down her legs, their eyes never leaving one another's.

"God, Kelly, you are the most gorgeous woman I've ever laid eyes on."

Kelly's cheeks got red with that compliment. Susan knew her buttons and was pushing them in all the right places. She reached for Kelly's hands and situated them so they were kneeling in front of each other. Kelly cupped her face with her right hand as Susan mirrored the gesture. They stared deeply into each other's eyes, drawing their faces even closer, Kelly searching Susan's face one last time looking for any reservations or doubts. She found none.

Leaning forward, she captured Susan's lips with her own, the kiss soft and unprobing. They relished the feeling for many moments. The softness of their lips just tasting each other was making Kelly thirsty for more, and she gently slid her tongue to Susan's lips and laved the texture that she found there.

Susan's mouth opened wider, accepting Kelly fully within her. She tasted wonderful. Their kisses became hotter with each moment that passed. Lips and tongues sought out their mates, trying to slake the need that was beginning to burn out of control.

They took turns taking off the remainder of the other's clothing, leaving nothing but their nakedness between them. When their bodies came together, Kelly's eyes rolled into her head, the feel of Susan's flesh sending chills through her body. The warm, smooth skin against hers felt like everything she'd thought it would, and more. Kelly knew that heaven was just around the corner.

She softly kissed Susan's cheek and then over to her ear. Feeling Susan's grasp tighten, Kelly breathed softly against her neck. Nipping and sucking the soft skin she found there sent goose bumps down Susan's body.

"Mmm..." she sighed.

"You make me so crazy, baby. Do you have any idea?" Kelly said hoarsely, not expecting an answer.

She felt Susan's reply when a warm tongue trailed down her shoulder and over her collarbone, setting her body on fire, inflaming her to heights that she'd never reached before. She couldn't stifle the sighs and moans that were coming from her mouth.

Tilting her head back, Kelly gave Susan access to more of her body. Susan took full advantage as she slid her tongue lower to capture a nipple in her mouth, swirling her tongue over the sensitive peak and wrapping her arms tightly around Kelly.

"Oh, God..." Kelly sighed heavily; her body began to tremble with need, a need to be one with Susan. She brought her hands up to stroke Susan's breasts as Susan continued to love Kelly's with her mouth. Finding Susan's nipple, she began to roll it between thumb and forefinger while caressing the other with her palm.

"More..." she breathed into Kelly's flesh.

That was all the encouragement she needed. Kelly eased Susan down onto the blanketed floor and laid on top of her. She placed her thigh between Susan's legs and groaned at the unbelievable sensations it caused, her skin tingling from just the contact of their bodies. Kelly leaned into her, pressing her leg against the warm, wet apex and watching Susan's rapture as she moaned softly. Their eyes locked, intensifying every emotion they were feeling.

Kelly's eyes never left Susan's as she took an erecting nipple into her questing mouth. Susan's eyes stayed with her, watching every movement of Kelly's tongue. Kelly was spellbound as Susan brought her hand into the dark hair and began urging her on. Kelly sucked harder on the turgid flesh, which brought a louder response from her lover. The rate of her breathing increased, as did Kelly's, who was getting greatly aroused by observing Susan while she loved her breasts. She bit down tentatively, awaiting Susan's response, and wasn't disappointed.

"Oh, God, yes," she moaned. "Harder."

Kelly's hips begin to thrust harder against Susan as

she suckled her nipples with every ounce of passion she was feeling. She switched breasts often, trying to give her as much pleasure as possible. The thrusting of Susan's hips was in sync with her own; she could feel the sweat begin to form and roll off of her back. Their fingers intertwined as Susan gripped Kelly's hands with a surprising strength.

Body sliding even lower, Kelly's sex straddled Susan's thigh. Their bodies moved as one as their passions rose. Kelly could feel Susan's wetness against her leg, which ratcheted her desire even higher. She wanted to love Susan with her mouth; she needed to taste her release.

"Turn over, baby," she whispered.

Susan nodded and Kelly lifted herself slightly to give her room to roll onto her stomach. She moved up to her neck and began to lick slowly down her spine, Susan's body arching in response to her actions.

"Oh, Kel... you feel so good," she murmured into the pillow.

Susan grasped the edges of the pillow as Kelly traced her spine down to her buttocks then kissed each cheek reverently, feeling more love for Susan with each stroke of her tongue. Kelly knelt between her legs and gently spread her cheeks.

Susan's breathing hitched as she felt the tip of Kelly's tongue run along the crease of her buttocks. She tongued each of Susan's orifices tenderly but thoroughly, and felt Susan's hips grind into the floor in response.

"Please..." she begged throatily.

Kelly lifted her head from her task and teased, "Please what?"

"Please go inside of me, Kelly. I want to feel you deep inside of me," she answered huskily.

"Anything, baby. I'll give you anything you want," she whispered truthfully. Bringing obliging fingers down to her wetness, Kelly found her opening, and filled her lover completely, causing her to scream out.

"Yes!" Susan cried out, raising herself to her knees.

Kelly wrapped her left arm around Susan's waist, thrusting her fingers in time with the movement of lunging hips. Kelly prolonged the interaction, taking great pleasure in hearing Susan calling her name. The sound was bringing her close to her own release.

Without disturbing the rhythm they'd created, Kelly swung herself onto her back, turning so that her head was between Susan's legs. With the hand that was free, she pulled down on Susan's hips, bringing the swollen clitoris to her mouth.

Susan whimpered at the contact. "Jesus!"

Kelly began to bathe her clitoris with wild abandon, her tongue and fingers working in tandem to send Susan into oblivion. She could hear her partner's breathing quicken with each digital thrust, could taste her impending climax.

"Omigod!" Susan groaned as she started to buck against Kelly's face.

Kelly moaned loudly as she felt her own orgasm crest along with Susan's.

Their bodies continued to thrust blindly until they could no longer move. Kelly lay there kissing the insides of Susan's thighs until she'd worked herself out from under her. When the smaller body collapsed onto the floor with an ungainly thud, Kelly crawled up next to her and spooned against her side.

Kissing her cheek and ear, Kelly began to speak from her heart. "God, I love you. I've never met anyone that makes me feel the way you do."

Susan rolled over on her side to face her lover, staring into blue eyes as her own began to well with unshed tears. "Oh, sweetheart," she breathed. "I love you, too."

Kelly's heart melted at the admission and they reached for each other. Resting Susan's head on her chest, Kelly held her as tightly as she could without hurting her. Susan's leg was thrown over the top of Kelly's, and her arm wrapped around her waist as if she were going to fall off.

"Easy, baby. I'm not going anywhere, I promise," Kelly whispered into her hair. She rubbed Susan's back tenderly as she felt the grip loosen. Peppering the blonde head with many kisses, Kelly tried to convey everything that she was feeling. She could feel Susan's sobs as well as her tears on her bare chest. "Shh... what's wrong, baby? Can you tell me?" Kelly soothed.

Susan moved her head so her face was looking squarely into Kelly's, searching her face for any hint of insincerity. There wasn't any. Kelly had finally found someone to spend her life with, someone that would guard her heart as if it were her own.

Susan looked into her eyes with watery affection. "If someone had told me a year ago that my life would be like this, I would've told them they were crazy. I never imagined myself being this happy ever again. Sometimes I wonder when I'm going to wake up from this wonderful dream. Things like this only happen in dreams and storybooks," she sniffled.

"Well, if this is a dream, then I don't want to wake up, either. I never thought I'd find anyone as wonderful as you. I'm so glad I was wrong. You are the most incredible woman I've ever met." Kelly placed her fingers over Susan's lips to forestall any rebuttal. "Before you say anything, it's true. I love you; and I never thought I'd find anyone who I'd want to say that to ever again."

Susan took Kelly's fingers from her lips and kissed them one by one. "I was only going to tell you that I love you, too. I've never had this much love in my heart before. I just hope it doesn't go away."

"Me too," Kelly agreed.

"Say it again, Kelly. Tell me you love me again, please?" Susan asked.

"I love you, Susan. I love you with all that I am."

"I love you, too, so much. Thank you for loving me. I can't imagine my life without you," she said, looking as if she were going to cry again.

"I know the feeling. Every thought that I've had in the past weeks has been about you. Anytime I think about something that I'm going to do or need to do, you're in the picture as well. I hope to have you by my side for a long time, Susan. I mean that."

"I'll be here as long as you want me."

"Good. I like you here."

Their embrace became more relaxed as they caressed each other gently. Kelly felt goose bumps rise on Susan's cooled skin and knew they needed to get into the warmth of her bed.

"Are you ready for bed? I'm getting kind of chilly," Susan confessed.

"With you by my side, I'm ready for anything," Kelly said with a smile as she kissed the damp forehead.

Chapter Twenty-Two

After closing the glass doors to the fireplace and turning off the lights, they walked arm in arm up the stairs towards Kelly's bedroom. Susan's body was still reeling from what they'd shared. She had known that making love with Kelly was going to be special, but had had no idea how much so.

I will never feel as loved with anyone else again. I know that I've found the other half of my soul in Kelly. We just fit so well.

"You want to wash up first or shall I?" Kelly asked.

"I'll go first. I have to pee anyway," Susan said sheepishly.

"Okay, darlin'. I'll be waiting for you when you get out," she whispered, as she leaned in and kissed willing lips.

Susan walked into the bathroom and looked at her reflection in the mirror, wondering if she would see a change. She felt different; she had been loved like no other. Nothing would change her feelings for Kelly. They were in it for the long haul. That she knew for certain.

She used the facilities and brushed her teeth before returning to the bedroom, where she found Kelly lying on the bed, wearing nothing but a smile.

"Penny for your thoughts," Susan giggled.

"Oh, I'm pretty sure you can guess what I'm thinking right now."

"Yeah, I think I can. It's probably what I'm thinking right about now."

"Well, hold onto that thought until I get back," Kelly said as she got up and walked towards Susan. She leaned down and kissed her deeply before going into the bathroom. The door clicked shut and Susan felt her heart jump once again. The woman had a hold on her like a vise grip.

She hopped onto the large bed and assumed her position under the covers. The scent of her lover was everywhere, sending fresh chills down her body. It was something she was growing to love more and more with each day that passed. Kelly had such a clean, fresh smell all the time, a major change from the people she usually hung out with.

Who'd have thought my life would end up like this? I know I never thought I'd be this fortunate again. Never in my wildest dreams did I think a woman like Kelly could ever love me. Boy, am I glad I was mistaken. I can't imagine my life without her now.

Susan heard the water from the faucet turn off a second before she heard the door open. Her naked, beautiful lover walked to her as if she were on the prowl, and Susan felt like prey under Kelly's smoky gaze. She was powerless to look away, and had no desire to do so.

Kelly's long frame found its way into the bed beside Susan. She clicked off the light on the nightstand and shifted closer to her bedmate. "Miss me?" Kelly purred as she brought her hand to one luscious breast and squeezed lightly.

"Oh yeah..." Susan whispered, unable to keep the desire from her voice.

"I'm glad. I really want to make love with you again. I don't think that I'll ever get enough of you."

"Don't worry, I'm not going anywhere any time soon," Susan said as she grasped the hand that was rubbing her breast. She squeezed gently, letting Kelly know she was very much in favor of another round of loving with her.

"I like how you think," she growled playfully, as she tugged a little on Susan's breast.

"I like how you feel," Susan countered.

"Well, I *love* how you feel."

"Yeah, well, I love you," the young blonde said, landing the winning blow.

In the darkness, Kelly chuckled into her ear. "I love you, too."

"Merry Christmas, sweetheart," Susan whispered.

"Merry Christmas, baby," Kelly said as she moved her body on top of the smaller one beside her.

Her kisses told Susan that they weren't going to be sleeping any time soon, but she wouldn't have had it any other way. She was starting to think that 'dreams coming true' wasn't such a load of shit after all. She had the proof right there in her arms.

Right where she belonged.

A Saving Solace

Chapter Twenty-Three

As she opened her eyes in the early dawn light, Susan felt a warm, pleasant weight on her, and wondered how she'd managed to sleep with Kelly resting almost fully on top of her during the night.

Kelly's breathing was deep and even, telling Susan she was still asleep and allowing her some unguarded time to just watch her. *God, she's gorgeous. And she loves me. Me! She told me so herself. How lucky am I to have a beautiful creature like Kelly want someone like me?*

Words weren't enough to convey what Susan was feeling. She stroked languid fingers down Kelly's naked back and felt her nuzzle deeper against her, the soft sigh of contentment almost melting her very soul. It also cemented the fact that the previous night had really happened.

So, this is what love is all about.

She had wondered what all the fuss was about. Though she had thought she was in love with Cindy; what she felt with Kelly was completely different. She knew she'd found her life partner, and it felt good.

She took a deep breath and felt Kelly shift again. This time she locked eyes with sleepy blue ones and smiled softly.

"Good morning, sunshine," Kelly whispered.

"Merry Christmas, sweetheart," Susan said with a tiny smile.

Kelly moved up slowly until her soft lips captured Susan's in a tender, loving exchange. Their lips melded and allowed them to express anew how much love they had for each other.

They broke apart and Kelly gave Susan a slow grin that made her heart swell. "Did you sleep all right?" she rasped in her sleep-filled voice.

"Like a baby." Susan couldn't keep the smile off her face.

"You're my baby," she stated.

"I hope so."

"You *are* so." Kelly sealed her testimony with another searing kiss that curled Susan's toes.

God she has a knack for that. Susan's stomach took that moment to announce its emptiness, which elicited a throaty chuckle from her lover.

"What was that?"

"Three guesses, and the first two don't count," Susan teased.

"Hmmm... I'll guess that... you're... I don't know... hungry?" Kelly joked.

"Give that woman a prize!" Susan said, in her best game show host voice.

Giggling, they began to wrestle under the covers. Kelly pulled Susan on top of her and brushed errant strands of blonde hair behind her ears. She said nothing as she gazed deeply into Susan's eyes, then exclaimed, "God, you are so beautiful."

Susan swallowed convulsively as she nodded. *I will not cry. I will not cry. I will not cry.* She mentally chanted the mantra, but felt the tears betray her. As a rebellious tear ran down her cheek, Kelly brushed it away with a gentle thumb.

"I love you," Susan choked out before resting against Kelly's body.

Loving hands stroked her back, and then tightened into a strong hold. "I love you, too."

After a while, they broke apart and got dressed to go eat breakfast. Susan was so hungry she felt as if she could eat the house. It was going to be a long day, too. As much as she enjoyed going to the kitchens and helping feed the homeless, it would always be an ugly reminder of what her life had been.

The trio walked downstairs, and Susan sat down at the kitchen table, while Kelly smiled widely at her pup and asked Mattie, "You gotta go out, girl?"

Mattie's tail wagged frantically as she waited for her mistress to open the back door. Kelly let her out and watched her as she ran through the backyard. "She's so pretty when she runs." Kelly looked over at Susan with love in her eyes.

"Yes, she is," her young houseguest agreed. "So, what's for breakfast? Would you like me to make something? I can make eggs or…"

"Not so fast… It's a Christmas tradition that I make omelets and sausages for Mattie and myself; but since you're here with us this year, I'll just have to make enough for three."

"Well then, by all means, cook away," Susan said as she gestured to the stove.

Kelly playfully smacked her thigh as she passed. "You're lucky you're sitting on what I wanted to slap."

"Ooh, I'm *not* so lucky, then. I'd like it if you smacked my ass." Susan laughed at Kelly's reaction.

"Are there… um… some things you like that you didn't mention last night?" Kelly asked with wiggling eyebrows.

"You'll just have to wait and see, dear chef."

"Oh, now that's something to look forward to." Kelly smiled her toothy grin, and Susan knew she was serious.

Lucky me.

~~*~*~*~*

They eventually made their way down to the church where they would be helping feed the hungry for most of the day. It was their second venture to the church that day, the first having been to attend Mass. Kelly had been very happy that Susan wanted to go; it was nice to attend Christmas Mass with someone special. It made the day even more memorable.

Never having done any volunteer work of that particular nature, serving up a holiday meal to those less fortunate was going to be an experience for Kelly. It was going to break her heart to see such destitute people, but on the other hand, it was always good to have a reality check. It also made her appreciate how amazing Susan was. Despite her own experiences, she still had such a beauty inside of her, more than she even realized herself. It took a very special person to do what Susan did.

"I've um... got some questions, if you'd be kind enough to help me out," Kelly said, looking at Susan and the road.

"Sure, honey. What about?"

"About the soup kitchen and such. Is that okay?"

"Shoot. I'll be more than happy to answer them. You're so great to come with me today." Susan beamed at her lover.

Kelly couldn't help but smile back. She had a surprise for Susan that she knew she'd love. "Okay, first of all... do they really still call them soup kitchens? I thought that was an outdated term, and I want to make sure I don't insult anyone."

"Yes, it is an old term, but most everyone knows what that is. I guess they kept it for that reason alone."

"I see. Now what about food vans and such - I remember you telling me about Carol coming to you out in the streets on Christmas."

"Yeah, she did, bless her soul..." Susan stared blankly at the road. "Oh... sorry, sweetie... um... oh yeah... food vans... Well, the church has rented one that we will use later in the day. They usually have warmers for the food and built-in shelves in the back. It's a great way for us to get to the people that don't venture out of their 'homes.'"

Kelly visualized Susan and Carol meeting for the first time. Just picturing Susan out there sent sadness through her. *I won't ever let that happen to her again. No way. I would work fifty jobs if I had to, to keep her from the streets again.*

"Anything else, honey?" Susan asked, recalling her from her thoughts.

"Umm... I guess I wonder why they do the cafeteria style versus just handing out Styrofoam containers with food already in them."

"Well, we use the cafeteria method to serve the food to keep costs down. The plates or trays we can wash and reuse. They're made of plastic, so no one could use them to physically harm anyone else if something were to happen, and believe me, something always does. Holidays are a very emotional time."

"What do you mean? What happens?"

"Well, I remember hearing about an addict who caused a big scene a few years back. Generally, they're not allowed to participate if they're using, because violent things can happen. Apparently, this guy fooled someone into believing he was straight and broke a glass or a plate and threatened to cut another person if he wasn't given money or something for drugs. The poor guy he attacked got stitches in his neck, too."

"Wow, that's horrible!" Kelly couldn't believe people could do such a thing to one another under the auspices of peace and good will. She decided that she must be more naïve than she'd thought.

"Yeah, it was bad. So, we try to keep everything to a minimum so that the people that do accept our food will be able to eat in peace. That is our main goal."

"Did you ever eat at one of these?" Kelly wasn't

A Saving Solace

sure whether Susan wanted to talk about her experience, but she really wanted to know.

"Well, like I told you before, it took a lot for me to even accept food from Carol, who actually took food *to* people. I was one of the proud who didn't like to accept assistance, so, no, I didn't. I thought it made me stronger, knowing I could survive on my own." She looked out the side window and sighed deeply. "It was really stupid to think that way, though. I could've died out there, with no one to blame but myself. I'm so thankful Carol found me."

"So am I, darlin'. So am I." Kelly laced their fingers together as they drove the rest of the way to the church in comfortable silence.

When they arrived at St. Mary's Church, there were quite a few people already waiting to get down to the basement. That alone made Kelly happy about what she'd arranged. Susan was going to be so excited.

As they got out of the car, Susan eyed her warily. "Why are you smiling like that, Kelly?"

"You'll see, baby."

"Okay. You never cease to amaze me. Why should now be any different?"

"Exactly. Come on, let's go inside."

She directed Susan by placing her hand at the small of her back. They walked into the church just as Reverend O'Malley finished rearranging the altar from the last Mass held on Christmas Day.

"Kelly!" he said with a large grin on his face. He descended from the altar to greet them.

"Hello, Father O'Malley, Merry Christmas. How are you?" Kelly asked, extending her hand to him.

"Good, my dear, thank you. Merry Christmas." He looked over at Susan beside her. "This must be the woman you told me about. Susan, is it?"

Susan's eyes widened at his knowledge of her name.

"Yes. Merry Christmas. It's good to meet you. Miriam, at the office, spoke highly of you. Thank you for allowing us to use the basement this year."

"You are very welcome, Susan. Miriam is a sweet lady and a wonderful parishioner. We've known each other for several years."

Susan nodded and smiled at the friendly priest. "She mentioned you've known each other a while."

Father O'Malley gestured to the basement door. "Well, let's get down there. There is quite a group already."

"Really?" Susan asked, surprised. "I thought we told everyone two o'clock."

"Oh, we did. I guess this year they didn't want to miss the spread."

Confused, Susan looked at Father O'Malley, then at Kelly.

They walked downstairs and Kelly watched with anticipation as Susan's eyes opened wide as she looked around the tables.

The volunteers were everywhere; and people were sitting at tables, eating quietly. "How did we afford this?" Susan asked softly, noticing the warming units on the tables with all kinds of foods heating above them.

"Why don't you ask her?" Father O'Malley directed, pointing at her companion.

"You?" Susan choked back a sob as she looked into Kelly's smiling face. She wrapped her arms around her and hugged her tight. "You are the most wonderful woman! Thank you, Kelly. How did you do this?" she mumbled into her chest.

"Well, most of the volunteers work for Maxine's. I asked some of my employees if they'd help out for a few hours on Christmas. I knew the ones I asked wouldn't mind at all. But as far as the food went, I just contacted a few restaurants until I found the best deal." She smiled at Susan as the tears streamed freely down her cheeks. "I think that Christmas should be happy for everyone. At least, as much as possible, considering the circumstances of their lives."

"Thank you so much. You have no idea what this means to them… and to me."

"I think I do." Kelly leaned down to her ear. "I love you, baby."

This was undoubtedly one of the best Christmases of their lives. Susan hugged her again, and then walked towards the tables to greet everyone. Kelly watched her girl interacting with everyone, and felt a tear sneak down her own cheek. It would only take one other person being there to make the day perfect. And Kelly knew she was smiling down on her right at that moment.

Merry Christmas, Momma.

~~*~*~*~*

They were able to send some people off with extra food since Kelly had purchased too much. *God, she is incredible. What an amazing gift she gave these people. I'm so damn lucky. I don't know how I became so fortunate, but I don't want to jinx it by asking too many questions.*

Even the press showed up again. The same woman that had interviewed Kelly at Maxine's the day before was there, interviewing the town hero once more. Kelly refused to take much credit, but Susan could tell she was happy about what she'd done. And Susan was more than happy to sing her praises.

"Miss McGovern? Can you add anything to this joyous occasion?" the newswoman, Tina Simkins, asked.

"Yes, I can. Kelly Cavanaugh has proved once again that she has a heart of gold. I have lived the life that most of these people are living now, and I would've been much better off had someone donated money for food like this every year. This is a wonderfully selfless thing she's done, and I would hope that everyone watching would follow her example. She's made this a very happy holiday for everyone here," Susan concluded, as she looked at a blushing Kelly with love in her eyes.

"Indeed she has. The Christmas spirit is alive and well here in the town of Northshire, and the St. Nicholas responsible is once again, Kelly Cavanaugh. I'm Tina Simkins, reporting from St. Mary's Church. Back to you, James."

The interview went until a little after five o'clock and ended just in time for them to get into the van to spread more Christmas cheer throughout the homeless community. Susan was proud of Kelly, and she wanted to make sure the rest of the city knew just how proud she was.

A Saving Solace

Chapter Twenty-Four

"...I'm Tina Simkins, reporting from St. Mary's Church. Back to you, James."

The television clicked off as the tears streamed down Elise McGovern's face. Seeing her daughter twice in two days, she finally took the step she'd been hesitating over for years.

"Oh, Susan, I'm going to get you back, I promise you. I won't give up on finding you this time."

Mrs. McGovern went into her kitchen and opened the cabinet containing her phonebook. She leafed through the pages until she found the listing for Maxine's clothing store.

"General information... Store hours... Shoes... Accessories... Regional Office... Yes, that's what I need," she said to herself.

She nervously picked up her phone, keeping her finger on the number in the phonebook. As she dialed, she felt her heartbeat increase tenfold. The number she had dialed began to ring, and she started to fidget and pace through her kitchen. The answering machine clicked on, as she knew it would.

After the click, she heard, "Hi, you've reached the office of Kelly Cavanaugh, regional manager for Maxine's. I'm either on the phone, or away from my office at this time. Please leave me your name, a number where you can be reached, and a brief description of the reason you are calling. Thank you, and have a wonderful holiday." The beep indicated that the machine was ready to record her message, but Elise paused, not knowing how to begin. She finally opened her mouth to speak just as the machine switched off.

"Dammit!" the woman screamed, angry with

175

herself for hesitating. "This is your daughter, Elise McGovern! Don't make that mistake again."

She redialed the number and waited for the message on the machine to finish. After the beep, she mustered her courage and spoke. "Hello, Miss Cavanaugh, my name is Elise McGovern. This is going to seem very strange, but I saw you on the news over the holidays and you were with a woman I believe to be my daughter, Susan. I... I would really like to talk to you, so if you could please call me when you get this message, I'd appreciate it more than you know. My number is 487-555-7820. Please feel free to call me any time, day or night. Thank you again, Miss Cavanaugh. Merry Christmas."

Elise exhaled loudly as she rested the phone's receiver in its cradle. "Oh, please call. Please," she whispered as she rested her face in her hands.

Chapter Twenty-Five

Susan drove the van into the heart of the homeless community. Kelly looked around in disbelief as some of the makeshift homes were shown to her for the first time. Boxes and Styrofoam crates sheltered the people in the alleys, while others lay deathly still in doorways of the closed businesses in the neighborhood.

"Jesus..." she heard Kelly breathe.

"Gives you a whole new appreciation for the life you have, doesn't it? And I don't mean that in a snarky way, either."

"I know, baby. But, yes, it really does." Kelly took Susan's hand in a firm grip. "It just tears me up to picture you out here."

They had reached the alley where they were going to be distributing meals, so Susan put the van in park and turned a little in her seat to look squarely at Kelly. "Don't, then. I'm right here with you now. Just imagine me in your arms, like we were last night," she said with a hint of desire in her voice, and Kelly looked at her intently with want in her baby blues.

She leaned over in her seat, grabbed the back of Susan's neck, and kissed her hard. Susan was relieved that they were stopped at the time, knowing that if they had been in motion, they would've crashed. Susan sank into the kiss, and before she knew it, their tongues met in a rhythm that was nothing short of erotic. She could feel her arousal building, but remembered where they were and pulled away breathlessly.

"Kelly..." she exhaled sharply, "we need to stop before we end up doing something in this van that we really shouldn't. Well, not here anyway," she said, with hopes of continuing their kisses after their mission was over.

Kelly rested her forehead against Susan's and breathed in the same air, trying to control her own need. "You're right. God, I just look at you and I want you so badly, Susan. I can't help it." Kelly smiled sheepishly.

"It's quite all right. I love that you want me as much as I do you. Perhaps we'll finish early enough to play a little later on."

"Oh, I think that's my new mission," Kelly chuckled.

"Good." Susan squared her shoulders and took a deep, cleansing breath. "All right. What we'll do is take turns – one taking the food out to the people, while the other stays by the van in case others show up. Does that sound good?"

"Sure, it sounds fine. We'll be safe enough, right?" Kelly sounded a little uncertain.

"We should be. I can't promise anything, because I know what it's like out here, but I'm pretty sure we'll be fine. If not, we do have the intercom thingy." She gestured at the two-way radio they had in the van. Father O'Malley had the other one, and knew that if he heard any signal from them he was to call the police.

Kelly laughed at Susan's description. "It's not a thingy, it's a Nextel phone. It's like a walkie-talkie. They are the best things ever to have been invented. I'm just glad I bought a set. I'm gonna give you one when I'm in the office. That way I can talk to you whenever I want."

"Maybe you're not so selfless after all, Miss Cavanaugh." Susan smiled, crossed her arms over her chest and squinted her eyes.

"No, darlin', I'm just extremely selfish when it comes to you." She leaned over and kissed Susan again. This time it was a chaste kiss that indicated she was ready to start working. "Come on, let's go." She opened her door and got out into the cold winter air.

Susan got out of the van, walked around to Kelly's side, and opened the side door. They'd packed the warmers with food containers for the needy people they might find. The shelves they'd stocked with more containers to replace the ones they handed out. There was plenty to serve about fifty people or so. Hopefully that would be enough.

"Okay, I'll make the first foray into the alley. Stay here and give containers to anyone that may wander to the van. Most people expect to see us this time of year."

"All right, but take the phone with you. If you run into trouble, please call Father O'Malley and yell loud enough for me to hear you."

"Kelly, I'll be fine." Susan knew her companion wouldn't let it rest, and there was always an element of fear about going out into the streets, so she took the phone that was held out for her, hoping she wouldn't need it.

"I love you," Kelly said as she turned to hug Susan.

"I love you, too. You've made today very special for me. I can't thank you enough for what you did for these people." Susan couldn't hide the pride in her eyes.

Kelly blushed a little at the compliments. "It was my pleasure. It really felt great to do something for them. I'm glad it made you so happy."

They pulled from their embrace and Kelly loaded Susan up with as many containers of food as she could carry.

"I'll see you soon," Susan said, as she walked towards the alleyways that she had once called home.

"Be careful," Kelly called after her.

~~*~*~*

Kelly waited by the van and handed out several

A Saving Solace

containers of food to people that approached. They had such gratitude in their eyes as she gave them the hot meal. She couldn't even imagine living that way - not knowing where their next meal was coming from.

She leaned inside to move some of the containers from the shelf into the warmers. When she turned around, there was a disheveled, unkempt older man standing in front of her.

"Ah!" she hollered in surprise, then apologized. "I'm sorry, you snuck up me and I didn't hear you." The man didn't respond and was standing a little too close for her comfort. "Would you like some food? I have some for you, if you want it."

"You think you can come 'round here, all high and mighty, doing your duty for us unfortunates?" he spat angrily.

Kelly didn't know what to say. "No, not at all. We just want to spread some Christmas cheer and give you some good nourishment. You don't have to take it, but it's here if you change your mind."

He looked her up and down, giving her the willies. "I know what I want, and it ain't in them boxes." He leered at her, licking his dry, cracked lips, making her want to vomit.

"Look, buddy, you've got about two seconds to turn and walk away if you don't want what I *am* offering. Because what you want, sure as hell ain't on the menu." Kelly stood to her full height and she could tell he was debating what to do next. She looked down and saw his hand in his coat pocket and something causing a protrusion.

"I don't think you get it. This ain't a request," he snarled.

He aimed his bulging pocket at her and she began to rapidly sort through her options, which weren't very many. She tried to talk some sense into him. "Whoa, okay, buddy. Calm down for a second there. Is that any way to treat a lady?"

"No, but I's gonna show you how." He grabbed his crotch, moved his hand around in a circle and groaned. "Oh, yeah..."

Nice going, Kel. Wrong choice of words there.

"Look, I don't... um..." She saw Susan coming towards the van and watched as her expression changed from happiness to fear when she saw the confrontation. "I um..." She looked back to Susan, who motioned for her not to look in that direction.

"What! Come on lady, I don't got time for this. Let's go!" he yelled. He grabbed Kelly's forearm with his free hand and started to pull her away from the van.

"Now put your hands up nice and slow, mister. I really don't want to hurt you," Susan hissed in the man's ear as she poked the phone unit into his back. He immediately raised both hands over his head, letting the comb fall from his fist.

"I...I...I...didn't mean no harm! Don't shoot!" He stood with his hands up and eyes wide as Susan walked around to face him. "It's only a comb! "

Recognition dawned on Susan's face as she looked at the man in front of them. "Switch? Is that you?"

The man looked at Susan with curious eyes until finally his recollection set in. "Little Ray? Holy Sweet Mother o' Jesus!"

Susan nodded as she embraced the man in her arms. He hugged her back for a long time, while Kelly stood and stared, her mouth open. "I thought you was dead, Little Ray. I haven't seen you in so long."

Kelly watched in awe as the two friends reunited. Susan finally pulled away from the man. "Switch, what are you doing bothering this lady friend of mine? I don't remember you being like that."

"I didn't mean nothing by it, ma'am, really. I didn't

know you was friends with Little Ray." He looked back at Susan with shame in his eyes. "Time's is rough these days, Little Ray. I dunno what come over me." He looked back to Kelly. "I'm sorry if'n I scared you."
She shook her head in confusion and smiled at him. "Don't worry about it. But I wouldn't recommend doing that again. You could get killed that way."
"What happened to you, Little Ray?" Switch asked, holding Susan's hand.
"I got out, Switch. A couple years ago I met a woman who offered me some food. A little while after that, I got really sick, remember? " Switch nodded. "Well, she came back and saw how sick I was. She brought me to the clinic and told them I worked for her, and they kept me for a couple of weeks until I got better. I got pneumonia and almost did die, Switch. That's probably where the rumor got started. Anyway, Carol took me in and gave me a job. Now I've got my own place and I work for a living."
"You's lucky, Ray. But I knew you was different than ol' Switch. I been out here for twenty years now. This's my home and always will be." He shook his head in acceptance of his life. "This ain't no place for a soul like yours, Little Ray."
The two hugged again and Kelly offered Switch a container of food, which he accepted. They offered him a seat in the back of the van to eat his Christmas dinner.
"Kelly, let me introduce you to the man that was my guardian for a while when I was out here. Switch, this lady here is my partner, Kelly."
They shook hands, and Switch smiled at her for the first time without lust in his eyes. "Nice to meet you, Miss Kelly. Little Ray always liked the ladies. I see she got herself a good one."
"Thanks, Switch. I feel pretty lucky myself." She gazed at Susan and felt the love she was sending. For

her, Kelly tried to make conversation with Switch. "So, um... you took care of her out here?"

"I tried to. I finds her one day curled in some box over in that alleyway." He nonchalantly hooked a thumb in the general direction. "She was cryin' her eyes out. Thought I was the devil hisself," he chuckled. "After that, we was like peas in a pod. I'd tell her stories, and she told me what she was gonna do when she got out." He looked up at Susan and smiled. "I'm so happy you did, Little Ray."

"Um... can I ask why you call her that?" Kelly asked, hoping she wasn't getting too personal.

He smiled when he looked at her. "She was my little ray of sunshine in 'is dark place." Susan went to him and hugged him again. "You always was my Little Ray, and you always will be."

Kelly felt her heart break for him. She could tell that they had shared quite a bit in the time they'd had together and that he still loved her very much. *How could he not? Hell, she's my sunshine, too.*

~~*~*~*~*

Susan would always remember that year as her favorite Christmas. First, Kelly sponsored the food drive, and then seeing Switch again put her over the top. "Are you okay, sweetheart?" she asked Kelly, who was very quiet as she drove them home.

"Yeah, I'm just thinking about the day. So much to take in, you know? I mean, what would've happened if it wasn't a comb in Switch's pocket? What if it was a knife? What if you hadn't known him?" Kelly paused and took a deep breath. "I can't believe you made it out there for so long. I wouldn't have lasted a day." Kelly shook her head and tightened her grip on the steering wheel.

"Honey, don't do that. Just know we were fortunate that things worked out the way they did. He *did* have a comb and I *did* know who he was. And we are both safe and sound. Don't worry about the 'what ifs'; they'll make you crazy."

"You're right. But when I saw you come for him... God!" Kelly shook her head. "You're right! That'll make me nuts. Okay, so um... tell me, do you plan on seeing Switch again?" Kelly tried to change the subject a little.

"Oh, yes! Now that I know he's still around, I'm gonna visit him. Sadly, I'd forgotten all about him. I don't even think I mentioned him to you before; I'm sorry." Kelly looked at Susan, an unspoken question on her face. "Don't worry, I'll go during the day." Susan saw the relief flood through her partner, and knew she'd settled the issue.

Kelly shrugged airily, as if unconcerned. "I'm glad you said that. I got worried for a second."

"I could tell. Don't worry, I'm not willing to play that game again any time soon." Susan patted her thigh gently with their entwined hands.

They finished the rest of the drive home in silence, holding each other's hand and just letting themselves feel. It was so nice to be able to do that with someone. They'd each had an incredible day, though for different reasons. All Susan wanted to do with the rest of it was to snuggle up with Kelly and be held until morning. She knew Kelly had a big day at work the next day, because it was the day after Christmas – which meant Christmas returns. She could tell her partner was dreading it.

They entered the house through the garage and were greeted by a hungry Mattie. "Hey, girl!" Kelly cooed as she stroked the happy animal. "I bet you gotta go out, huh? We were gone a little longer than I'd planned." Kelly opened the back door for Mattie and watched as she ran into the backyard.

"I'm going to change into my sweats, if you don't mind. I want to be comfy and just cuddle with you on the couch. Does that sound okay?" Susan asked a smiling Kelly.

"That sounds wonderful. I'll make us some tea." She leaned in and kissed her gently, and Susan sighed deeply when it ended. "Hurry back."

"I will." She ran upstairs and into Kelly's bedroom. She could hear Kelly letting the dog in and the sounds of the can opener heralding Mattie's dinner. Kelly began to sing *The Christmas Song,* and Susan hummed along with her as she got changed.

Susan used the bathroom and trotted back downstairs to find Kelly had plugged in the tree lights, started a warm fire in the hearth, and had tea ready for them on the coffee table. She was sitting on the couch with her legs pulled under her and her head resting on her arm that was lying along the back of the couch.

"Hey there, sexy," Susan said in a hushed voice. "You waiting for someone?"

"Yeah," she said as she reached for her arm. "You." She pulled Susan onto the couch with her and held her in a long embrace.

Susan rested her head against the sturdy shoulder and pressed her cheek to Kelly's breast. Being cradled like an infant, she felt incredibly loved.

Kelly leaned down and kissed her head. "I love you, so much. I can't tell you how good it feels to say that to you." She kissed Susan's forehead.

Susan looked into dark blue eyes and pulled her head down into a long, fiery kiss. As she sucked on Kelly's tongue, she heard the dark-haired woman moan. Kelly glided her fingers through Susan's hair as the younger woman explored the depths of her mouth. They could both feel their desire building with each passing moment and knew there wasn't going to be much talking.

A Saving Solace

Susan didn't really care. Her body was Kelly's, and she could take it any way she wanted. And Susan knew that that night, she would.

Chapter Twenty-Six

Beep beep beep beep... The raucous noise of the alarm broke the silent morning.

Kelly slammed her hand down on the snooze button of the alarm clock, hoping not to wake Susan. The younger woman was snuggled into her body, one thigh thrown over Kelly's legs and her head resting on Kelly's chest. Kelly could still smell their essence from the night before. *God, she was insatiable. My body has that hum going this morning, reminding me that it was put through its paces only a few hours ago. I lost count after three orgasms. Susan is an aphrodisiac to me. All I have to do is think about her and I'm aroused as all get out.*

She yawned and involuntarily began to stretch. Susan moved to hold her tighter. The grip on Kelly's waist tensed then eased, and Kelly's thoughts drifted to the upcoming day for a few moments. It was her least favorite day of the year. She got the nastiest phone calls on *Return Day*, or 'the day after' as she liked to refer to it.

With a sigh of regret, she managed to wriggle out of Susan's grasp and head to the bathroom. She needed a shower and caffeine, in that order.

After her shower, Kelly threw on a robe and went downstairs to make some tea. She wanted to check her voicemail before she went in to the office, liking to be forearmed on days like the one that was about to begin. Letting Mattie outside, Kelly watched for a moment as she frisked around the backyard. The teakettle was still on the stove from the previous night, so she added fresh water and set it to boil.

Waiting for the shrill cry that would signal the

water was ready, Kelly sat at the kitchen table, picked up the phone, and dialed her office. Grabbing her planner, she jotted down some notes from the messages she was receiving.

"Tina needs new fixtures...Ralph needs employees... Yeah, like I can fix that... Marta needs to see me..."

She broke the tip off her pencil and stopped writing as she heard the woman's voice on the machine. *Susan's mother wants me to call her? Oh boy. This could get sticky.* She jotted the number down in her book just as Susan appeared in the kitchen.

"Good morning," she whispered as she kissed Kelly's cheek. "Whatcha doing?"

Kelly closed her planner and hung up the phone, trying not to panic. When the teakettle shrieked, it almost knocked her over. She was panicking big time.

"Uh... I was checking my um... voicemail to get a headstart on the day... Do you um... want some tea?" She stammered badly, crossing over and taking the kettle off the hot stove.

"Kelly? What's wrong, honey?"

"Nothing... nothing. I just got a message from my... boss, and she's going to be coming in to check on the stores next week. That's all. I always get a bit rattled when she calls."

"Ah, I gotcha. Let me take your mind off of her for a few minutes," Susan husked sexily, and Kelly had to gently stop her before she passed out from hyperventilation.

"As much as I'd love to, I really have to get going soon. Will you uh... need anything today? I'm really jealous you don't have to go back to work until tomorrow."

"I wish you could stay home today too, sweetheart. But no, I'll be fine. I'm actually going to lounge about, if that's okay."

"That's totally fine. My house is yours, you know that," Kelly said, sounding more like herself. The shock of hearing Susan's mother's voice was slowly dissipating. She turned to Susan and gave her a large hug and kiss. "Mmm... good morning."

"That's better. I was beginning to wonder who you were earlier; you were so jumpy."

"I know, I'm sorry. You surprised me just as I finished with her message. I got spooked is all; don't mind me. I think it's because someone's been keeping me awake long past my bedtime the past few nights. I might be a little sleep deprived."

"Oh, poor baby." She kissed Kelly gently. "Okay, scoot. I'll get Mattie in and fix your tea while you get dressed."

"Thanks, darlin'." Kelly shared another kiss, then quickly made her way upstairs into the bathroom where she promptly threw up. "Oh, God..." She rested her head against the cool porcelain of the toilet bowl and tried to calm her nerves.

A Saving Solace

Chapter Twenty-Seven

After role-playing her return call to Mrs. McGovern over a hundred times in the car on the way to work, Kelly walked into her office with a tumultuous headache. *And it is only 8:30 in the goddamned morning. Not a good way to start December twenty-sixth.*

She looked at her phone and the message light was already flashing. "Jesus, I just cleared them!" She collapsed into her leather chair, rested her elbows on the desk, and put her head in her hands. "God, this is going to be a long fucking day," she grumbled.

The phone rang, and Kelly considered whether or not to answer it, wishing she had Caller ID. Since it was her business line, she knew she had to answer it, she just didn't want to.

"Good morning, Maxine's regional office. This is Kelly, how may I help you?" she answered cheerfully.

"Hi there, sexy."

She felt her insides shift at the sound of Susan's husky voice. "God, I'm glad it's you," Kelly sighed. "How are you? Do you miss me already?"

"I'm missing you terribly, and you've only been gone about twenty minutes."

Kelly could just picture the pout on Susan's luscious lips. "Mmm. I wish I was home. My head is killing me. I'm starting to see little birdies floating around my head." She chuckled mirthlessly.

"Honey, are you okay? You looked awfully pale when you left here."

"It'll pass. I've just gotta get going and I'll be fine. Don't worry."

"If it involves you, I'll always worry. You'd better know that right now." Susan's voice was calming her head.

"Thank you, baby. I hope you have a nice day. You're not upset that I didn't take you home, are you?"

"Oh, right. Leaving me here in this delicious house with food and a television and whatever else at my disposal... Yeah, Kel, I'm really pissed."

Kelly heard her chuckle. "Okay, I just wanted to make sure. Eat whatever, watch... you know, whatever and... God, listen to me. Just act like it was your home too, okay?" she stuttered.

"Thanks, sweetheart, I will. Thank you for your hospitality. I'd much rather be here than in my tiny box of an apartment. I will have to go back tonight, though; I'm running out of undies." Susan whispered the last part in such a cute voice, Kelly couldn't help but laugh.

"Okay, okay. I'll get you back there. Then we'll have to see about getting you some things that will stay at my place. Okay? I mean... that's not too much too soon is it?" *God, I sound like such an idiot!*

"No, honey. We're fine. I promise, if I was uncomfortable, I'd let you know. Frankly, I love the attention," she admitted.

"Good, I love giving it to you," Kelly replied softly.

"Good. Then it's a win-win situation."

"Okay, baby, I gotta run. I should be home around five or five thirty. Okay?"

"Okay, honey. I love you."

"I love you, too. Talk to you later."

"Bye."

"Bye, baby." Kelly hung up the phone feeling much better. She knew she still had to call Susan's mother, and she'd have bet a million bucks that Susan would kill her if she ever found out that she had made that call.

Why me?

The afternoon arrived without much angst generated by customers. There were the usual *"I'm not satisfied with my service. What will you do for me?"* sort of calls. Kelly expected those, and just laughed at the ridiculousness of those people. They asked for so much, sometimes it made her head spin.

When she took a break and looked at her watch, she found it was already 2 in the afternoon. She still needed to eat lunch, but the call to Susan's mom was becoming a huge weight on her shoulders. Kelly sighed loudly into the air as she reclined in her chair with her hands behind her head and finally made the decision to call.

Kelly opened her planner to retrieve the number she'd been given, which she dialed. As the phone began to ring, she felt her nerves kick in again.

"Hello?" The voice sounded very much like Susan's.

"Um... hi, Mrs. McGovern?"

"Yes?"

"This is Kelly Cavanaugh; you left a message on my machine regarding your daughter, Susan. The woman on the news with me." She swallowed audibly.

"Oh, my God, yes. Then, she *is* my daughter?"

"Yes, they're the same person."

"Thank you for calling!"

Kelly could hear the relief in her voice. "You're welcome. What can I do for you?"

"Well, Miss Cavanaugh, I'm sure that Susan has told you about our... uh... situation."

"Yes, she told me what happened. What does that have to do with me?" Kelly wanted her to squirm a bit. She wasn't so sure she wanted to risk having Susan hurt without knowing just what her mother wanted.

"I know I have absolutely no right to ask anything of her, but I really would like to see her." Kelly could

A Saving Solace

hear the strain in her voice. "I'd like to meet with you and discuss this face to face rather than talking over the phone. Is there some place I can meet you?"

"Well, I'm in my office today. Would you be able to come to Maxine's? My office is inside the Lawrence Avenue store." *What am I doing?*

"Of course. It's only a few miles from my home. I can be there in fifteen minutes, if that's okay with you."

"Yes, that would be fine. Just go to any of the counters and tell them you have an appointment with me. They'll direct you to my office."

"Thank you, Miss Cavanaugh, I really appreciate it. I'll see you soon, then."

"I'll be expecting you. Good-bye."

"Good-bye."

"Oh, Kelly. I hope you know what you're doing," she muttered into her hands after she hung up the phone.

She busied herself for the interim until she heard a knock on the door. Opening it, she found one of her employees, Therese, and a woman who had to be Susan's mother. *They look so much alike, it is uncanny.*

"Kelly, this woman has an appointment with you?" Therese questioned.

"Yes, thank you, Therese." Therese smiled and walked away, leaving Kelly with Susan's mother. "Mrs. McGovern?"

"Yes, Miss Cavanaugh. Thank you for seeing me." They shook hands politely.

"You're welcome." She gestured to the office. "Please, come in and sit down."

"Thank you."

Mrs. McGovern looked around the office as Kelly watched her closely. The resemblance between her and her daughter was remarkable. Kelly flushed in embarrassment when the woman caught her staring. "Pardon me, but you look so much like your daughter.

It's really amazing."

"I'd hoped she'd look more like me. Her father had some traits that just wouldn't have looked good on a woman," she said with a smile, which Kelly returned easily.

"Well, now that we're here, what can I do to help you, ma'am?" Kelly leaned forward on her desk and laced her fingers together. She maintained the intimidating pose for several moments, waiting for Susan's mother to start the conversation.

Mrs. McGovern began to fidget with the strap on the purse in her lap. "Well, as I started telling you on the phone, I'd really like to see my daughter. I was hoping that perhaps you could help arrange a meeting."

"Well, I can't guarantee that she'd want to see you or her father. I'm not sure if you have any idea where she's been for the last five years, but it hasn't been a pleasant life for her. In fact, I'd say she's come back from living in hell." Kelly really wanted to make sure Mrs. McGovern knew she wasn't happy with what they'd done to the woman she'd grown to love very much.

"No, you're right. I don't know where she's been, but believe me I've been looking for her. I'd given up all hope of finding her until I saw her on the news." She began to cry.

Oh, no. Why did she have to cry? Kelly leaned over the desk to pick up the box of Kleenex and handed it to her.

"Thank you," she said as she wiped at her eyes with the tissue.

Even though she was starting to feel sympathy for the woman, Kelly remained unbending. "Mrs. McGovern, Susan has been through hell and is now finally piecing her life back together. She's become a damn fine woman without any help from you or her father."

"I know... I know..." she sobbed. "It was my fault. I couldn't fight him. He... he was so... Well, I just never could stand up for myself. I dutifully stood by his side, and it cost me my daughter. I was so selfish. I miss her so much. God, I'm so sorry," she sobbed desperately, breaking Kelly's heart.

"All I can do is ask her if she'll see you. I can't promise anything. She's a very special person in my life, and I won't do anything to hurt her, ma'am. Not even for you," Kelly warned.

"You and she are... together, then?" Mrs. McGovern questioned through her tears.

"Yes, Susan is my partner. I love her very much. She is one of the most incredible women I've ever met."

"I'm glad she has you," she sniffled. "And it won't be me and my husband. It'll just be me. Jonathon...he uh... passed away last January."

Oh, God. "I'm very sorry, Mrs. McGovern. Can I ask what happened?" Kelly asked in a gentle voice.

"Heart attack. He worked himself to death," she said flatly. "It's all he really cared about - his job... his status... money... I was such a fool to indulge his lack of humanity. Miss Cavanaugh..."

"Please, call me Kelly."

"Thank you. Kelly, I'm not at all proud of the woman I was, but I've never stopped thinking about Susan, not for one day. She is my only child, and I love her very much. I didn't have much when I married her father, and I was afraid of losing everything by going against him. If I could go back and change how things happened, I would in a heartbeat."

"I'm sure you would, ma'am. Well, like I said, I'll ask Susan if she'll meet with you. That's all I can do."

"Kelly, thank you. You have no idea what this means to me. I've been separated from my daughter for far too long."

Kelly thought about having the opportunity to spend even one more day with her mother, and her eyes welled with tears. "Yes, I think I have a good idea of what you're feeling. When would you like this meeting?"

"Whenever she'll see me."

"Okay, I'll talk to her for you. Do you want me to tell her about her father's passing?"

"No, I think she should hear it from me."

Kelly shook her head doubtfully. "I'm not sure that's the best course of action, but it's your decision to make."

"Thank you, Kelly. Thank you for meeting with me. You've given me a ray of hope that I've not had in years."

"You're welcome, Mrs. McGovern."

"Please, Kelly, call me Elise. Mrs. McGovern was my mother-in-law, and I never really liked that woman." She chuckled, trying to lighten the mood.

It was easy to see where Susan got her sense of humor. Kelly couldn't help but smile at her. "All right, Elise. I'll call you after I talk to Susan."

"Thank you, again."

"You're welcome. I'll walk you out; I need to grab some lunch anyway."

"That'd be great."

They both stood, and Kelly walked her to the door. When she opened it, she found Susan standing on the other side, just about to knock. The expression on Susan's face changed from joy to shock when she saw the woman in Kelly's office.

Under Susan's scrutinizing stare, Kelly was extremely uncomfortable all of a sudden. Susan looked back at the woman in the office, who hadn't moved since her daughter had appeared.

"Mother?" Susan choked back a mix of several emotions.

Her mother took a step towards her. "Yes, Susan, it's me."

Susan's face became a mask of anger. "What do you want?"

Elise froze in her tracks and her eyes filled with tears. "Oh, Susan. I've been looking for you for so..."

"Don't!" Susan growled, then turned on Kelly. "What are you doing? Trying to rip my heart out?"

Kelly attempted to calm her. "No, baby, please. She called me after seeing us on the news. She's been looking for you."

"Whose side are you on? That woman kicked me out and left me to die!" Susan gesticulated angrily at Elise, who had begun crying in earnest.

"Please, come in here." Kelly gestured to her office. "Please." She pleaded with Susan with her eyes.

Susan sighed heavily and walked past her mother and Kelly, and stood in the far corner of the office.

"Susan, I'm so sorry. Please... can I have a few minutes to talk to you?" her mother begged.

"Why should I give you anything? You just stood there and said nothing while Daddy threw me out. You did *nothing* to help me."

Elise sobbed as Kelly watched the two uncomfortably. "I'm sorry, Susan... I'm so sorry," Elise kept repeating.

The only sound for several minutes was Susan's mother crying. Susan's silence was killing Kelly. The way Susan was staring at her, she felt as if she had betrayed her. The day just wasn't getting any better. Her headache had now returned in full force.

Chapter Twenty-Eight

What the hell did Kelly think she was doing anyway? How could she? I wasn't ready to see my mother.

Susan had no desire whatsoever to see her mother, and yet there she was - sitting in Kelly's office having a stare down with Kelly *and* her mother. She had come to have a late lunch with Kelly, surprise her by taking a cab in, and then had planned to hang out at ForOthers until Kelly was ready to go home.

Well, it looks as if the person surprised here was me. Fuck.

She looked at the woman who had given her both life and death, in a manner of speaking. Her face was very drawn and her hair had grayed. *God, she looks much older than I remembered. I wonder how Daddy is.*

No! I don't want to talk to either of them. I made it out of hell without them, and I don't need them now.

"I don't need you," Susan gritted out, starting to pace in the back of the office like a caged animal. Kelly's eyes hadn't left hers since they'd walked into the office. Even when Susan wasn't looking at her, she could feel the heat of Kelly's stare.

Why did she do this? Dammit, I wasn't ready for this!

Susan heard her mother's voice talking. "Please, Susan. All I'm asking for is a little time to explain things to you. Please."

She looked up at her mother's face and felt the tears she was crying. She knew those tears quite intimately since she'd cried plenty of them herself. *Why do I still have to care?*

Susan could feel her resolve cracking. *I guess it*

would do me good to finally find out what the hell happened five years ago - why they decided that social status was more important than their child; why it was so easy for them to toss me out like the trash; why they never looked for me. I think I want to know. So, yeah, I'll give her the meeting... for me... not her, but for me.

"Fine. When?" She was curt and to the point.

Her mother and Kelly both looked surprised that she'd come to that decision. Susan eyed them, hoping her mother would give her an answer before she changed her mind.

"How about tomorrow night?" her mother suggested.

Susan crossed her arms over her chest. "Fine. Where and what time?"

"Well, you could come to the house if... if you wanted. How about, around seven?"

The uncertainty in her voice was satisfying for Susan to hear. She wanted her mother to feel like she'd felt the last five years. "Fine, I'll be there."

"I'll take you if you want," Kelly offered quietly. Their eyes stayed locked on each other and remained that way until Susan heard her mother speak again.

"Thank you, Susan. Thank you so much." She gazed at her daughter with relief apparent in her eyes. "You have no idea what this means to me." She looked at Kelly and Susan once more. "I'll see you tomorrow at the house around seven, then." She wiped her eyes with a tissue and left the office.

Kelly and Susan were left alone and the younger woman had no idea what to say. She was very angry with Kelly for stepping in where she didn't belong.

"Susan... I'm sorry that it happened this way. I wanted to talk to you first before you saw her. I had no idea you'd be coming here."

"Yeah, well, I guess we're even, because I never in

my wildest dreams ever expected to see my mother coming out of your office." Susan just stared at her, not really knowing what else to say. She needed to get out of there and be by herself. "I'm gonna go home," Susan said quietly as she moved towards the door. Kelly reached for her arm but Susan pulled away.

Kelly attempted to stop the hasty exit. "Susan, please... I'll take you. Just give me a couple minutes."

"No." Susan looked at the concerned face. "I really just want to be alone right now." She could see the hurt in Kelly's eyes, but just then she couldn't think about that. She had too much else to think about. "If you want to drive me tomorrow, that's fine, but I can't guarantee that the mood I'll be in will be light and cheery."

"I don't care about that. I just want to be with you. Please."

Susan nodded her acquiescence. "I'll see you tomorrow, then."

"Okay. I am so sorry," she choked out.

"That seems to be the word of the hour, doesn't it?" They shared another glance and Susan watched as the tears began to spill down Kelly's cheeks, feeling the urge to flee, and quickly. She looked at the sad and solemn face once more, then hurriedly left the office and headed towards the train station. Susan made her way to the station in time to catch the four o'clock Metra to take her home. *Home.*

Jesus, what does that word mean to me? Oh, Carol, I wish you were here right now. I'm so confused. I thought I'd found everything in Kelly; now my mother has come back into the picture and thrown a monkey wrench in my happiness. What could she possibly say that would change the way I feel about them? I have no idea what to say to my father without spitting in his face. And why didn't he come with her?

God, please give me control over my actions

tomorrow night. *I just don't know what I'm doing anymore.*

~~*~*~*

Susan checked her clock again. This time it read three forty-five. She wasn't going to be able to sleep, no matter what. Her head was filled with far too many scattered thoughts to relax. Tonight, she was going to talk to her parents. *My parents. That's a funny term to use. Aren't they the ones that are supposed to love their children unconditionally? Ha! That was a laugh.*

Even though Susan was still angry with Kelly, she was glad her friend would be going with her. She had hated going to bed without Kelly. Susan's sofa bed wasn't even in the same category as Kelly's bed, or her arms. She threw the bedclothes aside and began to pace.

"Dammit! Why did she have to do this? If I'd wanted to see my parents, I'd have called them myself. Now I'm going to my old house to listen to their reasons for kicking me to the curb."

She walked over to the window and peered out at the night sky. The stars shone brightly above, as if they hadn't a care in the world. *What I wouldn't give to trade places with just one of them.*

She fell onto her bed with a thud and groaned in frustration. "Just a few hours of sleep, that's all I'm asking for," she pleaded. An hour's worth of wakefulness later, she groaned piteously, "How about just thirty minutes?"

~~*~*~*

God, I miss having her here.

Kelly had known that phone call was going to lead

to problems. She rued not telling Susan about her mother's call when she'd heard the message in the first place. *Now I'm in bed, alone, and I can't sleep because I know that she's hurting, but she won't even talk to me. I don't know what I was expecting when I called her tonight. I guess something other than the cold shoulder she gave me.*

~~*~*~*~*

"Yes?" *Susan answered in a not so friendly tone.*

Kelly knew that it was unlikely anyone else would be calling Susan, and it hurt to realize Susan didn't want to talk to her. "Hey, baby, it's me."

"Hello."

The frosty silence that followed was deafening.

"What are you up to?"

"Oh, nothing much. Just trying to figure out what to say to my parents, now that you've brought us together again."

Ouch. "Susan, your mother called me. She asked me to call her back, so I did." *Kelly wasn't much swayed by her own argument.*

"So you've said. Don't you think you could've let me know that she called you before you called her back? Did you ever think about that?"

"Well, they say hindsight is twenty-twenty." *Too late, Kelly realized that a flip response probably wasn't the smartest thing to say.*

"Your boss isn't really coming, is she?" *Susan's voice was flatly unemotional.*

Fuck. "No, she isn't."

"I didn't think so. After seeing you with my mother, it kind of made sense to me why you were so edgy around me this morning."

"I'm sorry," *Kelly said again.*

"What exactly are you sorry for? You keep saying those words, but I'd like to know what it is you are apologizing for."

"For everything. For not telling you that your mother called. For meeting with her before you had a chance to tell me if it was all right or not."

"How about lying to me?"

"Yes, that too. Baby, I just wanted to help."

Susan became silent again. Kelly didn't like it when she was quiet; she couldn't tell what she was thinking. All she knew was that Susan was pissed. And pissed at her, in a big way.

"Just do me a favor: in the future, when you want to help me, just think about the consequences before you do anything, all right? I was nowhere near ready to deal with this yet."

Kelly felt like a child being scolded. Jesus, I made a fucking mistake! "I won't make decisions that involve your life like that again, I promise. Just, please forgive me. I hate feeling like this." She could feel her voice starting to crack from the emotions wrenching her heart.

"I gotta go to bed, Kelly. I have a lot to think about... Good night."

"Goodnight, sweet..." There was a click as Susan hung up before Kelly could add "...dreams."

~~*~*~*

That was one of the worst phone calls Kelly had ever had. *I guess I didn't realize the impact this would have on her. I was stupid to do this.*

Stupid! her inner voice confirmed helpfully.

She rolled over again and tried to get comfortable. It was four in the morning, and there was no way she was going to sleep any time soon.

Oh fuck. Me and my big mouth.

Chapter Twenty-Nine

As Kelly drove to pick up Susan, she contemplated telling her about her father. She knew the news of his death would be one more unexpected circumstance for her partner to deal with. Kelly certainly didn't want to overstep her boundaries again, and Mrs. McGovern had expressly said that she wanted to be the one to tell her daughter. *As much as I want to tell her, I guess it's not my place to do so. I have no idea of how she'll react, I have no idea if she'll even speak to me again. This is such a mess!*

Kelly met Susan at six forty-five. Susan knew Kelly had left work early; so had she, to get ready for the meeting with her parents. Kelly pulled up in front of the ForOthers office and waited for Susan to get in and get settled inside the warm vehicle.

"Hi," Kelly greeted.

"Hi," Susan echoed. "Are you sure you want to come with me? I don't think this is going to be a very pleasant occasion."

The dark-haired woman took Susan's hand and kissed her knuckles. "I want to be there for you, Susan. You can still be mad at me, but I want you to know that I'll be there if you need me. Okay?" Her blue eyes pleaded with Susan's heart and won.

"Okay," she said quietly as she squeezed Kelly's hand.

They drove the rest of the way to the McGovern's home in a more comfortable silence. Susan was extremely nervous, and could tell Kelly was too. When they pulled into the driveway, Kelly turned off the engine, squeezed Susan's hand once in reassurance, and got out of the car. She circled around to the passenger

A Saving Solace

side, opened Susan's door, and offered her hand.

Susan accepted the assistance in getting out of the car, then stood taking in the view of her childhood home for the first time in five years, not counting the drive by of their second date. She felt her legs turn rubbery, and Kelly steadied her stumble with ease.

"Are you sure you're all right? We can see her another time, sweetheart."

Shaking her head, Susan said, "No, I want to get this nightmare over with once and for all." She felt the strength return to her body and walked with confidence to the front door. Kelly was next to her as she rang the doorbell.

Within instants, Susan's mother answered the door. "Hello. Thank you again for meeting with me."

"Mother," Susan said with a coldness she'd forgotten she had.

"Hello, Kelly."

"Good evening, Mrs. McGovern," Kelly returned.

"Please, come inside." She stepped aside and allowed them space to walk into the foyer of the house.

"May I take your coats?" Mrs. McGovern asked politely.

"No, we'll keep them. We won't be staying long. Where's Daddy?" Kelly and Elise shared a knowing look. "Is he waiting to jump out at me to tell me what a disgusting person I am?" Susan asked, steeling herself against the angry, disappointed glare she remembered so clearly from their last good bye.

Her mother looked at her strangely and gestured to the living room. "Won't you sit down; I'll get us some tea."

Susan felt Kelly's hand at the small of her back as they walked into the living room. The furniture was all the same. The neutral tones that covered the walls, the grand piano in the corner, the grandfather clock, they were all the same as they were when she'd been banished. *Apparently my parents never could get into change of any kind.*

Mrs. McGovern went into the kitchen and they heard her preparing tea. Susan could feel the tenseness of Kelly's muscles in her touch. *At least I'm not the only one uncomfortable with this. I can't wait to see Daddy's face when he sees my girlfriend sitting in his living room, holding my hand. Bastard.*

Kelly looked down and offered her a smile. Susan nervously smiled back, awaiting her mother's return.

"Are you doing okay?" Kelly whispered.

"Peachy," she said sarcastically, and then apologized when she saw the hurt on Kelly's face. "I'm sorry, I'm just really nervous."

"It's okay." She squeezed Susan's hand as her mother re-entered the room with a tray.

Mrs. McGovern put the tray on the mahogany coffee table and began passing out saucers and cups, fidgeting with them. She was nervous, as well. She took a deep breath, and then looked at Susan, taking a Kleenex out of her sweater pocket as the tears began to fall.

"Susan, before you say anything at all, I just want you to listen to me for a few seconds so I can get out what needs to be said." She exchanged looks with her daughter. "Okay?"

Susan nodded, but couldn't warm the indifferent look on her face.

"Okay... When your father and I first met, I was poor, with practically nothing to my name. As you know, my mom passed away when I was young, and I pretty much had to trust to my own devices to survive."

"Well, we have that in common now, don't we?" Kelly looked at Susan and she put her hands up in surrender. "Sorry! Please continue."

A Saving Solace

"Anyway, your father had his own business, he was handsome, and he took care of me. When we were married, I knew I'd never have to worry about anything ever again. I lived my life in his shadow. I played golf with the other wives of the club, I went to the restaurants where he liked to eat, I even went to his church because I didn't want to roil the waters, so to speak. We lived this life for a long time, until you were born.

"When you were born, everything changed for me. I finally had something that was truly mine. I don't mean a possession, but I'd created you and you counted on me for everything - to eat, to sleep, to be warm... You get the idea. Well, everything was great until..."

"Until, I wanted to be something you both weren't: my own person."

"Yes. You went against everything that had been drummed into me. I was taught that men were with women, women were with men, and that was it. Anything else was an abomination. End of story."

"Yeah, end of story," Susan mumbled.

"But it wasn't!" her mother exclaimed, surprising her. "I envied you so much, Susan. You wanted to live a life that *you* wanted, not some life that was already drawn out and just waiting for you to be inserted into the picture. You wanted Susan's life. I was so incredibly jealous that you had the will I could only dream of having."

"What do you mean? You had everything, Mother. What didn't you have?"

"I didn't have a voice of my own." Susan watched as the tears streamed down her mother's face. Kelly's eyes were welling with tears as well. "Your father had an image to uphold. He had the club, his clients, and his high society friends, all of which dominated his life. He didn't care what I wanted. He gave me what he thought I should have, and I was supposed to be happy with that."

"And you weren't?" Susan was stunned by her admission. Her mother had never seemed unhappy.

"Not until you came into my life. When we spent time together, it was real, more real than anything I'd ever had." Susan felt the tears begin to well in her own eyes. "You were my friend as well as my daughter, Susan. I knew what we shared was genuine and not fake like my other friendships. That's why it hurt so much when you were gone."

"Then why the hell did you let him get away with it?"

"I was afraid of losing everything I had."

"So you settled for the material things in your calculated life, while you turned your back on the one thing that made your life real and whole?"

"Yes," she said, as she hung her head in shame.

"Why, Mother? Why didn't you stick up for me? Why didn't you just tell Daddy that I wasn't wrong? Why did you let him throw me away like that?" Susan started to screech. "Why, Mama? Tell me!"

"Because I was a coward!" she cried out in anguish. "I knew as soon as I stuck up for you, your father would turn away from me just as he had from you. I was selfish and scared, and I let him run my life." She began to sob, which set off an anger in Susan towards her father.

"Did you ever tell him that? Does he know how you feel? Does he know how he kept you imprisoned in your own home?"

"No, I never told him," she sobbed quietly. "By the time I got up my nerve, it was too late." She looked at Susan, who felt as if she'd been kicked in the stomach.

"What do you mean, too late? Mama, where's Daddy?" Susan looked at her and her mother wouldn't meet her gaze. "Where is that bastard? He needs to know what he's done to me *and* to you. Stop hiding

from him, please. Where is he?"
"Your father's gone, Susan."
"What do you mean gone? Where'd he go?"
"He's dead, honey."
Kelly's hand tightened around Susan's as she registered her mother's words. "Dead?" she whispered in surprise. "When? How?" she asked numbly.
"He died last January of a heart attack. I buried him in All Saints Cemetery on January twelfth." Her gaze was soft, but her pain was so evident. The pain wasn't for him; it was for Susan. And perhaps for herself, as well.
Susan sat dumbstruck. *My father is... dead? My father is dead.*
She launched her body off the couch and ran towards the foyer and out the door. She didn't know where she was going, but knew she had to get out of there.
"Susan!" Kelly shouted from the doorway.

~~*~*~*

Oh, God!
Kelly could do nothing as Susan leapt from the couch and dashed out the front door. She and Mrs. McGovern quickly followed, but Susan was well on her way down the street by the time they looked out. Certain that Susan's hurt would carry her feet pretty far, and that she didn't want anything to happen to her distraught young lover, Kelly decided to go after her.
"I knew she was going to take this badly, but I had no idea it would be this bad. I'll be back," Kelly reassured Mrs. McGovern as she dashed out to her car to initiate her search.
Knowing that she couldn't have gotten far on foot, Kelly drove slowly through the dark streets of the

neighborhood looking for her. She picked up her cell phone and dialed Susan's number, willing her to pick it up. It rang several times and Kelly was about to hang up when she heard her answer.

"Susan! Honey?" Kelly could hear the runaway gasping for breath and her heart broke at hearing her sobs. "Baby, talk to me. Where are you? Let me come and get you."

She waited a few moments, but Susan didn't answer. "Susan, can you hear me?" She wondered if she'd hit the talk button by mistake.

"He's dead, Kelly," Susan sobbed finally. "My fucking father's dead!"

"I know, sweetheart. I'm so sorry." She waited a few seconds and asked, "Honey, where are you? Let me pick you up before you catch cold out there."

"I'm on Stevens. I'm walking towards St. Mary's."

"I'll be there in two minutes, baby. Just be careful, and don't walk in the street. I don't want anyone hitting you by accident."

Turning the car around and heading towards the church, Kelly quickly spotted the small form walking along the side of the road. "I can see you, baby. I'm just about behind you."

Susan turned at the car approaching and broke the phone connection. Kelly tossed her phone onto the passenger seat and pulled over to pick her up. Putting the car in park, Kelly flew out of the car to embrace Susan, holding her lover close as she collapsed into her arms and wept bitterly about her father's passing. Kelly cooed softly in her ear, letting her know she would do anything she could to make things better. She wasn't sure what she could do, but she was determined to do something.

Susan pulled away and wiped her eyes on the sleeve of her coat. "I'll never have closure with him, now. I'll

A Saving Solace

never know anything about what happened... how he felt, what he thought... nothing." Her expression hardened and her voice held no emotion. "He'll never know what he put me through."

She turned and went to the car, and Kelly followed to make sure she got in. Closing the passenger door behind her, Kelly went around to the driver's side and re-entered the car. "Do you want to go back to your mother's house?" she asked.

Susan shook her head frantically. "No, I can't see her any more tonight." Her staring eyes were straight ahead and very distant.

"Okay. Let me call her to tell her you're safe." Kelly got no reply from Susan, so she picked up the phone and dialed Mrs. McGovern's number, telling her she would be taking Susan back to her house. They said their good-byes and Kelly terminated the connection and turned to Susan, who hadn't moved since she'd gotten into the car.

"I'm taking you back to my house, okay? I don't think you should be alone right now."

Susan said nothing as Kelly turned the car around. They drove the rest of the way home with Kelly asking Susan questions that she didn't answer. She just stared through the windshield at the road. Kelly knew she was probably in shock and just needed some time to absorb the latest development.

As they pulled into the garage, Kelly tried to gauge Susan's mood, wondering whether she would want to go to bed right away, or talk, or watch television, or just sit and do nothing. Kelly had no clue what she was doing, she only knew that her love was hurting and she had to do whatever she could to help her.

They walked into the house and Mattie greeted them as usual. Surprising Kelly, Susan got down on her knees and hugged Mattie. She wept into Mattie's coat as the dog just stayed close, feeling her pain. Kelly knelt down next to them and waited to see what would come next, rubbing Susan's back as she cried into the pup's fur.

"Let's get your coat off, honey, okay? You're gonna get too warm in here."

Susan mechanically pulled away from Mattie and shrugged out of her coat. Kelly grabbed the garment and stood, walked into the kitchen, hung her coat on a chair, and added water to the teakettle. She knew some warm tea would feel good going down.

Susan was still on the floor petting Mattie who graciously accepted her attentions. She stopped rubbing Mattie's tummy and looked for her hostess. "Kelly?"

In answer, Kelly came out of the kitchen and back into the hallway. "I'm right here, baby."

"It won't always feel like this, right?" Her voice sounded so childlike, it broke Kelly's heart all over again.

She shook her head. "No, baby. Every day will get a little bit easier. It'll never fully go away, but today is probably going to hurt the most." She reached out for Susan, who molded her body into the comforting embrace. As her sobs lessened, she rose and walked into the living room and sat on the couch.

"I'm making some tea. Do you want some?" Kelly asked, hoping to get something into her stomach. Susan nodded a mute assent and leaned back against the couch cushions. Kelly sighed deeply and went to tend to the tea. *This is definitely going to be a long night.*

A Saving Solace

Chapter Thirty

Kelly watched over Susan most of the night. The younger woman no longer had any control over her tears. She watched television shows one after the other without recalling one thing that she'd seen. Her body felt so numb from everything she'd gone through, she wasn't sure how much more she could take. In the short span of two days, her lover lied to her, the mother who had abandoned her re-entered her life, and she found out her father was dead. It was too much to take in. She felt as if she wanted to be dead, as well.

Kelly stopped asking questions because Susan kept snapping at her. It came so naturally that she couldn't stop it. *I know she's hurt, but she hurt me, too. I may be acting selfishly, but right now, nothing else matters. I watched a movie once where a battered child asked someone if life was always so hard. If I were to answer that question tonight, I'd have to say, 'Yes, it's always this hard.'*

Trying to break through the wall of diffidence, Kelly asked, "Honey, do you think it would help if we went to the cemetery tomorrow so that you could say good-bye to your father?"

Susan tried to consider the question objectively. She supposed that perhaps if she could see his grave, she might find some kind of closure there. But she couldn't give Kelly an answer; she was just too tired to even think straight.

I'll just close my eyes for a little while and I'll feel better when I wake up, she thought, as she felt sleep pull her under.

~~*~*~*

Susan passed out on the couch. When Kelly

couldn't wake her, she carried her up to the bedroom. She struggled only a little as she was placed on the bed. Kelly could hear her murmuring, but had no idea what she was saying. She took off Susan's shoes but left her clothing on, having no wish to disturb her sleep. Kelly draped the blankets over the sleeping form and turned out the light.

Quickly changing for bed, Kelly got under the covers with her, moving a bit closer to feel the warmth that she'd missed so desperately the night before. She felt Susan roll over towards her and instinctively wrap herself around the willing form. Kelly knew Susan wouldn't have done that if she were conscious.

She has every right to be angry with me. Tonight I will just hold her gently as we surrender to sleep. Once morning comes, she'll be a different Susan.

~~*~*~*

The sun pierced the darkness that had held Susan asleep for several hours. Her body still hurt, but she felt more rested. She turned to find Kelly asleep next to her, studying her face and wondering what she dreamt while she slept. Other than Kelly sweeping her into her arms and taking her to bed, Susan didn't remember one dream she'd had the night before. Looking down at herself, she decided that it hadn't been a dream, but had actually happened while she watched through a sleep-induced haze.

She looked at the clock, which indicated it was nine o'clock. Rubbing her eyes, she stretched and swung her legs over the side of the bed to stand. She heard Kelly move, and her yawn told Susan that she was awake as well.

"Good morning," Kelly said quietly.

"Hi," Susan replied.

"How are you feeling?"

Susan shrugged noncommittally. "I really don't feel anything."

"I can understand that," Kelly said somberly, rising and walking into the bathroom.

When she returned, Susan agreed to go to the cemetery. She couldn't hurt any worse than she already did.

~~*~*~*~*

As they made their way through the cemetery, Kelly matched Susan's pace as it slowed. She could feel the trepidation flooding through her companion, realizing that the cemetery probably wasn't somewhere Susan had visited too often. To Kelly, it was a familiar place; she'd spent many afternoons just sitting near her mother's grave. For some reason, she felt her mother was closer there. Anytime she would find herself in a bad way, Kelly found it calming to just sit next to her mother's stone and talk to her. She was convinced that her mother knew she was there. She even felt the hugs she sent.

If there had been any way to lessen Susan's pain, Kelly would have done it in a heartbeat. She knew that there was no way to be prepared for finding out the man you once called daddy, the man who turned around and sent you away because you were gay, was dead. Kelly had been surprised that Susan had even agreed to the meeting with her mother in the first place, and the shock of hearing of her father's death had just been the final straw.

Susan is facing demons I can't even fathom. My mother never sent me away, and I never knew my father, but I loved my mother like no other and it nearly killed me when she died. Susan and I are definitely in the same

A Saving Solace

boat where pain is concerned. I hope she is not too angry to see that, so she will come to me for comfort.

Susan had not raised her head since they'd exited the car. She just stared at the ground as they walked through the wet grass. Kelly knew Susan was still angry with her, but hoped that one day soon it would blow over. She had hoped that by seeing her mother, things would get better for Susan.

Boy, did I blow it.

They followed the map they had gotten from the caretaker until they reached Mr. McGovern's headstone.

Jonathon Edward McGovern
April 5, 1940 – January 10, 2001
Father-Husband-Friend

Kelly watched the myriad of expressions wash over Susan's face as she read the stone's inscription. She wanted to reach out to Susan, but waited for an invitation. "Susan?" she attempted.

"I want to be alone," Susan requested stiffly.

"Baby, are you sure? I know what you must be going through." Kelly took a couple of steps towards her, only to have Susan stop her in her tracks.

"Don't!" she growled, extending her arm with her palm facing outward. "Don't you come near me! You have *no* idea what you've put me through!" Susan shouted. Kelly's eyes widened in shock, completely flabbergasted at the outburst. "We said we loved each other! That means I'm supposed to be able to *trust* you. You had *no right* to go behind my back! Wha... wha... what was it - your good deed for the year? Help the poor homeless worker reunite with her long lost family? Well, happy fucking reunion, Kelly!" Susan screamed, her crimson face filled with rage and betrayal.

Kelly tried to quell her ranting. "I made a terrible

mistake and I'm sorry, but Susan, you can't believe that..."

"I can't believe what? That you weren't doing your duty for the community, to make yourself a better person? You take a young girl under your wing... invite her over for dinner... seduce her with your money... fuck her... make her believe you loved her... help her feed other destitute people at a soup kitchen that you personally funded out of the goodness of your heart... then go one step further and reunite her with her parents that threw her away like garbage?" Susan accented each accusation by poking Kelly in the chest. "What's not to believe? You hear about shit like this all the time. I just never thought I'd see it coming from you." Susan's breath was labored as the tears ran down her cheeks.

Kelly's eyes filled with unshed tears as Susan's words struck her like slaps in the face. "You know I didn't do all of that because of some need to fulfill a civic duty. It's crazy to even think that!" She stopped to take a deep breath, then looked into Susan's eyes. "I *do* love you... and I know you're upset. Believe me, I know what you're going through." She tried to soothe Susan with soft words.

"You don't have a *clue* about what I'm going through! You weren't thrown out of your own home by the people you loved the most. You didn't have to sleep in shit with rats for three years, not knowing where your next meal was coming from." Her voice was low and accusatory, and tears stained her face. "You didn't get raped because you had shoes that fit some guy that was passing through the alley. I had NOTHING left in me, Kelly, NOTHING! That life took everything from me when I was only twenty years old! How the fuck could you possibly know what I'm going through?"

Kelly felt her tolerance reach its limit and couldn't stop the words that spilled from her mouth. "How could

I possibly know, huh? Let's see: you had nothing at twenty? How about being fifteen and watching your mother, the one person you loved more than life itself, deteriorate into nothing before your eyes without being able to do anything! How about trying to feed her because she couldn't do it for herself because her arms didn't fucking work, and then turning around to find that she'd vomited everything you'd just fed her all over herself because her stomach wouldn't digest anything anymore! OR how about having to wipe her ass because she'd shit her pants because her whole fucking body was breaking down more and more with each passing day; and still you prayed for more time with her, begging for more of the same just so she would still be there!" Through her tears, Kelly glared icily into Susan's eyes and tried to control her shaking body. "How about watching as her last breath was taken from her body, turning her the ugliest gray you've ever seen...You're right, Susan, I don't have a FUCKING clue what you're going through. I'm just an asshole, right? A fucking bitch with no heart, just a lot of cash, doing my civic duty. You know what, Susan..." She couldn't bear to say the rest, *Fuck you!* so she ran towards her safety zone - away from Susan and her father's grave.

"Kelly!" she heard Susan scream, but she couldn't stop. She just kept running until she knew she was far from sight. She hadn't hurt so much since her mother had left her. *I know what abandonment feels like, no matter what she fucking thinks.*

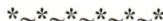

"Kelly!" The scream ripped through Susan's throat as she fell to the ground. "Oh, God, what have I done?" She cried miserable tears with her face resting against the wet blades of grass. Her whole body ached from their exchange. She'd never meant to say all that she had. *It just hurt so much to see... to see...*

Susan looked up through the angry tears in her eyes and glared at her father's headstone, feeling the rage within her as it tore through her chest.

"YOU BASTARD!" she sobbed as she turned on the ground to kick his stone. "You will not take anything more from me, DO YOU UNDERSTAND! You took everything from me before, but no more, Daddy. I won't allow you to take Kelly from me, too. You won't win this time!" *I will die first.*

She choked back the sobs that desperately sought release. She had to find Kelly. That was the only thing she was sure of at the moment. "Kelly!"

A Saving Solace

Chapter Thirty-One

Kelly sat by her mother's stone for at least a half an hour after her confrontation with Susan, not believing what had happened. She wept as she stroked the cement engraving of her mother's name.

Dorothy Ruth Cavanaugh
September 24, 1955 - December 28, 1990
Mother – Daughter - Friend - Angel

"What I wouldn't give to have you with me right now. I need you so badly," she sobbed. "What do I do now?" She was crying so hard, she couldn't think clearly. She was feeling as if the last few weeks didn't matter, her love for Susan didn't matter. Nothing mattered.

How could Susan think so little of me? How could she think so little of what we shared?

Kelly's mind was racing through a million thoughts a second. The tears hadn't stopped since she'd run to her safety cocoon. She felt like she couldn't breathe, like someone had knocked her down, picked her back up, and then knocked her down again at least a thousand times. Her heart was hurting beyond words. She never would have thought she'd be capable of being so cold towards Susan. *God, I loved her with my life! I laid so much of myself out there for her. For what? She turned around and stabbed my heart in places I didn't even know existed.*

This is why I stopped extending myself. This is why I stopped dating. This is why I didn't share my mother's pain with her. I knew this would happen eventually. That's what all women do to me: they love me, and then break me. I just can't do this anymore. "I just can't,"

A Saving Solace

Kelly whispered through her tears.

Kelly's phone rang, or rather, vibrated against her hip. Considering her state of mind, she contemplated not answering it but knew that she probably should. Reaching through layers of clothing to extract it, she plucked it open. She wiped her eyes and stared at the number display in confusion. Expecting it to be Susan, her mind was assailed by new possibilities for which she was not prepared. She drew in a much-needed breath, then hit the talk button.

"Hello?" she answered shakily, waiting for the return greeting. "Yes, this is Kelly Cavanaugh." Listening to the voice on the other end of the line, her heart stopped cold. "What room is she in?" She closed her eyes in silent prayer as the tears rolled down her face. "ICU number four? Okay... yes. Thank you for calling."

Kelly quickly closed the connection and looked down at the grave marker. "Oh, Momma." She sadly shook her head and ran to find her car.

~~*~*~*~*

Walking around the cemetery for nearly an hour, Susan couldn't find Kelly anywhere. She knew her friend was hurting and desperately needed to find her, to apologize. *I was so wrong in yelling at her the way that I did. I had no idea she'd been through such hell with her mother. If she had told me, I might not have behaved the way I did to her.*

Her inner voice picked that most inconvenient time to pour salt in her wound. ***Who are you kidding? You were out of control, plain and simple. Now you've wounded the woman you supposedly love with all your heart.***

God, I am such an asshole.

"Kelly!" Susan shouted again, still hoping to find her, though she'd have thought she should have found her by that time. Believing that Kelly would have gone to her mother's grave, Susan had found a caretaker on the grounds, who was kind enough to show her where Mrs. Cavanaugh's plot was. But there it was, and Kelly was nowhere to be found. Susan looked down to the engraving on the stone. The date of her death brought her a new realization.

December twenty-eighth. Jesus, that's today! No wonder she wanted to come here today. I'm even more of an asshole now. I'm sure she was feeling incredibly sad and vulnerable with this being the anniversary of her mother's death. And I added to that nice, excruciating pain. I can't imagine how she feels right now.

Nice going, Susan.

The discovery brought on a fresh bout of tears, and Susan felt about two inches tall. *I wouldn't be surprised if Kelly never wanted to see me again.*

I think you've just fucked up the best thing that's ever happened to you.

"God, Kelly, I'm so sorry. I had no idea," Susan whispered to herself sadly.

The rain had begun to fall and the cold temperatures were starting to chill her. Kelly was there somewhere; of that she was certain. But Susan knew that she had to leave and find a way back home soon. She reached in her pocket, tracing the antenna of her cell phone with her finger. She tried calling Kelly's phone, but there was no answer. Hesitantly, Susan began to dial a number she thought she'd never dial again.

"Hello?"

She almost hung up when she heard the answering voice, then took a deep breath and spoke. "Mother?"

"Susan?" came the tentative query.

"Yeah," she answered, then stopped, trying to figure out why she was calling her mother, but she thought of Kelly's pain and she knew why.

"Honey, are you all right?"

Hearing the gentle voice again brought a welling of tears to Susan's eyes. "Oh, Mom, I really screwed things up," she began, emotion clouding her voice.

"What? Honey, where are you? Can I pick you up somewhere?"

There was another pause as Susan tried to collect herself enough to answer. "I'm at the cemetery," she said through her tears. "Kelly, um..." She couldn't stop herself from sobbing. Her heart was breaking with each and every moment away from the one she loved. "Kelly and I had a fight, and uh... I... I can't find her!"

The maternal instinct in Mrs. McGovern took over, even though they'd practically been strangers for five years. "Shh, honey, it'll be okay. Stay where you are, and I'll come and get you. The weather is going to be awful the next few hours. I don't want you getting ill."

Susan couldn't bring herself to refuse the offer. "I'll be by Dad," she said, knowing her mother would know where to find her. Her eyes scanned the cemetery, looking for any sign of Kelly and finding none. "Thanks, Mom," she said into the phone, and then they said their good byes.

She clicked off the phone and began to walk towards her father's grave, worrying about Kelly. If she had left the cemetery, her emotional state was nowhere near as calm as it needed to be to drive safely.

"I'm so sorry!" Susan screamed into the now powerful storm. The raindrops had already thoroughly soaked her hair, and the sky didn't look like it was going to calm any time soon. She knew that the storms raging without and within were both going to need very large rainbows.

~~*~*~*

Susan waited for her mother by the side of the road. She had no idea what kind of car to expect, so when she saw headlights approaching, she hoped it was her, and was thankful to find that it was.

The black Acura made its way slowly towards her, as if not to splash. When it stopped, she saw her mother's face and was waved inside. Grabbing the door handle, she quickly opened the door and got inside the warm automobile. As soon as she was seated, she recollected how wet she was and cringed. "Oh crap! I'm sorry, I'm going to ruin the leather!" she said through chattering teeth, wiping away her unceasing tears.

"Nonsense, it will dry," her mother replied, patting her forearm. "And so will they." She pointed to the tear soaked face and gave her daughter a warm sincere smile, which set her off again.

Mrs. McGovern immediately reached over to the glove box and pulled out some Kleenex , which Susan gratefully accepted to dab at her eyes and cheeks. Her mother turned in her seat to face her daughter, stroked an arm tenderly. "Wanna talk about it?"

"Can we go home first?" Susan answered automatically. When no answer came, she looked up to find a confused look on her mother's face. "What's the matter?" she asked.

"Whose home do you want me to take you to? Mine or yours?" her mother asked wistfully.

"Yours, please. If that's all right."

"Of course it's all right. It will always be your home, Susan," she said with as much love as she could muster. Susan could feel the tears threatening again and could only answer with a nod of her head.

Mrs. McGovern turned back in her seat and put the

car in drive. Their trip back to Susan's childhood home was very quiet. She gave her daughter the space and peace that she needed to think about what the things that had happened. Susan was very grateful for that. *She always knew when I needed to just think. I missed this part of our relationship. No one knew me like she did.*

'You were always an introverted child, Susan.' Susan remembered her saying that more than once in her life. *I guess some things never change.*

They pulled into the driveway and Susan watched as the garage door opened, welcoming them home. It had been too long since she'd felt like that. Sighing, she thought that perhaps there was hope for her and her mother, after all. There was still much to talk about, but for the moment, Susan was willing to let her mother take care of her. They both needed that more than they would ever admit.

Her mother's touch drew Susan back from her thoughts. "You coming? Or do you want to stay in here for a little longer?" She smiled.

"No, I mean, yes. I've got to get out of these clothes." Susan shook her coat as she got out of the car, spraying rainwater onto the floor.

"I kept everything of yours, honey. I'm sure you can find something warm to wear upstairs," her mother said as she opened the door leading into the house.

The smell of her old home warmed Susan instantly. She knew things were going to be hard and slow going, but she had reason to hope again. Susan nodded to herself and walked into the family room. The same furniture rested on the same carpeting her parents had had since she was in high school. She shook her head and grinned at her mother, who was watching her with interest.

"What?" she asked with a curious smile of her own.

Susan looked around the room again. "It's just that

everything is the same as it was when I left or um..." She paused, not wanting to be harsh with her mother anymore.

"You can say it, honey," Mrs. McGovern said with shame. "When your father and I kicked you out."

"Yeah," Susan breathed out, closing her eyes against the memory of that night.

~~*~*~*~*

"*Get out of my house!*" *Susan's father screamed.*

"*You're kicking me out?*" *Susan asked incredulously.* "*I'm your daughter!*"

"*You are* **no** *daughter of mine!* **My** *daughter isn't queer!* **My** *daughter isn't a freak!* **My** *daughter isn't an abomination to God!*" *he spat, within inches of Susan's face.*

"*You're right. Your daughter isn't any of those things. I am a human being who happens to love another woman.*" *When Susan's father turned a deaf ear to her, she began to show her anger.* "*I'm sorry, Daddy! You can't change who I am!*"

"*No, I can't; but I don't have to look at you, either. You disgust me!*"

Tears were streaming down Susan's face as she looked to her mother for support. "*Mama? Are you going to let this happen?*"

Her mother looked at her feet, not meeting her daughter's eyes.

Jonathon McGovern didn't wait for his wife's answer. "*Your mother is just as disgusted as I am! Don't look to her for acceptance, because you won't find any here!*" *he continued to rage.*

"*Mama, say* **something***!*" *Susan pleaded with her mother as her father grabbed her arms and moved her towards the door.*

A Saving Solace

Elise McGovern never looked up from the floor. Susan could see the tears soaking through her mother's blouse. "Please, Mama, don't let him do this!"
Her mother turned and walked into the kitchen - away from her daughter, away from her cowardice.
"Don't even think about coming back or I'll have you arrested for trespassing!" *Jonathon screamed.*
"Daddy, no! Please!" *Finally, Susan was shoved out of her home. With one final breath she called out to the one person she had always counted on.* "Mama!"
Elise shook with sobs as she heard Susan's last call to her. She heard the front door slam and knew she would never see her daughter again.

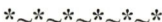

"That was the worst day of my life, Susan," her mother said. "I never thought I'd turn my back on my own flesh and blood. I can never ask you to forgive me."
The family room was quiet as Susan listened to her mother's voice. She knew that her mother was sorry, but she also wished that her father had been.
"You'll find dry clothes in your closet. They should still fit you. I don't want you to catch cold in those wet things. I'd like to talk…"
"We'll talk more. I'm just going to go upstairs and change, if that's all right?" Susan looked into her mother's sad eyes and she nodded. "I'll be right back."
Susan walked through the foyer and up the stairs leading to her old bedroom. The same floorboards creaked as she made her way down the hallway. The bedroom door was slightly ajar, so she pushed it open to reveal her room. It hadn't changed one iota in five years.
The same pictures still hung on the walls. The two twin beds had the same sheets and comforters on them.

She walked towards her closet and opened the sliding door, instinctively reaching for the switch just inside the doors to turn on the light. She grabbed a sweatshirt and a pair of jeans from the shelves, turned the light off, and closed the door.

Removing her wet clothes, she hung them on her desk chair. She fit easily into her old clothes, with a little room to spare. She sat on her bed for a moment, absorbing all that had happened in the previous 72 hours. *A wonderful Christmas spent with the most wonderful woman on the planet. A reunion with the woman that allowed her husband to disown me. Visiting my father at his gravesite. Screaming vicious words at the same woman who had made passionate love to me only days before. Now I am sitting on my bed in the home where I wasn't welcome for five years.* Susan's body turned to jelly and she found her head on her pillow.

She sobbed endlessly for several minutes as she reflected on how badly she had hurt Kelly. *She meant well, I know she did. God knows, I know that. I just let my emotions take over, and then BAM! I lost complete control, and now I've probably lost Kelly, too. Why does life have to be so hard?*

Why does life have to be so hard?

Kelly looked at the still form that was her grandmother. She was seventy-four years old, but her face was so pale and looked so much older than Kelly remembered. She tried to imagine her without all the tubes running through her, but when she looked at her grandmother, all she saw was her mother. Dying.

Her grandmother was dying. She'd had a stroke and her neighbor, Sally, had found her in her apartment. Kelly's grandma was a stickler for punctuality, so when

A Saving Solace

she didn't show up for lunch, Sally knew something was wrong. *If you're late, I won't wait,* she'd always say in her singsong voice.

"What I wouldn't give to hear your voice now," Kelly said through her tears. She gently grasped a frail hand and sat in the chair close to the bed. "I love you, Gram." Kelly kissed her hand and rested her cheek on it.

It must have been the emotional toll the day had taken, because she didn't realize she had fallen asleep until she woke to the loud beeping of the monitors and felt the weight of something on her head. Her grandmother had put a hand on her head while she was asleep. The sound of feet approaching quickly drew Kelly out of her slumber-like trance.

"Code Blue!" she heard one of the nurses cry out. The nurse looked at Kelly and took her arm. "Miss, you'll have to leave, now. I'll let you know something as soon as I can, I promise." She escorted her gently out of the area.

Kelly looked back at her grandmother and the hospital staff working to revive her. She knew they wouldn't be able to. This was what her grandmother had wanted since the day her daughter had died. Kelly was incapable of stopping it. *No one should have to bury a child. I can't even imagine what that felt like.* Kelly couldn't fathom living day to day after losing a child. *Apparently Gram couldn't either, and eleven years to the day, she finally got her wish.*

Kelly mutely walked into the waiting room, waiting to have someone confirm the news that she already knew in her heart. Her grandma was gone.

"We did everything we could for her. I'm sorry," the doctor finished as Kelly stared into his sympathetic eyes.

"I know you did. I'm just glad I got to see her one last time," she said, almost to herself. The physician put

232

his hand on Kelly's shoulder, gave it a light squeeze, and then quietly walked away. She sat back down and stared dumbly at the walls of the waiting room. Alone.

A Saving Solace

Chapter Thirty-Two

Kelly hung up the phone after speaking with the funeral director at Scott's Funeral Home, wondering if she could ever do that kind of work. It took a very special person to run a funeral home. Their job was to help everyone say one final goodbye to the people they'd loved in their lives. They made the last visit as painless as possible. She really admired that.

"One last call to make and I'm out of here," she said to herself, pinching the bridge of her nose to ward off the migraine she knew was coming. She picked up the phone and called her boss to let her know she was taking some time off. "Shannon? Hi, it's Kelly."

"Hello, Kelly. How are you?" she said cheerfully into the receiver.

"I'm not well, actually. My grandmother passed away yesterday, and I'm going to need some time off," Kelly said as she fiddled with the papers on her desk and tried hard not to cry again.

"Oh, Kelly. I'm so sorry," Shannon said with genuine regret.

"Thanks."

"You take whatever time you need. I'll have Brad watch over your market until you get back. Don't worry about anything, okay?"

"I'll do my best." Kelly paused and took a breath. "Thanks, Shannon. I really appreciate it."

"You're welcome. Again, please know how sorry I am. When you get a chance, can you let me know where the services are? I'd like to send an arrangement."

Kelly's eyes welled up at her boss's kindness. "Thank you, Shannon. I'll send you an email before I leave today."

"You're at the office? Go home, Kelly. Whatever you're doing can wait until you get back." When she didn't respond, Shannon repeated herself, "I mean it, Kelly. Go home. Please."

"I will," she acquiesced.

"Take care of yourself."

"You too, Shannon. Bye."

"Bye."

Hanging up the phone, Kelly collected her things. She looked at the paper on which she'd been writing and sighed. "You'll never forget about her, so stop trying," she said to herself as she grabbed the piece of paper, crumpled it, and threw it towards the trashcan. Kelly missed the can, but left the wad on the floor, not wanting to waste any more energy on it. Or Susan.

~~*~*~*

Susan had fallen asleep, and woke to feel a light touch on her head. Her mother was sitting next to her, stroking her hair and humming a tune she used to sing to Susan when she was a child. It always had a calming effect on her, and today was no different.

Susan groggily looked into her loving eyes. "Must have fallen asleep. Sorry, about that."

"Oh, honey, don't apologize. You obviously needed it," she said as she continued to play with her daughter's hair. "You know, I've missed this… missed you."

Susan looked into guilt-ridden eyes and realized that her hell had been out in the streets, while her mother had never left hers. Not long ago she would've been happy to know her mother was hurting as badly as she had. Now she wasn't so sure she'd want anyone to feel that way. She sighed in contentment. "Me too, Mama. Me, too."

Susan closed her eyes and just let her mother try to

banish the demons she'd been keeping inside herself for so long. She wasn't sure why she was so readily allowing her mother to touch her. She wasn't sure about anything at that point. All she knew was that she'd hurt the woman she'd intended to spend the rest of her life with. Hurt her badly.

She hadn't left a message when she called Kelly's cell phone. In hindsight, she wished she had. Her heart began to race, not knowing exactly how much time had passed since she'd heard Kelly's voice. "What time is it, Mama?"

"You slept through to tomorrow, honey. It's a little after ten."

Sitting up abruptly, Susan noticed that she was in the clothes she'd changed into, but under the covers.

Her mom put a calming hand on her shoulder. "When you didn't come back down last night, I came in and found you asleep on top of your bed. I maneuvered you under the covers, but obviously you were too wiped out to remember," she explained.

Susan rubbed her eyes in disbelief; she'd never slept so long. "I have to find Kelly, Mom; I do. I said some awful things to her. Things I shouldn't have ever said, least of all yesterday."

"What was yesterday?" she asked.

"The anniversary of her mother's death," her daughter revealed regretfully.

"I see," she acknowledged, without commenting further.

"Would you mind if I borrowed the car? I'm sure she's at the office. I won't be long, I promise."

"On one condition," her mother negotiated.

"Yes?"

"You take a shower and come downstairs to eat some breakfast. You haven't digested an ounce of food since God knows when. I might not have seen you in the last few years, but I sure remember how you can get if you haven't eaten." She smiled playfully.

"You've got a deal." Susan smiled back at her mother as she stood to leave her to shower. "Mom?" Her mother turned with a questioning glance. "Thank you for coming to get me yesterday. It meant a lot to me." Susan could feel the emotion building again as her eyes teared up.

"You don't have to thank me, sweetie," she almost whispered, then looked her daughter in the eye. "Thank you for calling me. That meant the world to *me*."

Susan stood up and did something she hadn't done in five years. "Can I hold you?" she asked in a childlike voice.

Mrs. McGovern stretched out her arms and Susan fell into them desperately, hugging her mother for all she was worth. The older woman wrapped her arms around her daughter tightly. Susan could feel their twin heartbeats racing. She had truly missed that feeling; she wasn't going to let it go for anything in the world.

They parted with a watery smile for each other. Susan's mother squeezed her forearm and walked out into the hallway, closing the door on her way out.

~~*~*~*

In keeping with their agreement, Susan showered, dressed, and ate before her mother turned over the keys to her father's old BMW. Susan wondered why it hadn't been sold, but her mom said she liked the car too much to get rid of it. Looking up at the convertible top, Susan couldn't have agreed with her more. She backed out of the driveway and made her way towards Maxine's, unsure of what kind of reception she was going to get but determined to do her damndest to let Kelly know how sorry she was. Susan didn't care if Kelly punched her square in the face, she was going to say her piece.

She pulled into a parking spot on Lawrence and went into ForOthers. Entering, Susan greeted Miriam, who looked up from her paperwork.

"Hey, stranger. How are things going for you? Any better?"

"I know I didn't really tell you much when I called, but I was really out of it. I've had a pretty traumatic few days."

"You wanna talk about it now?" she asked.

"Well, I do, but I can't at the moment. I came in here to see if you guys can do without me for a little while. I really need some time off."

Miriam looked at her with wonder. "Wow, this must be serious. Is there anything I can do?"

"Yes. Just say you'll give me this time, and I'll be okay in a couple of weeks."

"You know I wouldn't deny you anything. From the looks of you, something big must have happened."

Looking down, Susan considered the clothes she was wearing - designer clothing, something she'd not worn in a long time. "Yeah, I stayed at my mom's last night."

Miriam's eyes got wide. "You're kidding! Susan, that's great!" she cried. "Is everything going okay?"

"Well, it's going to take a lot more time for us to try and work things out, but Mom and I have always had a closeness that even our past couldn't take away. I also found out my father died in January."

"Oh, honey, I'm sorry," she started, but Susan raised a hand to stop her.

"Don't be sorry. The only thing you should feel for my father is pity... I won't miss him." *But I'll miss the man who used to be my daddy.*

Looking down at her boots, Susan realized she had stayed longer than she'd intended. She had to get to

Kelly. "Hey, I really have to get going. Thank you for the time off. I really do appreciate it."

Miriam circled around her desk and enveloped her in a hug. "You're welcome, honey. You come back when you're up to it. We'll be here." She smiled as she pulled away from Susan.

"See you later," Susan responded, and left the building.

She walked down the sidewalk towards Maxine's, her stomach in such knots, she thought she was going to lose her breakfast. Taking a deep breath, Susan walked into the store, immediately spotting Kelly's favorite employee, Therese, behind a counter sorting ties. She looked up and saw Susan and gave her a friendly smile.

"Hi, Therese. I was looking for Kelly. Is she in?"

"Mmm... I haven't seen her in a while. You can go back and check, though. She looked pretty beat; I know seeing you will cheer her up." She winked.

Susan challenged Therese's knowledge of their relationship. "It will, huh?"

The saleswoman rose right to the challenge and knocked her on her ass. "I was there, you know," she said, chuckling. Susan's face instantly blushed, remembering the kiss they had shared on a very live newscast. "Don't worry about it. You guys look good together."

"Thanks, Therese." *Now I know why Kelly likes her so much.* Susan walked towards Kelly's office and found the door closed. After a few moments of breathing deeply and trying to calm her nerves, she knocked. Receiving no response, she knocked again. Finally, she grabbed the doorknob and found the door was unlocked.

"Kelly?" Susan said as she entered the office. There was no sign of Kelly or her belongings. She had apparently left for the day. Susan turned to leave, and a crumpled piece of paper lying on the floor caught her eye. Instinctively, she picked it up to throw it into the trashcan, when she saw her name written on it. Curiosity got the better of her, and she carefully smoothed the piece of paper. Her name was written several times on the page, but what she also found shattered her heart.

Untitled

I'm looking in a mirror
Where a window used to be
Instead of looking outside
All I see is me
I stare at my reflection
And I begin to cry
What used to give me inspiration
Won't look me in the eye

How did this change abruptly
I begin to question now
One day I'm feeling more than loved
Today I wonder how
I'm trapped inside my anguish
It's trapped inside itself
I know I can't endure more pain
Release me from myself!

Please hear me as I whisper
Please hear me when I pray
Please free me from this hellish ache
That fills me now today
I've plunged into this new abyss
That plagues me with despair
Erase this fragrant memory of
The sunshine in her hair.

A Saving Solace

As the tears rolled down Susan's face, she was startled by Therese's reappearance. "You find her?"

Wiping her eyes, she folded the piece of paper and put it in her pocket. "No, I think she's gone for the day."

"Was the door unlocked?" Susan nodded. "Well, we should lock it when you leave, because she would freak if she realized she left her office open all night."

"Good idea." Susan motioned her towards the door. "I'm done; we can go."

"All right. If I see her, I'll tell her you were looking for her."

"Thanks."

Therese locked the door handle and pulled the door closed. "You guys have plans for New Years?"

That question brought incredible sadness to Susan's heart. "I don't know yet. Haven't really talked about it."

"Well, if I don't see you, have a happy New Year."

"You, too." Susan waved at her as she tried to exit the store nonchalantly. Outside, she ran to the car and got in and just stared out into the street. She pulled Kelly's poem from her pocket and reread it, over and over.

God, she's devastated. I have to find her.

Susan cranked over the engine and put the BMW in drive. If Kelly wasn't home when she arrived, she was going to wait for her. *All night if I have to.*

Chapter Thirty-Three

As she approached her house, Kelly saw a black BMW convertible in the driveway. She had a feeling it was Susan. She had so much going on in her head, she wasn't sure what she would say to the younger woman. *I really don't want to see her, and yet I really want to see her. How's that for a paradox?*

As she drove into the driveway, the driver of the BMW opened the car door. It was, in fact, Susan. "Dammit," Kelly said, shaking her head in disbelief.

The headlights of Kelly's car highlighted the waiting figure as Susan looked up at her and waved, a small smile on her face. Kelly hit the garage door opener without acknowledging Susan's presence. As the door slowly opened, Kelly felt eyes burning her with the fierceness of their stare. She used every Jedi mind trick in the book not to look at Susan. And failed.

Seeing the questioning brown eyes, Kelly knew it was going to be a much longer night than she'd bargained for. Emotionally drained from having met Sally at her apartment earlier in the evening, Kelly just wanted to sleep.

~~*~*~*

Kelly pulled up to her grandmother's building and parked the car in her space. Since she never owned a car, Connie's space was always empty. She much preferred public transportation. Somehow, Kelly didn't blame her.

She buzzed Sally's apartment and her grandmother's friend met her at the door. Sally Jenkins was a forty-something woman with short, deep red hair and beautiful green eyes. Her small frame was heavily overlaid with bulk. Kelly's grandma had always tried to get her to lose some of that weight, not wanting to lose her friend to a 'heart attack or some such nonsense.' Sally was the only one Kelly knew of that Connie had connected with since she'd lived there. Her grandma and Sally had been friends for at least six or seven years. Sally had a softness and warmth about her that always made Kelly smile.

"Hi, Kel." She leaned closer and hugged Kelly tightly.

"Hey, Sally. Thank you so much for everything you did for her. She loved you very much," Kelly said as she held her.

"It was my pleasure. Connie was a sweetheart, and I'll never forget her. She brought such color into my life," Sally continued, as they walked towards her residence. "She had a story to tell for everything."

Kelly smiled in remembrance. My grandma always did have a way with words. I remember having a hard time in History class. I couldn't remember what happened during what wars and who signed what. She would somehow turn a situation around and put it into the present and use names and places I knew, just so I'd understand it better. God, I'm going to miss her. *She turned her focus back to Sally.*

"That she did." Sally opened the door and motioned for Kelly to enter. The taller woman walked into Sally's living room and took a brief glance around. *It was quite charming. There were a lot of knick-knacks and family pictures throughout the room.* "You know, I don't remember if I've ever been here," Kelly commented.

"Mmm..." Sally thought for a moment. "I think you have, but it was a long time ago. When I first moved in, *if I recall correctly."* Kelly nodded as Sally walked into the kitchen area. "Would you like some coffee or tea or something?" she asked politely.

"Just some water would be great."

"You got it." Sally grabbed a glass out of her cabinet and filled it with water from the dispenser against the refrigerator. "Best damn thing I ever bought. I hate tap water from this place. Tastes like you're sucking on a nail." She handed Kelly the glass.

"Well, that can't be good," the auburn-haired woman said with a grin, taking a sip from the glass.

Moments passed as Kelly alternately stared at the floor and sipped her water, not knowing quite what to say. They sat in silence, and then Sally asked, "Would you like to go to her place? I have a key." She pointed to her key ring hanging on a hook by the door.

Kelly's head instantly popped up. "Would you mind?"

"Not at all, honey." She went to the hook and grabbed the key ring. Kelly set the water glass down on the coffee table and walked over to her. Sally handed her the key. "You go. I'm sure you'd like some time alone in there."

Eyes watering, Kelly leaned over to her and hugged her tightly. "I know why Gram always thought so much of you, Sally. Thank you."

They separated and Sally's eyes were full of tears as well. "She was like my own grandmother. I never had one of my own, but I was honored to have her step in as my surrogate. I know how sad she had been since losing your mother. I don't think she ever bounced back from that." She raked her fingers through her short hair. "She talked about your mom all the time. Losing her daughter killed something inside of her. I wish I had known her before she got so sad."

"So do I, Sally. It feels like we knew two different

women. I knew her before Mom died, and you knew the woman she became afterwards." Kelly stood and pondered that thought for a bit until she felt Sally's hand on her arm. Looking into wet, caring eyes, Kelly fell into her arms again and wept.

Sally rubbed her back and head, whispering sweet words. *"It's okay, honey. Let it out."* Kelly cried for a long while as she held tighter to Sally, the tears feeling like they would never stop. She felt Sally crying right along with her. They'd both suffered a great loss in their lives, so Kelly let her have her tears, too.

Kelly was the first to pull away and begin to wipe her eyes. My heart is completely broken. I am amazed that I have blood flowing through me at all, *Kelly thought.*

Kelly fiddled with the key ring she'd been given. *"I'm gonna go next door now, if that's okay."*

Sally nodded. *"You go and spend whatever time you need to there. I'll be right here if you need me."*

Kelly leaned over and kissed her cheek. *"Thanks, and if it gets too late, I'll just give the key back to you tomorrow."*

"Okay, honey. Take care."

"You, too."

She walked out of Sally's place and down the hall to her grandmother's. Kelly took a deep breath and put the key in the lock. Turning the doorknob and opening the door, her grandma's scent instantly greeted her. She had that scent Kelly thought everyone's grandmother would have. The smells combined from the cooking, cleaning, and fragrant plants but with every window nailed tightly shut to ward off any unforeseen chill. The images of her doing all of those things made Kelly smile. She refused to let anyone do anything for her. *'As long as I'm able to walk, I'm able to clean my own damn house!'* Kelly heard the memory in her head as if she were standing right next to her grandmother. I never offered to get her a cleaning lady again.

Kelly clicked on the light switch and looked around her grandmother's home. She noticed nothing out of place from the last time she'd been there. All of her pictures were still on the windowsills; all of her planters were hanging from the ceiling. Everything that was her grandma was right there in that apartment. She walked towards the couch and sat down and leaned her head back against the cushions. She sighed quietly as the tears began to cascade down her face again.

"Oh, Gram, I'm gonna miss you so much." She felt her chest grow tight and then fill with extreme warmth. Kelly smiled through her tears, feeling the hug that was sent to her. Whether it was from her grandma or her mother, she did not know; but she knew with absolute certainty that they were together again. And they were happy.

"One day we'll all be together again. You can count on that."

She leaned forward and rested her head in her hands and continued to cry. Kelly knew it would take a while before that inclination would go away. She welcomed the cleansing. She rested her head in her hands for several moments, trying to collect herself. Kelly knew her grandma was in a better place now. She was with the daughter she could never say good-bye to. That knowledge alone helped her greatly.

As she sat there starting to feel acceptance of her grandmother's passing, Kelly's mind once again went to Susan. What is going to happen with her? I know I love her, but she obviously doesn't know how she truly feels towards me. Otherwise, how could she have said all those things to me? They say that people say things in anger that they don't really mean. Well, those feelings came from somewhere, so there had to be a germ of truth in what she said. God, if she had all of that bottled up inside her, do I even want to know the stuff she didn't say? God, I hate mind games.

She looked at her watch and noticed it was almost ten. She was tired and only wanted to go to sleep. She rubbed her eyes and took another look around, knowing that the next time she came she'd be cleaning the place out. I want one more memory of the way it used to be.

Kelly rose from the couch and made her way towards the door. "I'll be back, Gram," she said as she opened the door and walked into the hallway. She put the key in the lock and secured the deadbolt. As she walked down the hall towards Sally's place, Kelly noticed the light that was under the door had gone out. Guessing that the woman had gone to bed, Kelly left the building and walked to her car. The night was almost over and she could almost feel the sheets of her bed on her skin, and she shivered in anticipation.

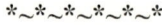

Pulling into the garage, Kelly got out of the car. She turned towards the driveway to find Susan waiting patiently by her car. Taking a deep breath, Kelly walked over to her. "Been waiting long?" she asked, sounding a bit harsher than she had intended.

"A little while," Susan said, leaning against the car.

Somehow Kelly didn't believe her. She looked at Susan, and then at the car. "Yours?"

"My father's, actually. My mother didn't want to part with it," she explained.

"What do you want, Susan?" Kelly asked, wanting to cut to the chase. She was exhausted and had no idea what was in store for her with Susan there.

"I want to talk, Kelly," she started.

"What, like yesterday? I'm not up for another

shouting match with you. I'm tired and the past thirty-six hours have been beyond shitty, so if you don't mind, I'd like to go inside my house and go to bed. Go home, Susan." Kelly started to push past Susan and the smaller woman grabbed her arm. Kelly didn't turn around to face her, but heard her voice from behind.

"Home? I don't even know where that is anymore. So much has happened to me, even in the last couple days!"

"I suppose that's my fault, too?"

"Please, Kelly. I don't want to fight. I want to apologize for my horrific behavior yesterday." At that admission, Kelly turned around and looked into sad, guilt-ridden brown eyes. "I went to find you today at your office, but you had left already," Susan continued without releasing Kelly's arm.

"Yeah, I had some things to deal with today." She didn't offer any information about her grandma. She was feeling mistrust for Susan, and knew she couldn't share anything too personal at the moment.

"Kelly, please talk to me. I know I was out of control. I didn't mean the things I said to you; I swear to God, I didn't." Susan could feel her teeth begin to chatter and her legs were getting icy cold.

"So, you're sorry. Well, I'm freezing. Now that we've established that, good night." She tried to pull free from Susan and go inside, but the blonde stubbornly refused to release her. Kelly was unable to listen to Susan's words; all she could hear were the hurtful words she'd shouted the day before. The anger that she'd felt at the cemetery was still very fresh in her heart. "Susan, I really don't want to get into this right now. Let me go."

Susan's eyes pleaded with her to believe her words. "I can't," she choked out. "Kelly, I love you!"

"You sure have a fucked up way of showing it." Kelly jerked her arm free. "Now if you don't mind, this civic minded person wants to get inside her civic house and sleep in her civic bed. Alone."

At those words, Susan crumpled to her knees and began to weep. She looked up at Kelly with tear-stained cheeks and begged her to listen. "Kelly, I'm so sorry! I freaked out at seeing my dad's grave. I didn't know what I was saying. Please... you... you have to know that! I can't lose you! Please don't leave me!" she cried out between sobs. Kelly's resolve was shattering as she listened to the piteous wailing. "I love you," Susan wept.

Kelly felt the knot in her stomach reestablish itself, and tried to walk away, leaving Susan in the same anguish she'd felt the day before. But she couldn't. The tears rolled down her cheeks before she could stop them, and Kelly's arms reached out to pick Susan off the ground.

Seeing the open arms, Susan lunged right into them, trembling terribly and clinging to Kelly like a lifeline. Her sobs were long and heartwrenching. Holding her close, Kelly kissed the top of her head. Susan's hair still smelled like sunshine. Kelly closed tear-filled eyes, willing herself to believe. She knew Susan hadn't meant those things she'd said. She was filled with all kinds of raw emotions that she was unable to deal with. In addition to everything else, Kelly knew deep down Susan was grieving for a man that had died long before his heart attack. She knew that feeling all too well.

"It's okay, baby. I'm right here," she whispered in Susan's ear. "Come on, let's go inside." Kelly felt the nod against her chest, but Susan didn't let go. Like Siamese twins, they walked clumsily through the garage and into the house. Kelly closed the garage and the door leading inside. Uninhibited by the emotional currents, Mattie met them with a happily wagging tail.

Susan turned in Kelly's arms and looked down.

"Hey, sweetie." She reached down and petted the pup, much to Mattie's delight. The trio went into the family room and sat on the couch. Susan's hold on Kelly didn't slacken at all, and Kelly relished the feel of the slight blonde in her arms again. She had missed holding her. Kelly knew they had a long night ahead of them, but the potential outcome was appealing. Very appealing.

A Saving Solace

Chapter Thirty-Four

Kelly's arms were warm around Susan, rubbing her neck and arms. *I never thought I'd be here again. I just hope she can forgive me.* Holding Kelly tightly, Susan continued to cry into her chest. *She is such a loving woman. How could I have said that she was doing this out of some sort of self-serving sense of duty? How could I have even thought that?*

Susan knew they were in for a long talk, and prayed that they could work through the feelings of hurt and betrayal. She had so much apologizing to do; she hoped that she was up to it. Pulling back from Kelly's embrace, Susan looked into her watery eyes. "Thank you, Kelly. Thank you for talking to me. I know seeing me probably wasn't tops on your list for the night."

Kelly looked down at Susan as the tears continued to fall down her beautifully sculpted face. "No, it wasn't. I really wasn't expecting you at all." Silence settled between them for a few awkward moments before she continued, "Now that you're here, we do have a lot to talk about."

"Yeah, we do," Susan agreed. "Please, if you'll allow me to go first?"

Kelly nodded as they pulled apart. They sat sideways on the couch in order to have a clear view of each other. Taking Kelly's hands, Susan hoped her lover would believe the words that she was speaking from her heart.

"First, you need to know how sorry I am for what I said. I know you didn't lure me into your clutches or your bed to procure a medal from the mayor. It was out of my mouth before I could stop it. When I saw my father's gravestone, I got so angry." As she spoke, Susan squeezed Kelly's hands. "I got angry because I will never be able to resolve anything with him now. He'll never know what happened to me because of his bigotry. He'll never know the hell he put my mom through, either."

"But what did that have to do with me? Was it that you were still angry about me meeting with your mother?" Kelly asked softly.

"I guess so. I was angry that you didn't tell me she called you. You lied to me about it to boot. I don't know if I was ready to see my parents, but I would've reacted better if I'd had a say in the matter. You went behind my back to decide *my* future with *my* parents. That was wrong," Susan said sternly, looking into Kelly's eyes.

As she collected her thoughts her head was bowed, looking at their hands, and then Kelly looked directly at Susan. "And I *apologized* for that over and over. I had *no* idea your mom was going to call me. I can't be held responsible for her seeing us on the news, Susan."

Kelly's voice was getting heated. Susan knew she needed to soothe the waters a bit if she wanted the discussion to be productive. "I know that, honey, I really do. I just wish you would've told me about it, so I could've prepared myself. Seeing her in your office was the *last* thing I ever expected to encounter." Watching Susan wipe her eyes with the sleeve of her coat, Kelly reached behind her to grab some tissues from the end table. "Thank you," Susan said, blotting her eyes.

"I didn't expect her there, either. When I returned her call, she asked to speak to me in person as opposed to talking on the phone. Believe me, had I known this was going to happen, I never would have agreed to it," Kelly explained, more gently this time. "I know I should've told you. You don't know how sorry I am for that."

Susan sat and listened to Kelly explain, trying to put

herself in Kelly's shoes. *Would I have said anything if our roles had been reversed? Maybe not, knowing the angst I felt for them at the time. Maybe she was just trying to protect me.* She mechanically slipped off her coat and rested it beside her on the couch.

"I see the wheels turning in your head, what are you thinking about?"

Smiling at Kelly, Susan replied, "I was just wondering what I would've done in that situation if I had been you. Realizing how hostile I got while just talking about my parents, I think I would've done the same thing."

Kelly's eyes widened. "You *would* have?" she exclaimed incredulously.

"Yeah." Susan nodded. "Now that I've had the time to think about it, I know you were just trying to protect me. I know I overreacted. You were only being the middleman, and you would've told me about talking with her after you found out what she wanted. Right?" she queried.

"Absolutely! You know I wouldn't have sent you to the front lines without a damn good weapon." Kelly smiled softly at Susan, completely melting her heart...and any lingering animosity.

Susan smiled gently back. "I know that now. I was just really freaked out, for lack of a better phrase. When you and I went to my mother's house the other day, it was like I was watching everything through someone else's eyes. It was surreal for me to be there again, a place I hadn't been welcome in for five years! Once I was seated in my living room and my mom told me how unhappy her life had been because of my father, I realized I wasn't the only one he'd hurt. I started to actually *feel* for her again; and it was something other than hate." Kelly rubbed Susan's wrists gently with her thumbs as the younger woman began to recount her view of the previous few days.

Taking a deep breath, Susan felt the pain of her next thoughts. "Then she told me he was gone. My brain went dead, Kel. I was so angry that I couldn't even think straight. I had to get out of there before I blew a gasket. As soon as I started running, I knew everything would be different. It's like this coldness came over me. I was so pissed that he was dead!" Kelly's eyebrows rose along with the volume of Susan's voice. "I know it sounds kind of whacked, but I wanted him to know what he'd done to us." She paused to collect herself so she would not start crying again. "He needed to know the monster he had become; and that he was no longer the man I used to call daddy." Her voice dropped in register with her last remark.

Kelly continued to stroke Susan's wrists with her thumbs, and her expression was extremely sad. Susan knew Kelly was hurting for her, for herself, and for the two of them. "Kelly, I'm sorry about yesterday. I know what a difficult day that must have been for you. It took me a while to put together that it was the anniversary of your mother's death. I felt like the worst person on the planet once I saw her stone."

Kelly's eyes met Susan's for a moment. "You saw her stone?"

"Yeah. I went looking for you after you ran away. I must have walked around that cemetery forever before I found a caretaker to show me your mom's plot. I had hoped you would be there, but you weren't. I saw that the grass was disturbed, so I figured you'd been there before me."

"Yeah, I was there." Kelly looked like she was fighting with something before she continued. "I um... I got a call that uh... made me leave." She paused again and started crying.

Susan's heart flooded with sadness and she threw

her arms around Kelly. "It's okay, sweetheart. Whatever it is, we'll get through it," she soothed as she stroked her back. "I'm never leaving you, Kelly. I promise."

Kelly pulled back abruptly. "You can't make that promise, Susan. You can't! Death takes whomever it goddamn wants to, whenever it wants to! Don't tell me you won't leave me; you don't know that for certain. No one does."

Her voice sounded so haunted, it scared Susan. She knew the pain had to stem from the call she'd gotten. "Kelly, what happened? Who called you?" Kelly turned and rested her back against the cushions of the couch and stared off into space. Susan gave her space to get out whatever it was she needed to tell.

"The saddest part about the call is that I'm not sure if I can tell you about it." Susan's eyes registered her shock but she remained silent, waiting for Kelly to make her decision. Kelly kept her eyes straight ahead, and her tears continued to fall endlessly.

"What happened yesterday hurt me more than I can tell you. I hadn't had anyone, anyone that mattered, in my life for a long time. I also hadn't trusted anyone with my heart until you. You shattered it yesterday, Susan. You may have been hurting, but you crossed a line. You said things to me I *never* thought I'd hear. *Especially* not from you." Kelly turned to face her. "You turned the love we'd shared into something dirty and calculated. You didn't even think about the effect you might be having as you ripped my heart out, did you? I was just someone to wipe your boots on, wasn't I? Well, guess what? I will not be a doormat for *anyone*, Susan, not *even* you."

Staring at Kelly through her tears, Susan could see the hurt reflected in the dark blue eyes, a hurt that she had put there. Kelly's heart was filled with such pain,

A Saving Solace

Susan wasn't sure if there was any room in it for forgiveness. "Can you ever forgive me, Kelly? If I could change everything that happened yesterday, I would. I'd do everything differently. I swear to God, Kelly! I can't apologize enough for the things I said. All I can promise you is that I won't ever treat you that way again. It wasn't your fault that my father kicked me out. It wasn't your fault that he died without knowing how I felt. It wasn't your fault that I hadn't tried to see him before now. None of it was your fault, yet I treated you as if you were him. I wanted to hurt him, but you were the one who was there, so I hurt you instead. I'll never forgive myself for the way I treated you, Kelly. I acted without thinking, and I'm truly, truly sorry for that. I didn't mean to hurt you."

Kelly blinked away her tears and rested her head against the cushions again, sighing deeply. "I know." They sat in silence for several minutes, neither knowing what to say.

A whimper from Mattie got Susan's attention, and she got up to let her out, Kelly giving her hand a light squeeze as she passed by to open the back door for the dog. "Come on girl, let's get you outside." Susan opened the door and let her out. Her arms wrapped around herself, she watched Mattie run around the backyard. Her grace and uninhibited joy had a calming effect.

"My grandma died," Susan heard a small voice say from behind her. Susan turned around slowly, not believing she'd heard correctly. Looking at Kelly's forlorn face, she knew she'd not misheard. Susan immediately knelt before her, taking her hands and rubbing them. "Oh, my God, sweetie. When?"

"Yesterday," she whispered hoarsely.

Susan drew Kelly to her into a strong embrace. "I'm so sorry, honey. I'm so, so sorry," she whispered over and over as Kelly cried out her grief. *And on the same day as her mother. God, how awful.*

Kelly clung to Susan; fresh sobs continued to well from deep within. Susan knew she was crumbling inside but could do nothing but hold her for a long time, waiting for her spasms to lessen. When they finally did, Susan pulled slowly from their embrace and peppered Kelly's face with tiny, loving kisses.

"I can't say it enough. I'm so sorry about your grandmother."

Looking at Susan with watery eyes, Kelly forced a pained smile. "I really wanted her to meet you."

Susan stroked her cheek with the back of her knuckles. "She knows me now, honey."

"I suppose. It's just not quite the same, you know?" Kelly sounded like a young child as she spoke.

"I do, sweetie, I do." Susan gazed at her, eyes trying to convey the love she felt.

"I love you," Kelly said before she embraced Susan again.

Susan's heart skipped several beats, knowing how hard that had been for her to say. "I love you, too, Kel. More than I can ever say."

Kelly pulled away from their embrace and cupped Susan's face gently with her hands. Their eyes locked with deep intensity and Kelly's lips devoured Susan's. Her kiss was demanding and strong, her tongue bathing Susan's with dominating strokes, looking for a connection they both needed like they needed air, needed so they could believe in each other again.

Rising from her kneeling position without breaking contact, Susan climbed into Kelly's lap. Kelly's fervor excited her incredibly, and Susan returned the heated kisses tenfold. They rolled into a lying position, Kelly peeling her coat off as they sank into each other. More articles of clothing were shed by both; they couldn't get close enough. Susan was bursting with such desire, she felt faint. She wanted to feel Kelly's skin against her own. Once they'd kicked off their shoes and stripped off their clothing, they began an age-old rhythm of love and passion.

Susan heard Kelly groaning in her ear while she moved against her. The sounds Kelly was making made her toes curl. Kelly's thigh moved deliberately between Susan's legs, and Susan's returned the favor. Their movements were rough, synchronized, and incredibly hot. Kelly's hand found Susan's left nipple and began to tug and twist it between her thumb and forefinger. Susan was close, but didn't want to come until Kelly was ready.

She grabbed onto Kelly's hips to urge her to move faster against the intrusive thigh. She wanted to feel all of Kelly's passion, needed all of it. Kelly looked down into her eyes, and Susan could tell Kelly was just about there. They drove into each other, desperately seeking release. The sweat began to drip from Kelly's shoulders and arms.

"Come on, sweetie, I know you're there," Susan said to her seductively. "I'm right there with you." She watched as Kelly's face began to contort with the pleasure racing through her. "That's right, honey. Let go. Let me feel you."

"Oh, fuck..." Kelly whimpered as she thrust blindly into her lover. They crested together and screamed out their gratification, continuing to move until the spasms left their bodies. Kelly's forehead rested on Susan's shoulder as she kissed the smaller woman softly around her collarbone and breast. "I love you so much, baby."

Susan held tightly to Kelly so she wouldn't see her new tears. They'd cried way too much that night already. "I love you. No more fighting, I promise," Susan managed to say as she recovered from her shattering orgasm. "I hate feeling like that."

"Me, too."

Susan could feel Kelly's body slow down as their breathing returned to normal. Their lips came together again, this time gentler and much softer. They parted and stared into each other's eyes until a soft bark was heard from the outside porch.

Kelly buried her head against Susan's chest and began to chuckle. She kissed her again and started to get up. "I'll get her." She pulled herself off of Susan and walked her beautifully naked body to the back door. Mattie came bounding inside, shaking her coat free of the frozen rain that had begun to fall. Kelly shrieked and jumped away as the icy droplets hit her exposed skin.

Sitting up, Susan chuckled as she watched the comic interaction between human and canine. They were a precious duo, and she hoped to see more of them on a daily basis. She had forgotten how long twenty-four hours could be. Susan knew she would do anything to prevent a separation from Kelly. Once was enough for one lifetime.

Kelly walked over to the couch and gathered their clothing. "Do you think we could continue this upstairs?"

That was music to Susan's ears. "Absolutely. I need to call my mother first and let her know I'll be staying here. " She paused to clarify Kelly's offer. "I am staying the night, yes?"

She leaned over Susan and gave her a soulful kiss. "Definitely."

Susan could feel the goose bumps start to dance all over her body. "Let me make that call before you make me forget."

"Forget what?" she asked, as she pinned Susan to the couch with another searing kiss.

"Mmmm... " Her young lover sank into her kiss, then pushed her back when she realized she'd been had.

"Go on. I'll meet you upstairs," she said breathlessly.

Kelly pecked Susan's lips again and smiled saucily. "I'll be waiting."

Susan watched the sway of her gorgeous ass until she'd walked out of sight. "Jesus," she breathed. She picked up the phone and called her mother, knowing she'd answer. Susan had called from Kelly's driveway earlier and updated her concerning the situation.

After letting her mom know her whereabouts, Susan turned off the lights and went upstairs to make up with her girlfriend. She was determined to show Kelly exactly how much she had missed her. Susan had a feeling Kelly was going to like her idea of reparations.

Chapter Thirty-Five

As she rested her head on Kelly's chest and listened to the slow, steady beating of her heart, Susan realized how close they had come to losing each other and all of what they could have together. But after the previous night, she knew they'd be all right...very all right. They were great together, much better than they were apart. Even though they'd only been together a few weeks, Susan knew that neither of them had ever experienced anything as special before. They were soul mates, nothing less; their connection was one that she knew she wouldn't find with anyone else. It would take a force greater than either one of them to pull them apart again. She felt very safe knowing that.

A smile came to Susan's face as she felt her bedmate stir beneath her. Kelly's hand unconsciously started to rub Susan's head in slow circles, sending gooseflesh down her body. A simple touch, an act of tenderness - Kelly did those things, and so much more, without even realizing she'd done them. That was what made Susan love her so much. *I was such a fool. Never again will I risk losing her... never ever again.*

"What are you thinking?" Kelly asked hoarsely.

"I'm thinking about how lucky we are to have this again." Susan smiled and inhaled Kelly's scent from the blankets wrapped around them.

Kelly's arms drew her even closer, and she kissed the top of the blonde head. "Thank you for coming over last night."

"You're welcome."

Not speaking, they lay together for several moments simply enjoying the feel of each other. In point of fact, they hadn't spoken much after they had gone upstairs the night before, either. Kelly had given Susan far better things to do with her mouth. The young woman smiled at the memory of their lovemaking, and the gooseflesh rose again at her recollection.

"Are you cold?" Kelly asked, gathering more of the blanket around them.

Susan shook her head against Kelly's chest. "No, just thinking about last night. It was fantastic, Kelly. I don't know about you, but I've never felt like that before."

She felt Kelly's chuckle rumble through her. "No, I can honestly agree that no one has ever made me feel what I felt last night."

Turning to look up at her, Susan's gaze locked on to gentle eyes. Their lips met softly as Kelly caressed her cheek with a thumb. As they drew apart, Kelly stared into Susan's eyes, and the former vagabond found a home again. Smiling softly, Kelly pulled Susan down against her, cushioning her head with her breast. The tender touches against Susan's back and shoulders made her sigh with contentment. She felt her body relax fully and knew she'd be asleep within minutes. It was still early; they had a few hours to kill.

By the time Kelly watched Susan pull out of her driveway, the weight of the world didn't feel so heavy anymore. She still had her grandmother's funeral ahead of her, but with Susan at her side, she felt like she could get through anything.

Her heart felt much lighter. She and Susan both knew there was a lot that needed to be discussed and worked out between the two of them, but there was something that hadn't been there the day before…hope. They had hope. It was a word that had been foreign to Kelly for such a long time, but now it was in her vocabulary again, and she truly believed it would remain there. *I still have a bone to pick with God about some things, but all in all, just having hope is a miracle to me.*

As Kelly sat on the couch flipping through channels on TV, she marveled at how much they'd shared in the short time they'd known each other. *It feels like we've been together for years. I can't say that about many people. Even though we hurt each other, there was a bond between us that couldn't be broken.*

And tomorrow is New Year's Eve. A new year. I need a new year, because this one is really starting to wear on me. Big time.

~~*~*~*~*

Elise McGovern was sitting on the couch waiting for Susan as she entered the family room. She smiled, and her daughter couldn't help but return the gesture.

"I take it things are okay between you two?" Elise asked.

Not hiding her excitement, Susan plopped onto the seat next to her mother and beamed. "We're going to be just fine, Mom. We have such a strong connection it would take hell freezing over to pull us apart."

She reached for her daughter's hand and Susan let her take it. "I'm so happy for you, sweetie." The look on Susan's face mirrored her doubt, and she was quick to add, "I truly mean that."

Looking into her eyes, Susan saw nothing but sincerity. "Thank you."

They exchanged smiles and Susan leaned into her, resting her head on her mother's shoulder. Elise reached up and stroked the blonde hair, and Susan sighed in response. "I've missed you so much, Mom. I really hope this is a new beginning for us. I missed having my best friend around."

She felt her mom's breathing change and knew she'd struck a chord. Turning her head, she saw a tear rolling down her cheek.

Brushing it away, her mother said, "Susan, if I have to pay with my soul in the afterlife, I will do everything in my power to make it right between us. I won't lose you again, to anyone." She slid her arm around her prodigal daughter and held her tightly.

After several moments, Susan pulled back and looked at her. For the first time, really looked at her. She'd aged so much in five years. Wondering what she'd been up to, Susan voiced the question aloud. "So tell me, what have you been up to while I've been away? I mean, besides losing daddy."

The familiar face registered a brief flash of pain, but changed into a sad smile. "After your father passed away, I tried to live the life I'd denied myself for so long. I took an art class, did some sculpting, and whatnot. It gave me some of the peace I'd been looking for."

"Mom, that's great. I'm so glad that helped."

She smiled in agreement. "It did. When he died, all the chains melted away and I was free to do what I wanted. I had freedom! For the longest time I'd had no idea what that was. Now I just take things day by day. If I feel the need to do something, then I do it. If I want to laze around all day, then by God, I do that too," she said with a confidence that surprised Susan.

Her expression was one of deep warmth and love. "Finding you has been the greatest thing of all, though. I prayed that I'd find you again, but I'd long ago lost hope of that. Then I saw you and Kelly on the news, of all places. Sucking face, I might add," she teased and nudged her.

"Mom!" Susan cried, feeling a blush creep across her cheeks.

"What?" She raised her eyebrows in question.

"Don't you kids call it that anymore?"

"It's not that; you just surprised me, is all."

She patted her daughter's shoulder and continued. "Anyway, after all of that, here we are; and I couldn't ask for anything more." She looked at her with such love in her eyes it made Susan's water. "Thank you for coming back to me."

Overflowing with emotion, Susan opted not to say anything, but rested her head again on the nearby shoulder. She felt her mother's breathing become more rapid and knew she had more to say. "What is it, Mom?"

"Will you tell me what it was like for you... out there? I want to know – I need to know."

Susan raised her head and looked into determined eyes. "It's not a pretty story. Let me simply say I wouldn't wish that life on anyone and leave it at that, okay?"

"No!" she exclaimed, startling Susan a little. Elise took a deep breath and composed herself before speaking again. "No, it's not okay, Susan. It was my cowardly behavior that put you out there in the first place. I want to know what happened to my baby. Please, Susan, please tell me."

Seeing the sad but unwavering expression on her face, Susan knew there was no way she could satisfy her without telling her the truth. The whole truth. "Well, if you let me grab something to drink first, I'll tell you. It's going to be hard on me to relive some of that again."

"I'm so sorry..."

"I know, Mom, I know." She kissed the side of her mother's head and walked into the kitchen that she knew so well. She grabbed a glass and filled it with water, then returned to her mom, who hadn't moved from her place on the couch. Sitting down and taking a deep breath, she began to relate the nightmare that had been

A Saving Solace

her life.

A couple of hours and five glasses of water later, she had told her mother more than she could've possibly expected to hear. She truly doubted she had been prepared to learn what her little girl had had to do to survive. Sometimes, Susan couldn't even believe she was still around. There were many times she'd thought death was imminent, with her staring at its ugly face so many times she thought for sure she was next. But Carol had made sure her number was nowhere near up. And Susan shared it all with her mother. Elise McGovern's tears never stopped from the time Susan started until at last she ran out of words. When her daughter became silent, she went to the bathroom to wash her face and try to compose herself.

God bless you, Carol. I hope you know how much I miss you.

Elise returned a few moments later, looking a little less pale. "You feeling a little better?" Susan asked gently.

Her mother nodded and sat quietly on the couch. "I had no idea people could live through things like that." She looked at Susan with respect and awe. "I'm so grateful you made it out of there alive and back to me." She shook her head over and over. "I can't believe I abandoned you to such a place. Can you ever forgive me?"

That was the million-dollar question. A few weeks earlier, Susan would've answered it negatively, without hesitation. Now, she wasn't eager to be mean, nor was she wanting to push the dagger of guilt deeper. She knew that her mother had not had it in her to protect her daughter back then, and she also knew her mother was devastatingly sorry. The retelling of her tale probably hurt her remaining parent more than she could imagine. What mother wanted to hear about the hell she'd put her own child through? She deserved an honest answer. "I'll tell you this much, Mom... And I'm going to be completely honest with you."

"Okay," she said softly.

"If you'd asked me that question a while ago, I would've told you to go straight to hell." She watched as her mother flinched at her brutal honesty. "Now that I'm here with you, and have heard about your own hell that daddy so nicely provided, well, I can't feel that anger anymore. I will never forget what happened to me, because it's made me the woman I am right now... but I can forgive you, Mom. It just might take me a while. I don't want any secrets or pain between us anymore. I just want you to promise me one thing."

Elise's eyes met Susan's, waiting like a puppy, wanting to please regardless of what she asked. "Anything, Susan."

"Promise me you'll never turn your back on me again." The tears rolled down Susan's face as the truth of her words hit her heart. "I couldn't bear to lose you again."

Elise McGovern reached across the empty cushion and grabbed onto her with a vise grip. "Oh, sweetheart, I promise you, I will never let anyone take you from me again. Nothing but death can take me from you. And even then, I'm not so sure." She sobbed into Susan's shoulder as they rocked away their pain.

Having her mother hold her again gave Susan peace, a peace she never wanted to leave again. She pulled away and just looked at her mom for the longest time, remembering her childhood, and how happy they had once been in that house. She looked around the family room and felt more warmth spread through her. It was so beautiful; it made her not want to return to her hole-in-the-wall apartment. Ever.

Elise looked at her with concern. "What is it,

honey?" she said, her voice matching her expression.

"I was just thinking about how happy we were when I was a kid. This house is in all my memories of my youth until that awful day. I loved it here."

"Well, sweetie, you know you are welcome here anytime you want. You could even..." She stopped and looked away.

"What were you going to say, Mom? Remember, no more secrets, okay?"

She cleared her throat and clasped her daughter's hands. "What I was going to say was that you could move back here if you wanted to. I mean, I know we've only just begun to work everything out, but I think it would be great to have you here with me again."

Susan's eyes teared up as she listened to the heartfelt offer. "My lease isn't up for a few months yet, but if things continue like this, I would love to move back here with you."

"You just say the word, sweetheart. This home will always be yours."

"Thanks, Mom. That means the world to me." Susan reached over and hugged her tightly.

They would've stayed like that longer, but the ringing of the phone startled them. Elise pulled slowly from Susan and reached for the cordless phone on the coffee table. Clearing her throat, she answered it.

"Hello?" She listened to the caller's voice and smiled. "Hi, Kelly... No, we're fine, just catching up... Yes, she's right here. Hang on a moment." She passed the phone to Susan, who couldn't help the excited grin that appeared on her face.

"Hi, honey," she greeted.

"Hey, baby, how are things going with your mom?" Kelly asked in a deliberately light tone.

"Things are fine... A little hard for Mom right now since she just heard an unabridged version of my time away from home." She gave her mom a comforting glance and grasped her hand.

"God, I'm sure that was hard for her to hear. Just from the few things I've heard, I know how awful things were for you."

"Yeah, her pallor kind of scared me at first, but she washed her face and came back from the bathroom looking much better."

"That's good to hear. Listen, we haven't talked about this, but tomorrow is New Year's Eve. Would you and your mom like to have dinner with me to celebrate the new year? I'm thinking of having Sally over, too."

"Sally?"

"I'm sorry, I guess I didn't mention her. She was my gram's neighbor and good friend. She found Gram... um...after her stroke." Kelly's voice sounded like it was beginning to cloud with emotion. "So um... I got to thinking that maybe we could all use a bit of family right about now, and um..."

God, she's adorable! "We'd love to!" Susan cut off Kelly's nervousness with her exuberant answer. She hadn't checked with her mom, but Susan was sure she'd want to participate. "I think it's what we all need right about now, " she echoed.

"Are you making fun of me?" Kelly teased.

Susan feigned outrage. "Absolutely not!"

"Good, then come to my place around five."

"What should we bring?"

"Just yourselves. You know how much I love to cook," she said with a smile in her voice.

"I do, and I remember how well you cook, too. I can't wait to see you." Susan said the last part in a whisper, watching her mother leave the room.

"I can't wait to see you, either." "I miss you," Susan whispered again.

"How much?"

"Very much."

"Can I see you tonight?"

"Well, Mom and I aren't doing anything except chatting, maybe watching a movie or something. Why, what did you have planned?"

"Well -"

Hearing the doorbell ring, Susan cut her off. "Hang on a second, someone's at the door."

"Sure."

"Mom? You want me to get it?" Susan called. Not hearing an answer, she called out again, "Mom?"

"Susan, hang up the phone," she heard her mother say from the other room.

"Why?" Confused, she walked towards the front door, where she found Kelly holding the cell phone to her ear and her mother smiling back at her.

"Because it's a waste of my minutes when I can talk to you face to face," Kelly said, ending their phone connection.

Lunging at her and hugging her with enthusiasm, Susan said, "You think you're so funny."

"I know I am, but looks aren't everything," she said into Susan's cheek.

She pulled back, staring at her like she had two heads. "You aren't the least bit funny looking, Kelly. I'll have you know I have excellent taste!" She mocked indignation, only to have Kelly laugh at her.

Mrs. McGovern cleared her throat, pointing at the still open door. "Can I close this now? I'm not heating the neighborhood, you know."

Their faces flushed at the motherly comment, and they both walked into the foyer of the house.

"Would you like to eat with us and maybe watch a movie?" Elise asked, smiling at Kelly.

"If I'm not imposing, I would love it." Kelly paused for a moment and looked back and forth between Susan and her mother. "I don't really want to be alone."

Mrs. McGovern reached up and lightly grasped Kelly's arm. "You can stay as long as you like. This is more company than I've had in a long time."

"Thanks, I really appreciate it." Kelly's eyes were red rimmed. She looked as if she had been crying.

"Are you okay, honey?"

She sighed deeply, and Mrs. McGovern took that as her cue to leave them alone. She smiled warmly at them and put out her hand for Kelly's coat. Kelly happily shrugged out of her coat and handed it over to be hung in the hall closet. Elise looked at them one last time and strolled into the kitchen.

Susan laced her fingers with Kelly's and gestured with her head to the stairs. "Wanna go up to my room? Um...my old room?" she corrected.

"It will always be your room!" her mother shouted from the kitchen.

"Boy, the walls have ears!" Susan countered, hearing a chuckle from the other room. Looking seriously at Kelly, she said, "Come on, let's go talk upstairs. You can get a visual to go with the stories I've told you about this place."

Kelly nodded and followed her up the stairs. She paused to look at the family pictures on the walls, smiling at each one. "You were such a cute baby!" she cooed at Susan's six-month-old picture.

"Were? Oh, the cruelty of some people," she said, pretending to be hurt. Grabbing Kelly's hand, she led her into her bedroom.

Looking around, Kelly's smile widened when she saw the twin beds Susan had spoken of. She sat down on one bed and bounced a little on the mattress. "So, this is the bed where it all happened, eh?" She winked at Susan when she caught the Cindy reference.

"Yep, the very same. Jealous?" She wiggled her

eyebrows.

"Of a memory? Not even close," she whispered, pulling Susan into her lap.

Humming softly with happiness, Susan accepted the tenderness Kelly was offering. It was bliss to be in her arms. The arms around her tightened, and Susan could hear and feel her breathing pattern change. "Honey, what is it? I can tell from your eyes you've been crying. You don't hide your emotions well, sorry to say," Susan said softly.

Childlike, Kelly sniffled quietly and shrugged her shoulders. "I thought I did an okay job masking my feelings until recently. I'm breaking down in front of everyone these days!" Susan looked at her lost expression and waited for her to continue. "When I saw Sally yesterday, I totally broke down at her apartment. I don't cry in front of just anyone, Susan; but there I was in Sally's arms, crying like a little baby."

Putting her fingers gently on Kelly's lips, Susan began to convince her otherwise. "First of all, you are *my* baby; and I love that fact. Secondly, sweetheart, you just lost your grandma, for Christ's sake! I know how much she meant to you. I'd be more concerned about you if you *weren't* upset by that. It's only natural to cry when you lose someone you love, especially on the anniversary of your mom's death. I mean, come on! There's only so much one person can take! I'd have lost it for sure!" Susan ran her fingers through silky hair, calming Kelly's frazzledness. The dark head rested on her breast while she continued to console her. "I'm sure Sally understood; she loved your grandma, right?" She felt the nod against her chest. "See? Don't worry about that stuff. You've heard the phrase, 'Don't sweat the small stuff,' right? Well, here it is again," Susan answered, without waiting for a response.

Kelly's head came up and their eyes locked

together. A small smile made its way to Kelly's lips. "I love you so much, baby. I hope you realize how much."

"I do, sweetie, I do." They hugged again and stayed that way for a few moments. "So, guess what? After talking with my mom, she said I could move back here whenever I wanted."

Their bodies separated enough for Kelly to look at Susan squarely. "Are you ready for that?"

"Honestly, I think I am. I know in my heart that we'll be fine. I was thinking that living with my mom could be a temporary thing, until you and I were ready to talk about that next step," she said with a wink, earning her a nod from her partner. "And God knows this place is heaven compared to my apartment. But unfortunately, my lease isn't up for a few months, so, I guess I'll just stay there until it is."

"Could you get out of it? I mean, if you wanted to."

Shaking her head, Susan replied, "I don't have the money. There is a penalty; and they keep my deposit if I break the lease. I'm not in a financial position to do that." Kelly smiled a goofy smile and Susan asked, "What?"

"Honey, if money is the only obstacle, don't you think we could get around that?"

"Meaning..."

"Meaning, if you wanted to come home, I'm sure your mother or I could figure out a way to get you here sooner. If that's what you wanted, of course," she reiterated.

"No way, Kelly. I don't want you doing anything like that. We're talking a couple thousand dollars. I'll stay there until it's up. I've been there a while already; it's fine."

"You deserve more than fine, baby." Susan started to protest, but Kelly silenced her by placing fingers on *her* mouth. "I'm just saying, it can be a reality if you want it to be. There... I'm done now," she said with a nod.

"As much as I appreciate the offer, I'll wait it out."

They grinned at each other until Susan's stomach growled loudly. Kelly laughed heartily at the sound. "I guess that answers my next question."

"Which was?"

"Are you getting hungry, because I'm famished and would love some dinner."

Susan smiled back at her. "Yes, I am hungry, thank you very much! Let's go harass Mom into ordering a pizza!" she said enthusiastically.

"You're on!"

They shared a tender kiss and made their way down to the kitchen.

Chapter Thirty-Six

Pulling the bread out of the oven, Kelly checked the time on the wall clock, 4:50. "They should be here soon, Mattie!" she called to her dog, who was happily thumping her tail on the linoleum floor.

Kelly rested the pan on the stove to cool before she removed the loaf. Lasagna had always been one of her favorites, so she was hoping it would work for the rest of the clan. She placed the pasta in the warmer on the dining room table and looked out the snow-bedecked window. The snow had been falling at a rapid pace. At least four inches of snow had fallen in just a few hours, and it showed no signs of stopping. It wouldn't stop her guests from coming, though. She was sad that Sally had made other plans and couldn't join them, but she was spending the holiday with her family.

I guess we all had the same idea.

The doorbell rang, and Mattie barked and ran to greet her friends at the door. Wiping her hands on a dishtowel, Kelly went to the foyer. Opening the door, the first face she saw was her angel's. With snowflakes adorning her head and shoulders, Susan looked up at Kelly, willing her to feel all of the love that filled her heart. For that one moment in time, Kelly felt complete - no troubles, no fears, no pain. She felt only love. And Susan was the reason for it all. *Never again will I let her out of my life.*

Pulling the smaller woman to her, she squeezed gently. Inhaling her scent, Kelly whispered quietly into her ear, "God, I missed you last night."

Pulling out of Kelly's embrace, Susan smiled. "You could've stayed over, you know. Mom said it was okay."

Smiling and waving at Susan's mother who was walking towards them, Kelly replied. "I know, but

A Saving Solace

Mattie is here, and I had a whole lotta shopping to do today. Thank God I got it done before all this snow fell."

Nudging Susan aside playfully, Elise stretched up on her tiptoes to give her hostess a hug. "Happy New Year, Kelly."

Kelly returned her hug enthusiastically. "Happy New Year, Elise." Belatedly remembering her manners and realizing her guests were still on the snowy stoop, Kelly offered them the warmth of her home. "Please, come in and out of this wet stuff."

"Thanks," they said simultaneously, then laughed at themselves.

"You're just in time. I just took dinner out of the oven," Kelly said, her stomach growling at the smells wafting in from the kitchen.

Both women took deep breaths and hummed happily in unison, "Mmmm."

Kelly looked at them with a crooked grin on her face. "Are you guys linked tonight, or what?"

They both answered, "Looks like it!" In tandem, they leaned down to take off their shoes, bumping into each other as they hunched over.

Rolling her eyes as the women laughed again, and taking their wet coats and gloves to hang them in the closet to dry, Kelly led them into the family room where Mattie would no longer be denied. Barking at her new best friend, Mattie looked at Susan pitifully.

"Oh, yes, my girl. How are you, sweetie? Were you a good girl, keeping mommy company last night?" Mattie shamelessly rolled onto her back, with Susan taking the hint to scratch her tummy.

"She's a pleasure hound, what can I say?" Kelly said, laughing at the display.

"Just like your mommy, right?" Susan cooed at the pup, making her wriggle with joy.

"She's beautiful, Kelly. Is she a golden retriever?"

Elise asked, also smiling at her daughter's antics with Mattic.

"Yellow lab, actually. She's really a great dog."

Susan returned her attention to Elise and Kelly. "So? I remember hearing something about food."

This time, Elise rolled her eyes. "That's my girl. Always thinking with her stomach first."

"Damn right. You of all people should know what I'm like when I haven't eaten."

"Don't remind me."

The subtle banter between mother and daughter brought a melancholy feel to Kelly's heart. She missed that part of her relationship with her mom.

I hope you and Gram are whooping it up tonight, Momma.

Feeling a warm hand on her forearm, Kelly looked into Elise's comforting eyes. "They're both here tonight, Kelly. You can be sure of that."

Swallowing the lump of emotion in her throat, she replied hoarsely, "I know. I'll never stop missing them. Mom especially. She loved celebrating the holidays."

They all exchanged sad smiles and, deciding to change the mood, Kelly suggested they go and sit. "If you guys take a seat in the dining room, I'll bring the rest of dinner out."

"Can we help with anything?" Susan chimed in.

"Nope. Just show your mom the way, and I'll be in shortly."

"Okay," she agreed, standing on her toes to give Kelly a tender kiss, then leading her mother to the dining room. Realizing she hadn't opened the wine, Kelly called after Susan, "Baby, you can do something for me, actually."

"Sure, honey."

"Will you open the wine on the table? The corkscrew is next to the bottle."

"You got it!" she said with a wink.

Watching Susan escort her mother into the dining room, Kelly sliced the loaf of bread, and placed it into a linen covered basket. The lasagna was on the table, as was the wine, so all that was left was the bread and herself. Walking into the dining room, basket in hand, Kelly saw her new family patiently waiting for her to join them. "Here's the last of it. Let's dig in!" she said with a toothy smile.

As she walked around to her seat, Susan stood and pulled out her chair. "Paybacks for our first date."

Kelly smiled at the memory of their first night together. Complete strangers breaking bread, sharing heartfelt memories for the first time. It seemed to her that theirs was a predetermined reunion of souls. How else could they explain their bond?

"Why, thank you, Milady," she said, pulling her chair closer to the table.

"It looks and smells wonderful, Kelly," Elise complimented, Susan nodding along in agreement.

"Well, I've always loved a good lasagna, so I hope you both do as well."

"One of my favorites, too. Let's tear into it!" Susan said with relish.

Laughing, Kelly handed her the serving knife. "Would you care to do the honors?"

"Absolutely!" she exclaimed, almost ripping the knife from Kelly's grasp.

Serving huge portions to all of them, Susan then filled everyone's glass with the Merlot that had been selected for dinner. Susan held her glass high in the air, her dinner companions mimicking her actions. "To old and new friends... new relationships and reconciliations," Susan began.

"Hear, hear!" Elise and Kelly started to toast, but were stopped by Susan's hand.

"Hang on, I'm not done yet." She took a deep breath and a flush suddenly colored her cheeks. Filled with emotion, she continued, "The similarities between you two are endless. I love you both more than I can say, and sadly, I almost lost you both. Mom, I did lose you when our lives were ripped apart by hatred and fear. Daddy acted out and did what he thought was best. Unfortunately, his best wasn't good for anyone but him. I lost my mom and my best friend the day he kicked me out. Now that we're together again, nothing will ever come between us. I feel sorry for anyone that even tries. We'll work this out and we'll be stronger because of it. I love you, Mama." Susan leaned down and tenderly kissed her mother's cheek. Wiping the tears from her eyes, Elise stood clumsily and leaned over to hug her little girl. The sounds of sniffling filled the room, with Susan and her mom locked in a tight embrace. Smiling as they pulled apart, Susan's mother handed her a napkin to wipe her tears. Looking over to Kelly, Susan's moist eyes locked with hers. "Your turn," she choked out.

"Be gentle," Kelly teased.

Clearing her throat, Susan captured one of her hands with her own. "Kelly, you are my heart and soul; and I will never be as grateful as I was the day you walked up to me. You've changed my life. When we met, I was a scared, tattered, and lonely young woman. I had a little voice in my head that would always be at war with me over any decisions I made. I was self-conscious, and I felt absolutely no self-worth. In the short time we have known one another, you've calmed my soul and erased my fears. Rejection had always been in the forefront in my life. Being away from real relationships and love for so long had really taken its toll on me. When you wanted to take me out, I was terrified that it was for some reason other than just you having an interest in me. Now before you think anything else, that was before I knew the woman that's in front of me. I was used to people using me for whatever they wanted, whenever they wanted, then discarding me like trash." Susan's mother's tears continued to fall during Susan's toast. Kelly's throat was constricting with so much emotion, she wasn't sure she would be tear-free by the time she was finished.

"You came along on your white charger and rescued me from a world that I never thought I'd escape. You freely opened your heart and showed me everything you had to offer. I would've been a fool not to accept such a gift. I'm so glad I'm not a fool."

Looking over briefly at Elise, she put down her glass and took her mother's hand, linking them all together. "You brought my mother back to me. You didn't think of anything or anyone but me and my happiness. Bringing her back to me was taking a huge risk, since you didn't know how I would react. Sadly, I reacted rather badly. I know now, in my heart, you did it out of love for me; and I will never be able to thank you enough. I know how much you miss your mom, and if I could bring her back to you, I would without hesitation. Instead, I offer to you the only thing I am able—me, Susan McGovern; and I promise you, that I will take good care of your heart from now on. I will love you for as long as you'll have me; and so help me God, I promise never to hurt you like I did at the cemetery. You are the most precious gift I have ever received, and I swear... I *swear* that I will treasure you until the end of our days," Susan choked out the rest of her toast.

Kelly jumped up to embrace the woman that had captured her heart completely. Feeling so many emotions roiling inside of her, she held tightly to Susan. "Thank you, baby. Thank you so much," she managed to squeak out. Looking over at Elise, Kelly saw that she hadn't stopped her own tears. "Come here, Mom," she said, extending her hand out for the older woman to take. Stepping into their group hug, Susan's mother held tightly to them. "Boy, when I asked you both over for dinner, I had no idea we'd be having a crying fest!" Kelly choked out through her tears.

Taking a cleansing breath, Susan's mom spoke softly. "I am so glad you are a part of my little girl's life. I know you will keep her safe and loved forever. I'm thankful you have found each other. It's pretty clear that the fates knew what they were doing when they matched you up. I have never met two people that were more deserving of each other than you. Thank you for loving my daughter so much that it brought her back to me, Kelly."

Kissing Elise's forehead, Kelly replied, "You don't have to thank me. It is my pleasure to love her. I pledge to you both, that I will continue to do so every minute of every day, until I no longer draw breath. Even then, I have a feeling we'll meet up again, one day. Like you said, the fates have a way of making things happen. I'm just grateful that I was on the receiving end of their offering to the love altar." They all chuckled at her lame attempt to be witty.

"Oh, that was bad, sweetheart," Susan groaned, sniffling away her tears.

"See what you have to look forward to? Years and years of my *glorious* sense of humor."

Pretending to try and break free of the circle, Susan teased, "You sure it's too late to run?"

Pulling her back, Kelly replied, "Yes, I'm very sure." Looking down at their cooling plates of food, she tried to resume her role as hostess. "If we're done snotting all over each other, I'd love to eat now."

Smacking her in the stomach, Susan cried out, "Eww! Kelly, that's gross."

"Just another of my wonderful qualities. All for

you, baby. All for you." Kelly kissed the top of her head and they all sat down in their seats to eat.

Dinner was wonderful, once their emotions were, at long last, under control. Susan's mother was charming and funny and all the things Kelly could see in her daughter. It was easy to see whose side of the family Susan took after. The snow prevented Susan and her mother from leaving after dinner, which was totally fine with Kelly. She loved their company, and knew it was something she would enjoy more and more with each passing day. Their evening together passed quickly and before they knew it, precisely at midnight, it was time for Father New Year to make his entrance.

Champagne flutes in hand, their glasses clinked in sync with the chimes on the clock. They sat in the family room with a warm fire blazing in the hearth and toasted the coming New Year and prayed for a better time for them all.

Some time later, the light snores coming from the small body nestled beside Kelly told her Susan was down for the count, with her mother right alongside her. Looking to the mantle over the fireplace, Kelly focused on the picture of her with her mom and grandmother and said a silent prayer of love and thanks to them for the new family she had found. She knew the pain of losing them would lessen with each day. Her grandmother's funeral might even be bearable with the love and support she was receiving from Susan and Elise. Kelly was learning to face up to the fact that life went on, even when she least wanted it to. It was the hardest lesson she'd had to learn. Wanting to shrivel up and just wait for her own time to come would never again be in her thoughts. That was a Kelly who was young and looking to find redress for a wrong she couldn't right. She had finally found a calm within herself, and with that came a love, a peace, and a place to call home.

The End

Diane Bauden is a sucker for a happy ending no matter what the tale or circumstance. She believes that things always happen for a reason in this life and that emotional journeys are a necessary means to an end.

With the release of her third book, *A Saving Solace*, new fans will quickly learn what hundreds of others discovered years ago: this woman packs more feeling in one book than some people experience in a lifetime.

"I'm big on feelings and emotions in my stories and I can't wait to see if someone felt my words while they read them. It's a great rush for me. If I don't get that reaction, then maybe I need to work a little harder," she said.

A loyal group of online fans frequently are treated to the author's stories before they are published. During the writing of her first book, *A Sacrifice For Friendship*, readers literally begged for updates. When the story was finished many had become so involved with the characters they needed to reread the story to maintain the connection.

"I have to admit," one reader said, "this was the hardest of your stories to read. Well worth it, but a little hard on the heart. But hey, it gets easier now that I'm rereading it for the fifth time."

Diane took up writing when she got to the point in life that nearly everything was an inspiration for a story.

"I write because I have so many ideas and stories in my head, I would burst if I didn't. I like being able to touch people with the stories I write. Everyday life inspires me. I've seen and felt many things in my thirty-five years. They say the best writers will write what they know and I'm trying to be no different in that aspect. I tend to get my best ideas from driving or dreaming. Something I see will spark my muse and she just runs free."

Diane has no shortage of life experiences to draw from as she and her long-time partner Lori, surround themselves with family and friends. Growing up as the seventh of eight children in the suburbs of Chicago, Diane has always embraced family as the foundation for her life and her work.

"I write about love and emotions and finding one's soul mate. That story to me is the greatest story ever told. I also tend to touch on death/loss and abandonment, since they appear in all of our lives at one point or another. Everyone feels alone sometimes and I like letting people know the opposite is also true: You don't have to feel that way. There's always going to be someone who knows what you are feeling, and maybe my writing will help them in their grief or healing. That would truly be wonderful.

"There's an amazing connection I feel when someone writes to me to say they have shared the same or a similar experience I've written about. I feel extremely happy if I've been able to reach even one person. If I can evoke emotion from them, then I feel I've written well. That definitely keeps me writing."

Contact Di:
E-mail: dsbauden@comcast.net
Notes: Bookmarks and bookplates are available. Please e-mail Di for details using the contact information above.

Order These Great Books Directly From Limitless, Dare 2 Dream Publishing

The Amazon Queen by L M Townsend	20.00	
Define Destiny by J M Dragon	20.00	
Desert Hawk, revised by Katherine E. Standelll	18.00	
Golden Gate by Erin Jennifer Mar	18.00	
The Brass Ring By Mavis Applewater	18.00	
Haunting Shadows by J M Dragon	18.00	
Spirit Harvest by Trish Shields	15.00	
PWP: Plot? What Plot? by Mavis Applewater	18.00	
Up The River-out of print ...While supplies last... by Sam Ruskin	15.00	
Memories Kill By S. B. Zarben	20.00	
Fatal Impressions by Jeanne Foguth	12.00	
	Total	

South Carolina residents add 5% sales tax.
Domestic shipping is $3.50 per book.

Watch for more and upcoming titles:

Visit our website at: http://limitlessd2d.net

Please mail your orders with a check or money order to:

Limitless, Dare 2 Dream Publishing
100 Pin Oak Ct.
Lexington, SC 29073

Please make checks or money orders payable to: Limitless.

Order More Great Books Directly From Limitless, Dare 2 Dream Publishing

Daughters of Artemis by L M Townsend	18.00	
Connecting Hearts By Val Brown and MJ Walker	18.00	
Mysti: Mistress of Dreams By Sam Ruskin	18.00	
Family Connections By Val Brown & MJ Walker	18.00	Sequel to Connecting Hearts
A Thousand Shades of Feeling by Carolyn McBride	18.00	
The Amazon Nation By Carla Osborne	18.00	
Poetry from the Featherbed By pinfeather	18.00	
Encounters, Book I By Anne Azel	10.00	Printer Error
Encounters, Book II **By Anne Azel**	10.00	Printer Error
Return of the Warrior By Katherine E. Standell	20.00	Sequel to Desert Hawk
Deadly Rumors by Jeanne Foguth	10.00	
	Total	

South Carolina residents add 5% sales tax.
Domestic shipping is $3.50 per book

Watch for these and more upcoming titles:
Visit our website at: **http://limitlessd2d.net**
Please mail your orders with a check or money order to:

Limitless, Dare 2 Dream Publishing
100 Pin Oak Ct.
Lexington, SC 29073

Please make checks or money orders payable to: Limitless.

Excerpt from A Sacrifice for Friendship

DS Bauden

The ride to the beach was a quiet one. I could feel the tension between these two, it was very thick. She sat between us in the cab of his truck. The closeness of her body was making me all twitchy. She needed to leave this bastard. And soon. Billy's pick-up stopped at Northeast Beach on the campus, right off Pratt Lane. It was truly an awesome day, and many other patrons felt the same way.

"Wow, how many days do you see like this in April, eh, Billy?" Annie said excitedly.

"Yeah, babe. Just point me in the direction of the keg. Corey said he was gonna have one down here today," Billy said, looking around, his eyes landing on his target. "There he is, let's go. I don't want to wait for a cup." And he bolted from the truck to find his nectar.

"It's nice to see a man with priorities," I joked. The look on Annie's face was forlorn. "What is it, Annie? Did I say something wrong?"

She turned slowly to look at me. "No, I just don't like him to drink so much. He won't listen to me. Every time I bring it up, we fight, and he gets really upset, and then he…Well, let's just say I don't bring it up anymore," she finished quietly.

I was really pissed off now. *If he has done **anything** to you, I will kill him where he stands.* My protective feathers were ruffled in the extreme. There was something inside of me that needed to protect Annie with everything that I had. I wasn't about to let her down.

There is such a sorrowful look on her face, when she was so excited just a few minutes ago. I need to shake her out of this sadness. It's too nice of a day to feel like that. I'll try to talk to her about Billy another time. She doesn't look like she wants to talk about this anymore.

"What d'ya say we find a volleyball game or something to watch?" I suggested.

Her face instantly lit up. "What do you mean 'watch'? Let's go kick some ass!" she said, with an amazing fire in her eyes. She dashed out to the game already in progress.

Annie ran up to some friends of hers and asked if they needed any more players. Standing at the sideline of the makeshift playing court, I waited for a signal from Annie.

Annie's face was beaming from the sunshine and the adrenaline rush of wanting to play.

She is absolutely adorable...and straight. I need to remember that.

I was shaken out of my thoughts by a set of fingers snapping in my face. "Frankie? Darlin', you okay?" she asked.

"Yeah, do we get to play?" I asked, hoping to be able to take out some aggression on an unsuspecting ball.

"Yes, ma'am. This is Betsy, she lives on my floor." Then she introduced me. "Betsy, this is Frankie; we just met earlier today. She is very nice." She leaned over conspiratorially to Betsy and in a stage whisper added, "And she is very attractive, don't you think?" My face instantly flushed, and I tried to turn away. Annie caught my face with her fingertips, and spoke directly into my eyes. "You are, darlin'. Don't take for granted what you have been given freely." God, those were words to live by. "Hell, you could have anyone here if you wanted."

They both started laughing, and Betsy chimed in," And we do mean *anyone*!"

Was that a hint for her, or Annie? I am rooting for the latter.

"Thanks. I guess I'm just not very good at accepting compliments," I said almost shyly, surprising even me.

"Come on, Frankie, let's go kick some ass!" Betsy said as she put her arm around my shoulders and led me towards the team.

The three of us took the net for our little squad and awaited the serve from the other team. I took the middle, Betsy was front right, and Annie the front left.

"Incoming!" screamed one of girls in the back row. I tracked the serve heading right for Annie. She watched the ball, connected solidly with it, bumping it to Betsy, who in turn set it up for my spike. I eyed the ball and leapt as high as I could.

WHACK!

"Yes!" the girls on my team shouted as my shot landed between two players in the back row on the other team.

Annie beamed at me. "Way to go, Frankie!"

I couldn't help but smile back. This was easy. Although, I think I had quite the height advantage over them.

"Annie! Get your ass over here!" Billy shouted from the sidelines.

"Billy, I'm in the middle of the game here. Give me a couple seconds, okay?" she asked.

"No, I want you now! Move it, girlie!" he ordered gruffly.

Excerpt from A Sacrifice for Friendship

Annie's face fell as she left the court. "Hey, sorry guys, I'll be back in a sec," she said.

Like everyone else in the area, I couldn't help but note the exchange between them. Billy was an asshole, plain and simple, I just didn't understand what Annie saw in him. She could do so much better than him; she deserved much better than him. He was just too stupid to realize what he had.

Annie walked over to Billy, and again he grabbed her upper arm roughly. "When I ask you to come over to me, you do it! Not in a few seconds or minutes. Now means now!" he sputtered.

"I'm sorry, Billy, what is it that you wanted?" she asked quietly.

"We need more beer. Go to the store and get another half barrel." He pulled out a wad of cash from his pocket and handed it to her. Annie took the crumpled bills in her hand along with his truck keys. She smiled weakly at him, and he leaned down for a kiss. He grabbed the back of her hair, roughly pulling her head back to face him. She whimpered slightly as she let him plant a sloppy kiss on her mouth.

She pulled back and started to walk towards the truck. Billy slapped her ass as she walked away, then downed the rest of his beer. He laughed with his buddies about his overbearing role in their relationship. "Damn bitch, never listens to me. I'll straighten her out later on. You think you can embarrass me in front of my friends?" he called after her. "I'll teach you some manners…" He trailed off when I approached him. "What do you want?" he asked as he staggered and tried to focus on me.

"Something tells me that even a dog wouldn't obey you. If she has any sense in her at all, she'll leave your sorry ass. Since I believe she has more sense than you'll ever have, it's just a matter of time." I really wanted to lay him out, but something told me that this wasn't a good time for that.

"Bitch. You sure don't know shit about women. Annie likes the way we are. Don't you, baby?" he yelled out to her, and she nodded slightly. I couldn't believe my eyes. "See? She ain't going nowhere. Not without me, anyway," he bragged smugly as his friends joined him in his snickering.

God, I want to make him eat the sand under my shoes right now. Calm down, Frankie. If Annie doesn't want your help, you can't make her accept it.

My thoughts took control and I didn't feel the slight tug on my sleeve.

"You want to come with me to the store, Frankie?" Annie asked. "I gotta pick up some beer for the guys." Her look pleaded with me to go with her.

"Sure," I said as I eyeballed Billy. "Asshole. Don't say I didn't warn you. She'll be gone before you know it." I smiled at him in a feral kind of way.

Pop taught me that sometimes if you smile just so, people will understand your passion without having to feel it smash against their skull. This was one of those times, but I wished I was smashing something against Billy's skull. It's not like he didn't deserve it. Bastard.

I smiled a sweet smile her way and turned towards the truck. "Let's go, Annie."

"Hey, Bets! We'll be back in a few, okay?" Annie shouted at our teammate.

"Sure guys. See you soon. Don't do anything I wouldn't!" she yelled back to us.

*That was an odd statement. This day is getting odder by the second. Who am I kidding? This is the oddest fucking day I have **ever** had.*

~~*~*

We walked to the truck in moderate silence. Annie looked distraught, and it wasn't hard to figure out why. Her so-called boyfriend had just humiliated her in front of her friends, and you can be guaranteed that it wasn't the first time. We got in the truck and sat in silence for a few moments.

"Hey, you okay?" I asked softly.

She looked up with tear-filled eyes that almost broke my heart. "I don't know why he has to drink so much. He is never like this when we are alone. I'm sorry that you had to see that, being that we just met and all. Thanks for sticking up for me, though," she added as she gently touched my forearm.

"Who wouldn't stick up for you? He was being a real jerk and he needed to be told off," I growled.

"Still, thank you. I really appreciated that."

"I'll do it again if I have to, Annie. He shouldn't treat you like that. Drunk or not, he was an asshole. Forgive me for saying so."

"No need to apologize, Billy *was* being an asshole. I need to stick up for myself more. It's just...," she trailed off, "well, let's just say he doesn't like those discussions," she said to the air above her,

Excerpt from A Sacrifice for Friendship

resting her head back against the seat and blowing out an exasperated breath.

"Annie, I know you and I really don't know each other at all, but can I ask you a personal question?"

Her eyes returned to mine. "Sure. I can't promise I'll answer, but you can ask." She smiled weakly.

"Okay, there is no easy way of asking this, so I'm just gonna ask."

"Okay." She focused on me fully.

"Does Billy hit you?"

She turned in the driver's seat and gripped the steering wheel until her knuckles turned white. I could see tears rolling down her face. When I reached up to wipe them away, she flinched at my touch. The expression on her face went from sadness to fear in a matter of milliseconds.

"Hey, Annie? You don't ever need to be afraid of me. I would never lay a hand on you. Please know that," I said in my most gentle, most reassuring tone.

"I'm sorry, Frankie," she started. She looked out towards the beach and took a deep breath before continuing. "No one...knows anything. No one has ever even bothered to ask. It took a total stranger to see it. You don't feel like a stranger to me, though. I'm so comfortable with you, it's almost scary." She turned to face me and shrugged her shoulders. "I don't know *how* to leave him. It's always been this way. My dad was the same way with my mom, before she left us."

"She left you with your dad?" I asked.

"Yeah. He had never hit me, so I guess she thought I would be safe. She just knew that she had to leave. She left me a note, though. Wasn't that thoughtful? That was over ten years ago. I've never heard from her since."

Somewhere in this conversation, I found a very sad and lonely girl. She was becoming a statistic. Raised by a father who beat her mother, who in turn started beating her; and now she was dating a man who beat her, too.

If I have anything to say about this, Annie, you will not turn into a battered statistic. I'll do everything in my power to make sure that you stay safe and loved. I'll make you see how much you deserve those things, and more.

"Frankie?" She broke me from my reverie.

"Sorry, kinda spaced out there for a minute. You know, my mom left my pop and me when I was two. So I kinda know where you are coming from. The only difference is that my pop didn't beat me," I said honestly.

"You were one of the lucky ones, that's for sure. It just makes you wonder 'why', you know?" she said rhetorically. I knew she wasn't looking for an answer.

"Well, if you need help with Billy, I'll be here for you. I promise," I added, as I noticed her rolling her eyes. I took her forearm gently, but firmly enough to make her face me. "A Camarelli never breaks a promise," I said very seriously.

"Thank you, Frankie, I think I might even believe you," she replied.

"Good, because I'm very serious about this," I finished, as she took my hand in hers and gave it a squeeze.

"I can't believe that they drank all of that keg already. This party only started a couple hours ago," she said in disbelief. "Let's get this damn thing over with."

Annie started the engine and we headed off to the liquor store. We drove down Sheridan Road, and I was still in shock from all of the differences that I was witnessing.

We drove past the 400 Theater, and I looked at the marquee. *The Godfather-Part II*. My head was spinning so badly I felt like I was in *Back to the Future*.

"I think I liked the third *Godfather* the best," I said without thinking,

"The third *Godfather*? Frankie, there are only two."

Dumb, dumb, dumb, Frankie!

"I meant I liked this one the third time that I saw it."

Smooth catch, idiot. Hi, Annie, I'm from the future, where you invaded my dreams with your voice. Remember me? God!

"Oh," Annie said as she eyed me suspiciously.

"I need some music. Do you mind if I turn on the radio?" I quickly asked.

"Sure, I could use some myself." She leaned over to turn on the radio. She was turning the tuning knob like mad. God, I'd forgotten how radios used to operate without a CD player or a cassette deck in them. I wouldn't have been surprised to have seen an eight track in there somewhere. She finally settled on Elton John's *Bennie and the Jets*.

Excerpt from A Sacrifice for Friendship

I had always had a soft spot for Elton John. It made me happy to see that she felt the same way. I watched her as she sang along with the melody when the chorus kicked in. She had a beautiful singing voice.

I smiled as I watched her slam out the sound of the B's in the word Bennie over and over again. Looking over at her, she started to look a little fuzzy to me. I rubbed my eyes and tried to sharpen my vision. I felt myself get extremely tired and was helpless to fight it off. I closed my eyes, thinking that if I rested for a second or two I would feel better. My eyes were shuttering closed, and I could see Annie talking to me, but I couldn't hear her voice anymore.

What the hell? Annie? Can you hear me? Annie? Annie? Why aren't you answering me? Annie? Annie?

"Annie? Annie?" I heard myself mumble.

"Frankie? Come on, sweetheart, wake up," I heard a familiar voice say. "Frankie? You're dreaming, hon. Come on, wake up." I finally recognized the voice, but it wasn't Annie, it was Crystal. Oh shit. No!

My eyes slowly opened to find concerned brown ones staring back at me. The curly brown hair and deep brown eyes were unmistakably Crystal. She looked down with a small smile on her lips.

"Welcome back, darlin'. Are you okay?" she asked, but I couldn't speak. After a couple of attempts, I finally took a deep breath and concentrated on forming words that were hard to speak.

"No...it couldn't have been...Goddamn it." I closed my eyes, they were filling with tears.

"Frankie? What's wrong? Shh...Why are you crying?" she gently asked, as she stroked my sweat soaked bangs.

"I can't believe it was just a dream. I just can't. She was right here. I touched her, Crystal. Oh God..." I rolled onto my stomach and began to cry mournfully. I felt a loneliness I hadn't felt since my pop passed away.

I really hope that the bastard playing with my emotions is getting a good laugh now, because if I ever find them, I won't be responsible for my actions.

This I guarantee.

Watch for **A Sacrifice for Friendship**, Second Edition by DS Bauden coming from **D2D** in 2004.

Printed in the United States
20529LVS00002B/142-144